THE BITE

ALSO BY MICHAEL CROW

Red Rain

MICHAEL CROW

THE BITE

A LUTHER EWING THRILLER

VIKING

VIKING

Published by the Penguin Group

Penguin Group (USA) Inc., 375 Hudson Street, New York, New York 10014, U.S.A.

Penguin Books Ltd, 80 Strand, London WC2R 0RL, England

Penguin Books Australia Ltd, 250 Camberwell Road, Camberwell,
    Victoria 3124, Australia

Penguin Books Canada Ltd, 10 Alcorn Avenue,
    Toronto, Ontario, Canada M4V 3B2

Penguin Books India (P) Ltd, 11 Community Centre, Panchsheel Park,
    New Delhi – 110 017, India

Penguin Books (N.Z.) Ltd, Cnr Rosedale and Airborne Roads, Albany,
    Auckland, New Zealand

Penguin Books (South Africa) (Pty) Ltd, 24 Sturdee Avenue,
    Rosebank, Johannesburg 2196, South Africa

Penguin Books Ltd, Registered Offices:
Harmondsworth, Middlesex, England

First published in 2003 by Viking Penguin,
a member of Penguin Putnam Inc.

10   9   8   7   6   5   4   3   2   1

Copyright © Michael Crow, 2003

PUBLISHER'S NOTE
This is a work of fiction. Names, characters, places, and incidents either are the product
of the author's imagination or are used fictiously, and any resemblance to actual persons, living or dead, business establishments, events, or locales is entirely coincidental.

LIBRARY OF CONGRESS CATALOGING IN PUBLICATION DATA
Crow, Michael, 1948–
    The bite : a Luther Ewing thriller / Michael Crow.
        p.   cm.
    ISBN 0-670-03222-0 (alk. paper)
    1. Police—Maryland—Baltimore—Fiction.   2. Baltimore (Md.)—Fiction.   I. Title.
    PS3563.O7714 B5 2003
    813'.54—dc21   2002193363

This book is printed on acid-free paper. ∞

Printed in the United States of America
Set in Giovanni with Jasper and Altemus Borders
Designed by Carla Bolte

For R.G., a constant gardener

ACKNOWLEDGMENT

With thanks, once again, to Doug Grad

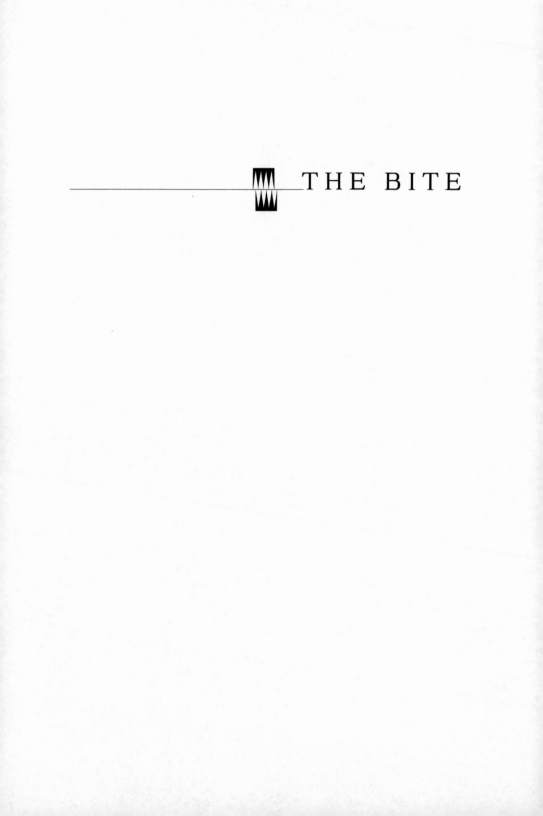

THE BITE

1. Call it a little love tap from God. Or whomever you figure runs things.

A heavy steel sledgehammer slams into my back, high on the left. I'm seeing matte black asphalt coming up to meet me before I hear the blast. By power factor, a .357 mag, minimum. But the deep boom says .45 hardballer. I can't feel a thing below the neck, just a sharp stinging as my face skids along that asphalt. I'm splayed helpless on my own parking lot, not believing this can be happening. But my face burns, ripped raw, in a spreading puddle of something warm and thick. It's not from the road rash.

Somebody I never saw just popped a cap on Luther Ewing. Something is very, very wrong here. Very, very nasty. Something's flipped. It's supposed to be the other way around.

Now, taken down hard, I'm thinking I'm going to learn the transcendent mystery I've unveiled to maybe a few too many people. And I'm thinking I don't want to learn it, don't want to find out exactly what it's like to have your brains blown out. Do you feel anything at all? Is there this great sudden flash of brilliant white light on impact? You read things like that. But it has to be imagined, because anybody who really knew could never write it, never tell it.

Dead people have serious communication problems.

It'll happen any second now. I'm scared. But I can't move. I hear the shooter take two deliberate steps toward me. The shit is wearing some kind of shoes with very squeaky rubber soles.

Gonna be now. Fuck. I cannot move.

Then I hear a crisp metallic snick. Like he thumbed on the safety lever of a cocked semiauto. My own piss begins to soak my jeans anyway. I hear Squeaky Soles take two deliberate steps back, then squeak quickly off, out of hearing range.

I'm lying there on that asphalt, all wet and messy as the thick warm pool spreads. Some's reached my mouth now, some's seeping into my nose. Maybe I'm not going to learn that great secret after all, not going to find out if you see some blinding bolt of light the instant a bullet splits your skull wide open and blasts splintered bone and gray brain tissue down your face. I'm going to die anyway, though. Just a slow fade, crumpled like a puppet with my strings all cut.

But it's in a nice suburban neighborhood, my parking lot. People who live in the condos around it punch 911 when they hear a gunshot. In the city, nobody calls anybody. They just check to see that none of their kids is lying in a blood pool, taken down by a stray bullet that crashed through a window. Bullets have such perfectly cold indifference; they don't give a damn where they wind up.

I'm about half-here, half-rational, images and thoughts racing randomly, when what must be an EMS wagon wails up and squeals to a stop. My attention is tenuous, slipping in, sliding off. I hear a lot of voices. Sounds like EMS guys, talking their way, and cops, talking another. That's cool. If it's real. It's cool if they're all doing what they usually do. Calmly but quickly taking care of business. Seen it, done it, stood around talking cop talk myself at scenes like this often enough.

There's some kind of sudden jump cut. A piece of time vanishes without a trace. Then, lying on something wet but much softer than grainy asphalt, I do see a brilliant radiance, strobing: surgical greens flickering all around, many hands heaving me off a gurney and onto a table, shifting me around, others sticking me with sharp things. Intravenous tubes dancing, some red, some clear. I'm naked, freezing. Trauma room. A hand puts a mask over my mouth and nose. When the anesthetic kicks in, I'll be sucked into that black hole, the one that's so tight you can't even squeeze in a dream for company.

Couple of nanoseconds, just time for some synapses to flash one last message: No problem, Luther. You've taken this trip before, remember?

Only thing is, you never know if your ticket's round-trip or one-way.

2. Round-trip this time, as the blackness thins to a wavery gray scrim some unknowable time later.

Or maybe not.

Feels familiar, at least. Feels like a place, a situation I've been in before. Soft plastic tubes up my nostrils, feeding oxygen to my lungs. An intravenous drip in my right arm. Wires patched here and there. A low whir of monitors, a muted beeping. My peripheral catches flashing red pin lights and yellow lines that jag across a ghost-green plasma screen, bump the edge, start fresh again at the opposite side. Over and over and over.

But I don't like what I see at the foot of my bed: a huge monolith, featureless, motionless. Light streaming around the thing from behind, like a full-body halo. No angel, that's for sure, this looming gray monolith, like the thing that kept appearing in that ancient sci-fi movie—what was it, *2001: A Space Odyssey*? Saw the video once. Apes gibbering in terror before a heavy slab, then picking up bones, tossing them high in the air when the monolith hums at them. The humming's a message they don't quite get. They hold the bones this way and that, until one finds a grip that makes his bone a club. The rest see, they find the same grip. They pound the dirt, they shatter some bleached white skulls lying around. Then they know. They go off and beat another bunch of apes to death. Ages of evolution later, men in white astronaut suits, moonwalking in front of the featureless gray slab, hear the same humming, get a message. Send a mission off to Jupiter in a spaceship run by a psychotic supercomputer named Harold or something. The computer talks; it's smarter than men. The computer starts killing astronauts. The last astronaut kills the computer.

It's as broad as it is tall, this thing at the foot of my bed. What's the message going to be? When it hums, what am I going to learn? Can't be about killing. I know most of what there is to know in that particular specialty.

"Hey, Luther? You awake? You hearing me okay?" Very weird, that nasal Baltimorese tenor from a hulk with a halo.

"What!" I hear myself bark.

The monolith laughs. It's high and fast, more like a giggle.

"Luther, you are one damned dumb lucky son of a bitch. Dumb to let yourself get taken down from behind. Lucky as hell the shooter only put an FMJ through the soft place above your collarbone. Just drilled a neat little hole clean through. Well, not so little. But clean through."

I know the voice. The gray scrim wavers away. Then there's this jack, this adrenaline dump, this shocky transition between dreamy sleep and total alert. My right arm automatically reaches for my pistol—pure reflex, muscle memory—but it's not where it should be.

Squelch that. Red pin lights, the cardiac wave on the ghost-green screen, the oxygen tubes. Now somebody's talking to me. Okay. I'm in a hospital and I'm hurt. I look hard at the monolith. Despite the dim room and the heavy backlight from what must be a corridor, the mass shifts, slides into focus. And I'm seeing Ice Box.

"Oh man," I say, all my muscles untensing. "Made it again. Oh man."

"What's that?" IB asks.

"There and back," I say. "The round-trip. Made it again."

"IB, I don't think he's quite ready. I don't think he's lucid yet." It's a woman's voice, off to my right. A soft hand, a woman's hand, takes mine and cradles it, gently squeezes it. It's clearing now. A sledgehammer slamming me from behind. Matte black asphalt coming up to meet me. EMS guys doing what they do. That bright light blinding me.

I don't even try to turn my head. No need to.

"He's right, Annie," I say. "I'm real dumb. And very lucky."

Ice Box and Annie. The best. Detective Sergeant Joseph Cutrone, universally known as IB because he isn't an ecto or a meso or any kind of morph unless they've got a special one for men the size and shape of restaurant-type refrigerators. Detective Lieutenant Annie Mason, head of the sex crimes unit, my personal ideal of the perfect woman—though I keep that deeply secret. We've been as tight as people ever get. They even backed me up on an operation four or five months ago that was so far over the line it would have cost them their careers if it'd ever come out. Lots of people had their suspicions about that op, after it was over. Lots of people wasted lots of time keeping the rumor running. Caged mice, racing around that wire wheel, sure they're going someplace when they're moving fast to nowhere at all.

IB and Annie think they know the truth of it.

But they don't. Nobody does. Except me and a drug tsar called Vassily. So nobody's ever going to know. Vassily has that communication problem.

Now I need to know some things from the living.

"Feel like I got run over by a truck. So can I ask a basic question here?" I say. "What exactly happened to me? Who, what, when, and where?"

"You got shot, Luther," Annie says. "Last night, sometime between 11:15 and 11:20. Sound about right?"

"Yeah. About right. But I need to hear details. Because everything seems a little fuzzy, a little disordered."

"Okay," Annie says. "You park your car in the usual place near your apartment. You lock it. You're walking toward the front entrance and somebody maybe twenty feet directly behind you fires one shot. Must be a total surprise, because you don't start to turn, you don't move to draw down. You just go down."

"I can't move. EMS picks me up. Then total blank, until people in greens are working me over. I think."

"You pass out on the way to the hospital," Annie says. "Blood loss, shock. Your heart's going just fine, though. You make it to the ER. The trauma crew gets busy. You're anesthetized."

"And I wake up now," I say. "When's now?"

"It's 6:45 the next morning. Out just a little more than six hours," Annie says.

"Damage assessment?"

"What IB said. You remember what IB told you a minute ago?" Annie says.

"Drilled clean through," I say. "Dumb and lucky."

Then that gray scrim drops down again, stiff and hard this time. I feel my eyes rolling back inside my skull. My body spasms. I'm gone. I'm back in that black hole.

But I don't stay there long. When my eyes open and refocus, a doctor and two nurses are just rushing into my room. They fuss with the drips, check the monitors. I see the doctor give Annie a thumbs-up when he leaves.

"Christ, Ewing. I'm gonna kill you myself, you scare me like that again," Annie says. I turn my head on the pillow and stare at her. She stares back. She's trying to stay cool, but she's wearing that crooked grin. The cutest grin going. Never figured out why it only shows up when she's distressed or really worried.

"Hey Annie, sorry," I say. "Promise I won't get shot anymore. Okay?"

"You think this is funny? You find it all real amusing, do you?" she says.

"Luther's got a really warped sense of humor—you ought to know that by now, Annie," IB pipes up. "The skinny little fuck likes to walk into bullets and shit like that every once in a while, just to pull our chains. He deliberately passed out just now."

"Sick. And it's contagious," Annie says. "Seems to me it was you that walked into something last time, IB. At least you had enough sense to be wearing a vest when you pulled that stunt."

"Now, Annie, I never did that on purpose. It was an accident," IB says.

"Yeah, he was planning to dodge, like the agents in *Matrix*," I say. "You know, bend this way, bend that way, faster than a speeding bullet. Only he got confused, bent the wrong way."

"It's all a movie to you boys, isn't it? Nearly getting killed is just entertainment?" she says.

"No. We need to maintain a certain distance. A certain point of view. That the guns only fire blanks, and the rest is all just special effects," I say.

"You are both seriously disturbed individuals, you know that? No, you obviously don't know that. You don't have a fucking clue. You're trapped in adolescence, the both of you." She's not grinning anymore. There's a hitch in her voice. "Maybe you should give some thought to getting professional help. Maybe you should find a good therapist who could help you grow up. You bastards."

Annie drops my hand, rises from the chair. "I'm glad you're alive, Luther. But you really piss me off," she says, bolting from the room.

"Shit, IB," I say. "Look what you did."

"Me?"

"Yeah, you. I needed that nice hand-holding I was getting. Then you go and spook her."

"Me?"

"I don't see anybody else in here."

"I got two things to say, birdbones. One, Annie doesn't spook. Two, I didn't get myself capped. Three, I'm not laying in bed tubed up like some drunk plumber mistook me for a bathroom that needed renovation. Four, I believe you did do that little croaking act on purpose. Lastly, you look like dog shit."

"That's two? Count much, IB?"

"Whatever." Ice Box grins. "Once I get started I inspire myself."

3. I've got to go back.

I've got to get way back, to when being a narcotics detective for the Baltimore County Police Department stopped being mainly a matter of busting suburban kids and their grass and Ecstasy dealers and started getting hard-core. Then take it forward, looking for any sign that someone slipped onto my path and shadowed me. Got to remember everyone I nailed, everyone I hurt, the how and the why and what happened to them. I can do that. The problem's going to be the ones I didn't personally hurt or bust. The invisible ones whose *interests* I may have threatened, the big players I never saw who got angry. Or worried I might be on them next.

I need to start now. But it isn't going to happen today. The painkillers are on the case too well. I keep sinking into a dreamy, comfortable lassitude, like a very tired man who's finally laid himself down on the softest, sweetest feather bed in the world. And people keep getting in my face. I resent the intrusions.

First it's Lieutenant Dugal, narc chief and my boss. Wake up, Luther. It's Captain Dugal now, still your boss but now head of a combined narcotics and vice unit. His reward, after I set up a sting that netted several million dollars of super-pure smack and six arrests. No convictions. No trials, even. They all made bail and then they all got dead. That was Vassily's doing. The fuck killed his own crew. So what if there was a short but very vicious little war after, and a bunch of cops—one of my guys and several city narcs who were working with me—got killed. No brass much cared in the end, because the bad guys went away. Dugal got the glory, got the promotion.

Now, sitting by my bed, he says, "We're going to get whoever did this to you, Luther. We are going to hunt him, find him, and take him down. You've got my promise. We will take him down."

I just nod, pretending to be more out of it than I am to keep from laughing at his bullshit. Dugal is a mediocre detective. But he's a smart, very ambitious suit. He knows exactly how much he owes me. He treats me like his star cop, overlooks my unorthodox procedures, and pretends he has no clue when I cross the line. As long as the results make him look good and he's sure there's no trail back to him when I go too far. Deniability, that's his only concern. He'd dump me in the meat-grinder without a thought if shit came down and he had to cover his own ass.

Not that I give a fuck. A scumbag like him is my ideal boss.

"The press got disinformation fast and thick, Luther," he says. "I personally saw to that. There is no way the jackals will ever make you. Your cover is secure."

I nod. He grips my right shoulder. He thinks that's some sort of manly gesture I'll appreciate, some tough-guy expression of caring. "Luther, is there anything you want? Anything I can do? Your parents, for instance. You want me to talk to them, let them know you're going to be fine?"

"Better if they don't know anything about it," I say.

"I understand," Dugal says, giving my shoulder another squeeze.

Then he rises to leave. "Anything you need, any little thing at all, I'll see to it, Luther. And we will get the fuck, believe me."

I just stifle a laugh. He can make his face look so sincere I'm sure he practices the expression in the mirror a couple of times each day.

The party's just started. But the rest of the guests who drift in today aren't carrying the shit Dugal learned in the management classes he takes at night at Towson State, and they don't overstay their welcome. Just quick drop-bys by Tommy Weinberg, Gus, and Petey from the squad. All decent guys, meaning well. A few other cops from HQ. And McKibbin, the department shooting instructor I'm tight with. Guy in his fifties, Irish, got his green card in the lottery. Ex–Royal Ulster Constabulary, the best hand with any sort of firearm I've ever seen. "Just a copper walking a beat in Belfast," he always says. I know he's got military training, probably SAS. He knows I know. But he just laughed at me like I was the village idiot or something the one time I mentioned it. I let it rest after that. Just like he let rest what he saw in me.

● ● ●

Modern medicine: don't let anybody lie there long. They might start feeling sorry for themselves. Or be assaulted by the mutated drug-resistant bacteria that are overrunning hospitals.

They get me up and walking around for a while just after lunch. My left shoulder and arm are immobilized in a rigid plastic casing that's got my arm bent so my fingertips are resting up around the old trache scar on my throat. I feel a little woozy, a little lightheaded when I first stand.

"How much blood did I lose?" I ask the nurse. She's a redhead, freckles everywhere, on the plump side.

"Gallons and gallons," she says, hands on my waist to support me. "You were just about empty when you got to the ER."

"I sort of figured that," I say, "since I was about to drown in the pool when the EMS guys got there."

"Oh, huge pool. You made a real mess on that parking lot," she says. "But the EMS guys found two wine-bottle corks near a dumpster. They just spit on 'em, wiped them once or twice on their coveralls, and corked the holes. Saved your butt."

I love nurses. They're so morbid.

"Then when you got here, we thought 'What luck.' We had a lot of blood sort of past the 'for sale by' date. Ready for the garbage. Would have been a shame to just throw it away. So we were set to transfuse it all into you."

"Glad I could be of help. Wouldn't want anything to go to waste."

"It did anyway, detective," she says with a grin. She's leading me in a sort of shuffling slow waltz around my bed. "Your large cubic friend made us give you a fill-up with the best we had. Freshly donated by eighteen-year-old virgins. He insisted. So don't blame us if your voice rises an octave and you don't have to shave for a while."

I start laughing hard. Mistake. Feels like some sadist is shoving a hot steel rod through my shoulder. White hot. All the way through.

"Ah, you think I could lie down for a while?" I ask.

"And I thought you were tough. Next thing, you'll be begging me for more of these," she laughs once she gets me back in bed. In her palm are a couple of Percosets. I swallow them dry. She gives me a cup of water as a chaser.

So I'm feeling fine when the surgeon drops by, except for an initial jolt when I see he's just about my age, thirty or so. Maybe Annie's right and I am stuck in adolescence. In my head somewhere I must still be seeing myself as the punk eighteen-year-old who believed the army's "Be All That You Can Be" TV commercials, joined the Special Forces, and looked forward to staying in thirty years. I always expect people like doctors and district attorneys and judges to be older than me, wiser. I'm always surprised when they're not.

"About as clean as it gets, detective," he tells me. "No bones broken, no tendons severed, no damage at all that'll limit your movements in any way. You'll need to do a little physical therapy to get your strength and coordination back, but that's it."

"Good news," I say.

"Frankly, it's amazing. I've never handled a gunshot wound that made so little mess. Hell, I've had kids here paralyzed from the neck down or doomed to wear a colostomy bag for the rest of their lives from a hit by a .22. And all you're going to have from a .45 is two scars."

"About the size of wine-bottle corks?"

"Two corks, on the exit," he smiles. "Couldn't help but notice this isn't your first time. That neat little in-and-out on your calf, and that dent in your head. They put a plate in your skull, didn't they?"

"Yeah," I say, my right forefinger involuntarily sliding along the dent, my mind going back instantly to a bad day in Sarajevo and jittering on the shock and the fear before I can shut that particular circuit down.

"We'll have you out of here very soon, though you'll need to wear that cast for another week after," the doctor says. "Unless you start running a fever or showing signs of infection, I'll just check the wound before you leave and when you come back to get the cast off. But I really hope I never see you again after that. Three times lucky—any more would be pushing it."

I've already pushed it too fucking far.

I try hard to stay cool. The Percosets help, but my mind's in a nasty place. I keep it hidden, like I keep it hidden every other time someone visits. But then all of them were trying just as hard to hide that strange feeling that comes over you when you see a friend down, that reflex of being glad it's him and not you that took the hit, and the shame and embarrassment over that reflex. I see it in their eyes, hear it in their voices anyway.

Except in Annie's eyes, Annie's words.

"Sorry I got hysterical this morning," she says when she comes ambling into my room just after I've eaten what passes for dinner. "I was so worried."

"And I was acting like a real asshole with IB. Defense mechanism, all that bullshit joking around. Got kind of giddy when I realized where I was, who was with me. Truth is, I thought I was going to die out there."

"You came pretty damn close," she says, taking my hand and stroking it. "I'm having a real hard time handling this. You're the best friend I've got."

"Poor you," I say.

"There you go, starting the bullshit again."

"Can't seem to help it, Annie. It's programmed. It's all I've got to put up against the fear."

"Yeah, I know. I mean I know it rationally. Shit, it's just Psych 101 stuff. But I can't *feel* it. So it gets to me. I guess I'm not helping you much."

"You are. In ways you don't even know."

"Luther," she says, dropping her voice to a whisper. "Was this payback for that thing last fall? Is it gonna happen again?"

"No way," I say. "If the guys who took Vassily down were after me, I would be dead. You know that."

"Then who?"

"I don't know. Some dealer I busted once? No way it was a professional hitter. No pro would've have walked away after one shot. He would've checked, finished it. But he walked away. Amateur, for sure."

"But who? Why?"

I shake my head. "It was a love tap, Annie. Now I have to figure who loves me so much."

$4.$ There's a monolith at the foot of my bed when my eyes flutter open the next morning. Only it isn't a featureless gray slab.

It's a guy stuffing an entire Egg McMuffin into his mouth, chewing maybe twice, then chasing the thing with a big slurp of orange juice. Small burp follows.

"MJ know you're still addicted to those?" I ask.

"I'm tapering off, tapering off. Can't just go cold turkey," Ice Box says. MJ is his wife. She's cool, we're great pals. But she had twins last September, and since then she's been on IB's case about taking better care of himself, about dropping twenty or thirty pounds. Hard for a man like IB, though, since he isn't fat and flabby. He's just naturally huge.

But he slips sideways like a bantamweight so an orderly can wheel in my breakfast cart and cantilever the tray over my bed. I thumb the button that raises my bed until I'm almost sitting up-right, only a slight burning in my left shoulder, snugged in that rigid white plastic casing. When the orderly's gone, IB squeezes into the chair on my left.

"So, how's it hanging, slick?" he asks. "You feeling real wounded today or what?"

"I'm feeling real hungry, and all I'm getting are MREs." IB's blank face tells me he is not getting the military term. "Meals Rejected by Ethiopians," I say, taking a forkful of scrambled eggs. They've been made from powder, they're barely lukewarm. "Take it back. MREs are better." IB laughs.

"Want me to run down to my favorite Scottish restaurant, bring you back some good stuff? Giant fries, Big Mac, whatever you like?"

"Maybe later," I say, sipping some hot brown water that's doing its best to impersonate coffee but isn't coming anywhere near to pulling it off. At least it washes away that grainy feeling the eggs left in my mouth.

"You gonna eat that roll there?"

"Nah."

"You sure? Looks like a cinnamon roll."

"Sure."

"Can I have it?"

"Yeah."

IB pops the roll into his mouth, chews once, chases it with another slurp of orange juice. No burp this time.

"You ready for what we got, Luther? Yeah? Okay, here it is. We got some footprints."

"On asphalt?"

"Yeah, it rained most of that day, remember? The perp's boots were muddy. The asphalt was still damp. So we got a couple of impressions. Pattern's like those L.L. Bean boots with the rubber soles and leather tops."

"That really narrows the field."

"Well, it's something, anyway. And the boots were very small. This guy must have tiny feet. Found some muddy tire tracks, too. Not twenty yards from your car."

"And?"

"Not much. Standard Michelin tread pattern. Could have been any Eurobratmobile, from Saab or Volvo to VW Jetta."

"Nothing you'd look at twice, correct?"

"Yeah. Unless you had reason to be hyperalert to cars in your lot you didn't regularly see parked there."

"It was late, I was tired, I had no reason to be scanning cars in my own fucking parking lot."

"Whatever. Anyway, we found the brass. Military surplus, made by Federal, the kind you can buy real cheap from any of those catalogs like *Sportsmen's Guide*. You know, $39.99 for two-hundred-fifty rounds, plus a free surplus ammo can. Doesn't get any more generic than that. It was dinged a little, but we got a partial print. This guy must have tiny fingers, too. Anyway, we've been running it through our system and the FBI's system and still no matches."

"That's it?" I ask.

"Saved the best for last," IB smiles. "Had the mud from the boot and tire prints analyzed. Same mud."

"That's the best? You're surprised by this?"

"Fuck no, numbnuts. If you'd listen instead of interrupting all the time you might learn something. It's interesting mud. Got a very heavy nitrate content, much heavier than you find in your ordinary household mud. Nitrates, nitrates, I'm thinking. Why's mud got nitrates? 'Bullshit,' the lab guy tells me. I think he's fucking around. Then he says, 'Or cow shit, pig shit, horse turds. Any kind of animal shit left on the ground breaks down. Nitrate is a big component.'"

"I don't think I'm going to be thrilled over what you're about to tell me, IB."

"Nah, you're gonna hate it. Some shit-kicking peckerwood who keeps a lot of cows or goats or whatever, probably using some really cheap old 1911-type .45, capped the famous Luther

Ewing, ex-master of military black ops." IB giggles. "You're gonna hate it worse 'cause it fits," he goes on. "Where's Luther been hanging the last couple of months? Out in the boonies up north, poking around farms and woods, looking for old double-wide trailers up on blocks where some rednecks are cooking up metham-phetamine. Correct? And some shit-kicker don't like this one bit, maybe figures you're coming a little too close. Maybe he doesn't even make you for a cop, just a competitor. Tracks you, pops you. I rest my case."

"Except why aren't I dead?"

"Hell, Luther, you've just spent too much intense time with those downtown gang-bangers and heroin mob shooters who know what they're doing. This country pumpkin is not a profes-sional, not an experienced assassin. He's a dumb lowlife hick with maybe a sixth-grade reading level. Which is all you need to read a meth cookbook. He probably thinks he killed you dead with his good ol' .45."

■ ■ ■

After IB leaves, I spend a while considering whether I'm one of the leading assholes of my generation, or simply retarded. Getting taken down like that? Double goddamn. I didn't just ease up after the Vassily business, which would have been stupid enough. I must have gone fucking semicomatose. But I'm clicking on things when my freckled nurse comes in, pulls down the covers, yanks my legs sideways so they're dangling off the bed, and slips these weird booties made of paper on my bare feet.

"Sit up," she says. I do. There's that burning in my shoulder but it isn't too bad. She drapes a bathrobe over my shoulders.

"Now get your feet on the floor and walk. Hope you can do better than yesterday," she says. "That was pretty pathetic."

"Anybody ever tell you you're merciless?" I say.

"Oh, sure! Every day!" She grins. "Pampering and coddling's reserved for pediatrics and geriatrics. Not hard-core guys like you."

I'm up and out of the room before she can lay a hand on me, shaking off that initial dizziness fast. I move down the corridor almost at double-time, turn when I get to the end, and almost double again down toward the far end. She's leaning against the wall just by my door.

"Oohhhh," she says. "I am impressed."

I think I grin at her as I pass, but she's barely registering. I'm too into those clicks I had just before she rousted me. First, IB's make on the shooter is too easy, too pat. Yeah, I'd been creeping around the rural parts of the county. Mostly all I'd found were lots of kids busy getting hooked on OxyContin, a new synthetic opiate for control of chronic pain. Available at any pharmacy, supposed to be safe from abuse because the twenty-, forty-, and eighty-milligram pills are time-release jobs. But kids are smart. Some of them, a year or so ago, discovered all you have to do is crush the fucking pills to powder and snort or shoot it up. Then you get a hit like fine heroin. Soon you get a heroin-grade habit, too. Hillbilly heroin, really took off in Appalachia and rural areas in the East well off the Interstate smack routes. Nobody has to travel to any dirty city, get down and dirty with any banger dealers. I ran into one really personable kid who was dealing, bought a couple of tabs from him. He'd simply charmed a dozen or two old ladies into selling him their prescribed Oxy. Mostly Medicaid patients, who paid only a dollar for a $250, ninety-pill Oxy script. He'd offer them $10 or $15 per pill. Then he'd sell a pill to his friends for $20 or $30. The old ladies needed the money, and the kid was keeping himself supplied and clearing a tidy sum every month.

Lately, though, his margins had declined, he admitted. He was using more and more, selling less and less.

I didn't bust him. He wasn't my target. He was just an idiot. If

I see him again in a month or so and he's still hooked, I'll get him into rehab, not jail.

The meth biz was another matter. Wasn't a trade run by personable kids. Wasn't a no-violence scam with Medicaid prescriptions. The meth guys were tough, biker-types. There'd been a couple of killings euphemistically called "possibly drug-related." There'd been a lot of export. But I'd only located two cookers out there in the boonies. I'd only given the humint to the local county police-station bosses. Never went on the busts—only one of which was good, the other trailer in the woods having been abandoned, the local cops thought, fairly recently. So they caught three guys and maybe $10,000 worth of speed. No big deal, but it made the local cops happy. I stayed at arm's length. Deep in the shadows as I could be.

So where's motive in IB's scenario? Why would some hick meth-head come after me? The fucks wouldn't even know I exist, let alone where I go home nights.

"Ahh, sir," the freckled nurse calls when I double past her for maybe the tenth time. The corridor is only thirty meters or so long. "I think you made your point. I think you've done enough for this morning."

I just blow by her. I'm thinking now of small feet, a small fingerprint. Maybe drives a Saab. Way outside the standard meth biz profile, not even a near fit with what IB's put together.

Freckles grabs me on my next pass and turns me into my room. She's a lot stronger than she looks. "Jesus," she says, pulling off the bathrobe. "Give guys like you a little nudge, it's like you feel your manhood has been challenged or something. Just get back in bed and watch a soap opera or something, huh?"

■ ■ ■

I watch eyelid movies instead. Rewind the tapes, adjust the tracking, start slow-forward. Go carefully along the trail that stretches out before me, the one I've already traveled, looking for a sign on either side. Indian stuff. That's a smile. But for a moment it takes me too far back, all the way to my Special Forces days, when my homies on the teams thought I was a full-blood Comanche. I'd played that up. It was easy. I look like one. Strange, but who knows what's going to pop out of the gene pool when your poppa's a black Marine lifer who did two tours in 'Nam and brought home a Viet girl as his wife and your mom?

Fast-forward a bit, get to the time that matters, focus on what matters. Late last summer something new started happening in the white-bread suburbs of the county: super-pure heroin, the kind you can snort or smoke. We start finding traces of new players in the heroin game. Russian mafia players, from up in Brighton Beach, Brooklyn. And, big surprise, we learn that the boss is an ex-Spetsnaz guy I know as Vassily, a guy who fought beside me when I was a CIA-recruited merc on the Muslim side in Sarajevo.

Nobody, especially Dugal, can quite figure out what's going on. I know, and I bring in a friend, a black city detective lieutenant of narcotics who goes by the name of Dog.

So Vassily and I, we have a big friendly reunion. He only knows me as Shooter, which was my merc name in Bosnia. He does not know I'm a cop, he thinks I'm into the drug trade now, just like him. So begins what the assholes in the BCPD call "The Russian Rattle." I go to Brighton with Dog, we do a deal with Vassily: his guys will supply wholesale, Dog'll take care of retail in the city and fuck the crazy gang-bangers who've been a pain in the ass for Vassily anyway, while I'll handle the 'burbs. Vassily's happy. His problems are solved. Until he has his guys bring down several million dollars' worth of heroin. It's a good trap: Dog and I and our crew and six Russians all get busted when we hand over the cash and Vassily's guys hand over the smack.

But it's a goatfuck. Vassily isn't there, like he was supposed to be. His guys walk on bail and disappear—except for the head of one, which winds up UPS'd to Dugal. Vassily still doesn't know that Dog and I are cops; he just thinks we fucked him and he's going to kill us. His shooters eventually get to Dog, who takes a bullet in the face and winds up in a coma.

Dugal wants to wait for the DEA and the FBI to nail Vassily. It might take those fucks a year or so. My life expectancy is days or weeks. So I go totally illegal. I go covert. I go up to where Vassily stays and Vassily gets dead. He dies very, very hard. I make certain of that.

End of story. No Russian payback, that forty-five slug to my back. I'm as sure of that as I am of anything.

And scratch some shit-kicker speed merchant IB's convinced did the job on me. So who? Who the fuck else is there that wants me dead but isn't smart enough to make me dead? And fucking why?

The movie wipes about there. Must be the Percosets my freckled friend gave me after the corridor march, finally reporting for duty.

■ ■ ■

Drowse away most of the day. The MRE man wheels in his cart, so it must be 5:30 or so. The meatloaf isn't all that bad. I'm finishing up some Jell-O of an artificial flavor and color I've never encountered before when I see a kid's face framed by honey hair peering into my room.

"Luther? Babe? You okay?" She's no kid, though everyone but MJ says she's way too young for me. She's beside my bed in two strides, this great girl with legs as long as nature ever makes them.

"Hey, Helen," I say with a smile. She's exactly the kind of sight I like to see, the kind I never get tired of looking at. We've been together maybe a year and half, since not far into her junior year at Goucher College.

"You're okay, right, babe? MJ called and told me. I came right over and it was really shitty. They, like, wouldn't let me in to see you. It was cops and that cop-ette of yours exclusively yesterday. IB saw me waiting, but he wouldn't get me in either. He just kept saying you were all right, doing fine."

She leans over and kisses my forehead, leaves her lips there. "You got shot, Luther! Oh Jesus, you got shot and they wouldn't let me in," she murmurs. Then she's crying, her cheek pressed against mine. "The fucks," she says. "They wouldn't tell me anything."

I stroke her hair with my good hand. "Hey, I'm good. Real good. Definitely not major."

"Getting shot's not major?" she sobs. "Are we on the same planet? Oh, Luther. I've been totally whacked since MJ phoned me. I figured she was lying, easing me into real bad news. IB, too, that big slob. Not major? What is, then?"

"Helen, Helen. It's really okay." I kiss her once, kiss her again deeply. "I'll be out of here and home tomorrow or the next day. Then I'll prove how all right things are. But, uh, you'll have to be on top 'cause I'll be wearing this for a while." I rap on the white plastic case. It makes a hollow sound.

"Is that a promise, or one of your slick Ewing lines?" she says, just before she sticks her tongue into my mouth, slides it around and in and out a few times, then pulls away and straightens up. She's smiling now, but her eyes are searching mine.

"Promise. Have I ever lied to you?"

"Oh, only a dozen times. That I know of for sure. Which means you've done it at least two dozen times," she says. "I'm going to be

real interested in finding out if you can live up to this one. I'm going to really dig it if you do. 'Cause I just love being on top."

"Now I'm hurt," I say.

"Oh, God. Your wound? Should I call the nurse?"

"No," I say. "I'm hurt because I always suspected you were only
interested in my body. And now you've proved it."

Helen laughs.

That wicked, half-mocking laugh.

I jack big-time after Helen's gone.

Take away all affection, add a hint of cold cruelty lurking just
beneath the surface, and it was remarkably like a laugh I'd heard
before.

In Dugal's office first, about a week after I'd got back from taking care of Vassily. Officially I'd been on leave of absence, and by
paper trail I'd been in Key West, not pulling a black op in New
York, thanks to an old Alpha teammate named JoeBoy who was
still in Special Forces. I'd sent him my credit cards before the op
and told him to make the most of his furlough, on me. The fuck
had done exactly that; I'd be paying off cards run up to the max
for the next six months or so. But JoeBoy'd also supplied me with
some of Uncle Sam's latest special equipment, besides perfect
cover.

Not a bad bargain, considering the stake: my life. And I was
sure I'd got away clean. Until that fucking laugh.

■ ■ ■

"Taxi service," IB says, barging into my room late the next afternoon.

"Taxi? Shit, Dugal pinching pennies again?" I say. IB just grins,
tosses me a pile of my clothes. They probably burned the stuff I
was wearing when I got hit. "I figured a white stretch limo at least."

"Take what you get, which is me and a dinged and dirty Crown Vic with rear shocks that died months ago," IB says. "And be grateful you're going home in that, and not someplace spooky in a shiny black hearse."

"Oh, I'm fucking full of gratitude to all concerned, man. I might burst into tears I'm so full of it," I say, twisting and shifting to get my jeans on, then managing socks and boots with one hand. Very early that morning, while I was still stuck in a comfortable web of dreams, they'd rousted me and taken me to an OR. I woke up pretty quick when the nurses none too gently removed the plastic casing that had immobilized my shoulder and arm, and started pulling out the drainage tubes. They generally leave bullet holes open for a while, to reduce the chance of infection. I could see the exit, about six inches above my left nipple. Not as big as two wine corks, the hole. Maybe not even one cork. But it had a dirty-looking black crust around the edges. The surgeon started looking inside with a penlight, then probed around a bit. It was worse than the fucking dentist. "Clean as a whistle. Let's close 'em up," the surgeon said. A bunch of stitches front and back, a tight-wrapped bandage and sling, and he pronounced me good to go. Right away, out of reach of those mutant bugs that want to eat you up. Hospitals may be the most dangerous place a sick or hurt person can be.

"But I got a question, IB. I'm supposed to walk out of here topless, or what?"

"See that nice big wooly thing? It's called a sweater. My sweater, so don't bleed on it or anything. Figured nothing of yours would fit over that truss you're strapped into."

"Hell, IB, I can't wear your favorite sweater."

"It's okay, man. Just take care of it."

"It's not that."

"Then what?"

"The color, man. The same ugly space-turd purple as your minivan. I mean, what if somebody I know *sees* me in this?"

"Got just two words for you, Ewing," IB says, easing the sweater over my head and my bandaged side, pulling it into place. "Just two: kiss my guinea ass."

"Fits like a fucking muumuu. Purple. Jesus, let's get out of here fast."

5.
IB has me home in maybe fifteen minutes.

It is not the same home I had before the Russian Rattle. That Cockeysville condo had been fragged during our little war. The grenades totalled almost everything I owned. But under one of the squares of parquet flooring, just where I'd stashed it, the only thing I cared about anyway had survived: a photo of my Alpha team and a few other teams in our loaded dune buggies, behind Iraqi lines. I'd retrieved that and just walked away from the rest.

Home now is a little one-bedroom rental on the top floor of a building on Padonia Road, a mile or two closer to HQ in Towson. I'd gone Zen with this place instead of duplicating a couple of pages of an Ikea catalog as I'd done with the Cockeysville condo. There are tatami mats on the floors, a futon and a couple of big cushions in the living room, a futon in the bedroom, some lamps with rice-paper shades, and not a whole lot else. All cheap imitations from Pier One, not the real Jap stuff. But it suits.

"Fucking sparse, Luther. Too austere. Molto depressing. Shit, why don't you at least hang some posters on the walls or something? A fucking Orioles pennant at least," IB says when he comes into the place with me. He says something like that everytime he comes here. He also always forgets to take his shoes off at the door.

"Shoes, IB?"

"Oh, yeah, sorry," he says, yanking off his size-fourteen Nikes without untying the laces. He walks over to the fridge. "You probably got Helen and Annie and whoever else is part of your harem already scheduled to come look after you, unless you figure you can steer that Audi with your teeth while you shift gears. But just in case that slipped your perverse mind, I stocked you up with your favorite stuff."

He pulls open the freezer. I see there's a stack of Stouffer's dinners: macaroni and cheese, Swiss steak, turkey, meatloaf. Things you just put in the microwave when you need fuel and aren't feeling particular, just in a hurry.

"Hey, thanks, man," I say.

"I'll call you, bud. Need anything at all, call me, okay?" IB says, leaving with his Nikes in his hand.

I lie down on the futon, feeling all at once very weary. I lie there for a long time, just practicing my breathing, just letting go. I've been hoping since I moved here that if I do this drill every day, one day I'll succeed in reaching that state where your mind is perfectly blank, not a thought or a memory or a regret or anything at all cluttering it up.

It hasn't happened yet.

Not this time, either. It's that laugh, that free, wild laugh of Helen's that reminded me of another laugh. I get up, go to the bedroom, remove a panel from the false wall at the back of the closet, open the heavy-duty safe bolted to the joists. I remove a single unlabeled tape. I go back into the living room, pop the tape in the Aiwa micro sound system, put on the earphones. Among other semiparanoid things I did immediately after the Russian Rattle, I wore a private wire a lot, recording every conversation I had with anyone. I'd listened and listened to all of them for a while, searching for any sign or signal or vague hint that someone seriously thought maybe I wasn't in Key West after all, that maybe I had something to do with Vassily's death.

I lie down on the futon now and listen to the only tape that includes that laugh. I listen twice, then shut off the tape and replay the scene from memory.

■ ■ ■

"Luther, this is Agent Braunstein and Agent Russo, DEA," Dugal had said when I walked into the office and eased the door shut behind me. It was about ten days after I'd returned to duty at the BCPD headquarters in Towson, after the Vassily incident. Dugal's voice was stiff, overly controlled, the way it always went when he was tense or unsure of himself. "They've got some interest in our Russian bust."

"Detective Ewing," Braunstein nodded. He was wearing a conservative, inexpensive charcoal gray suit, the kind Dugal favored, and he could have been anywhere between forty-five and fifty-five, with the wasted, pale face of a cancer patient. Russo, twenty years younger at least, was wearing gray, too: same styleless cut to the jacket, but it looked like fine merino instead of poly-wool. And a skirt that ended well above her knees. She said nothing, just crossed her legs. I heard that soft hiss women's stockings make when they rub together.

"Sit down, Luther," Dugal said, gesturing to the chair beside him at his fake rosewood conference table. Braunstein was pulling a manila envelope out of his briefcase. I could feel Russo's appraising eyes on me. Our Russian Rattle file was on the DEA side of the table. No doubt they'd been through it already, forward and back.

"As you might have guessed, Luther," Dugal started in, "the DEA and the FBI were keeping an eye on the crew in Brighton Beach before we did the buy-and-bust down here. A very close eye, I understand. And I believe they're somewhat cross with us for getting to these guys first. Is that a reasonable assumption, Agent Braunstein?"

"Oh, not cross. Maybe a bit chagrined, Captain Dugal," Russo said. It was hard to make her. She had the generic good looks and the generic, accentless voice of every anchorwoman you ever saw on local TV news anywhere in the country. "And now very curious about a few aspects of the case."

"Take a look at these, Detective Ewing. I understand this didn't make any of the media here," Braunstein said, slipping a few newspapers across the table to me. The story was front-page in the *New York Post* and *Daily News*, tucked back in the Metro section of *The New York Times*. It didn't require a long scan: Reputed Russian mob boss found slain at home. Execution-style, apparently professional, no leads or suspects, an NYPD spokesman said. Victim known as Vassily Ostrov, owned Palace nightclub in Brighton Beach. Ostrov a Russian citizen, but police found passports in other names and nationalities with Ostrov's photo. Two associates also killed at the scene. Police sources said they believe Ostrov's murder may be linked to warfare between competing factions of the Russian mafia over drug trafficking.

"Well, big fucking surprise," I said.

Russo had first laughed that laugh right then. "Surprise, detective?"

"If you'd been watching him, you'd have to've known this was coming," I said. "Vassily only showed up in Brighton a year or so ago. There's already a Russian immigrant mob in place. So how does Vassily get to the multi-million-dollar heroin deal level? He doesn't waste time trying to climb the local ladder. He just muscles business away from the Brighton Beach Russians. He makes a lot of enemies in the process. We bust his crew here, Vassily's suddenly vulnerable. Payback time."

"Not quite," Russo said.

"Yeah? What don't I know?"

"That maybe four or five years ago the Moscow bosses hosed the Brighton locals," Russo smiled. "Gave them a choice: work for us or die. Some of the locals said fuck off. They died. So there was no local ladder for Vassily to climb, and nobody local to muscle business from. The Moscow mafia had total control when he got here. He was just the new chief operating officer of one of Moscow's foreign subsidiaries."

"So I'm just an uninformed suburban narc. Sorry about that. We made a nice bust, we'd hoped to bag Vassily but he wasn't there. Now he's dead. What do you want from me?"

"Who took Vassily down?" Braunstein said sharply.

"How should I know? Agent Russo here's just punched a big hole in my theory."

"If that's really your theory," she said.

"The tone of that remark," I said, staring hard into her eyes, "irks me, Russo. I am getting very close to being seriously pissed off."

That laugh again. "And is it very dangerous to piss you off, Detective Ewing? You have a rather formidable background, we understand. Should I be worrying?"

"Goodbye," I said, starting to rise.

"Wait a moment, Luther," Dugal said, waving me back down into my chair. Then he surprised me. Amazing what a lot of good publicity and a big promotion did for the size of his balls.

"Agent Russo," he said in what he considered his command voice, "we can do one of two things here. We can talk in a professional, respectful, and cooperative manner about a matter of some apparent mutual interest. Or you and Agent Braunstein can get your asses out of my office right now. Your call."

She didn't hesitate for an eye-blink. She stood up, extended her hand to me. "I'm sorry if anything I said sounded offensive. I'm always getting my ass in a sling like this. I'm cursed with a loopy sense of humor that nobody but me ever seems to get. I should know better by now. I apologize."

I shook her hand. Then she said, "Can we drop all this 'agent' and 'detective' stuff? That's Dick Braunstein, from the New York office. I'm Francesca, your friendly local Fed. All right to call you Luther?"

"Fine by me," I said, letting go of her hand. I'd noticed a slight ridge of callous along the edge of her palm and little finger. Serious martial arts practice. A girl who likes to tussle.

Braunstein removed a sleek silver laptop from his briefcase and a very small digital videocam, wired the cam to the computer, then turned it so the screen faced Dugal and me.

"What we're interested in learning, Luther, is how you got so tight with Vassily so fast. He was not exactly a trusting soul," Braunstein said, hitting a key. One flicker, and I'm a movie star. There on the screen, amazingly hi-rez, is me and Dog sitting in my Audi TT on Brighton Boulevard. Three men approach the car. One stands directly behind it, one positions himself just behind Dog's door, and fucking Vassily starts tapping on my window. Then I'm out of the car, getting that big Russian embrace and a bunch of kisses. Next I'm walking toward the Palace with Vassily's arm draped over my shoulders. Big smiles all around, mouths going. If the DEA surveillance team had captured sound, which I was sure they had, Braunstein had the volume control off.

"Please don't read anything into this, Luther," Francesca Russo said after Braunstein touched a button on the camcorder and blacked the computer screen, "but that certainly does look friendly, doesn't it? Like you guys are old comrades? Best buddies?"

"We were, and you should already know why, since you checked my background," I said as evenly as I could. It took some effort. I hadn't reckoned any Fed surveillance was already in place when Dog and I made that first visit.

"Oh, we've got a little theory," Russo said. "Love to hear your version, to check if our speculations are correct. Or if we're just behind the curve again."

"Vassily was Spetsnaz, Russian Special Forces," I said, following the cardinal rule of lying: stay as close to the truth as you can without giving the game away. "Some Spetsnaz guys were riding very unofficially and very secretly with our Special Forces guys through Desert Storm. 'Observers.' You know, the Soviets becoming our new best friends and all that shit. My team got Vassily, I'm fluent in Russian, we got along great. So when he started moving into Baltimore, making contacts and stuff, my partner got a cell number from a snitch. I called, it's Vassily. Simple as that. Everything that followed is in the report."

"Yes, in the report. Very simple and straightforward. Except for what you just told us about Desert Storm," Braunstein said. I noticed Dugal was straining to keep his face set, to keep any surprise from showing.

"Nothing but history. Government-mandated secret history," I said. "Anyway, not relevent. We made the connection through my partner's source, then we did the sting."

"And Vassily's crew made bail, then conveniently disappeared," Braunstein said.

"Sure, and you must already know why, too," I said. "Vassily thought one was a snitch, couldn't get anyone to admit it, so he took them all out, top to bottom.

"In the Russian military," I went on, "dealing with a fuck-up like that is called 'the vertical stroke.' Though usually the offenders don't get dead, they just get demoted or fired."

"Vertical stroke? Love it. Maybe I'm working with the wrong people. Sounds like the Russians share my warped sense of humor," Russo laughed again. "You think perhaps the bosses in Moscow decided to include Vassily in this stroke too?"

"Since you say he had bosses in Moscow, why not?" I said. "He was in charge of an operation that failed."

"Would they have had to import a team to do it?" Braunstein asked.

"Maybe not. The Russians are suspicious fucks. Maybe they had guys here already watching Vassily," I said. "Or maybe not."

"Because we haven't found any trace of in-comers since your bust, and your war," Russo said. "How's your city narc friend? Dog, isn't it? Still in a coma from a Russian bullet?"

If the bitch's voice had been pitched one note differently, I'd have knuckled her thorax right there.

"And we have a pretty solid make on all the Brighton players who aren't dead," Braunstein said, hitting a camcorder button. "Except this guy."

A quick flicker, and I'm a movie star again, though the rez isn't so high this time and the face of the slob in the hooded sweatshirt standing next to Vassily's Mercedes outside the Palace late one night a few weeks after the bust is deep in shadow. I know the timing precisely because it's me in that sweatshirt, me that Vassily wraps in a bear hug when he comes charging out of the Palace's blue steel service door, me whispering to Vassily about calling off all the shooting, telling him we're even. And not meaning a word of it, just setting him up to be hit a few nights later.

"Any idea who the sweatshirt is?" Braunstein asked, making the video loop so I can watch it again and again. No sound, but this time I'm sure there isn't any. No tech I know of could have picked up what Vassily and I whispered. And no surprise either. I'd been stalking Vassily for days and spotted the Fed surveillance team at the start. The team was the only reason I went to the Palace that night. I knew Vassily must be aware of the watchers too, and wouldn't kill me on camera.

"Not a clue," I said. "Even if I could see his face, it wouldn't mean a thing, since every one of Vassily's crew I met is dead."

Braunstein turned off the computer, unplugged the camcorder, and stuffed both back into his briefcase. Then he shrugged at Russo.

"Too bad," she said.

"We were hoping, you see, that an ID or a lead on who killed Vassily might help us get on the trail of whoever is taking his place," Braunstein said to Dugal. "We're certain somebody is. There is no way the Moscow boys can let a power vacuum develop in Brighton Beach. It would cause them all sorts of problems with control."

"Yes, I can see that." Dugal said. "Very intractable problems. The Brighton locals might even start acting like, say, Chechens. Moscow could be looking at a very nasty situation in, what was the word you used, a subsidiary? Well, the best I can say is that if we get any more Russian activity in the county, we'll let you know at once."

"We'd appreciate that a lot. We appreciate your time today," Russo said. Then she turned to me, flashed what she must have thought was a winning smile. "Great work busting these fucks, Luther. I admire your tactics. And your technique."

Sure.

After Braunstein and Russo left, Dugal gazed thoughtfully at me for a while. "I'm concluding that it might be a good thing to lower your profile for a while, Luther," he said eventually. "It must have struck you that there was a subtext to what went down here just now. Some disinformation, too, about the DEA agenda. Nothing I can pinpoint, but very clearly present. Agreed?"

"Yeah," I said. "They're fucking with us, they're fishing for something."

"Exactly my impression. So what I propose is this. We're getting a lot of signals from the north of the county that some fairly major methamphetamine cooking and distribution is developing. How would you feel about spending some time in the sticks undercover, seeing what you can see about this?"

"Sure. Why not? I love humping the boonies," I said.

Which is why, I'm thinking now in my apartment four or five months later, shoulder throbbing, I'm in the state I'm in. One way or another.

. . .

I put the tape back in the safe. Then I go into the little kitchen, grind some beans, get a pot of coffee brewing. I slide Everlast's second CD, *Eat at Whitey's*, into the Aiwa. The beat's buckin', but some of the gangsta phrases come on and I start thinking about Dog. My best nigger, and one jammin' cop. Took a frangible bullet in the face from an AKSU-74. One of Vassily's shooters did it. At least Dog came out of that coma. But he'll never be the same again. Like me, after a countersniper clipped my head in Sarajevo. But much worse off, so far.

I drop a few Percosets with my first sips of coffee, try to wipe my mind blank. But I'm still in recall mode.

Not three hours after that meeting in Dugal's office, I'd gotten a call from Russo. Could we meet for a drink that evening, she'd asked, all easy and amiable. Fuck you, I thought. But then considered it'd be in my best interest to find out a little more about what the DEA was up to. So I said sure, told her to meet me at Flannery's. A nice pub near the stately old county courthouse, a place where no cops ever went, which is why Annie and I liked to hang there. Russo didn't know the place, but said she'd find it.

She did. I watched her come in from my usual table near the back. She was still wearing that gray suit. The skirt was shorter than I'd remembered. She flashed that anchorwoman's smile when she spotted me and walked over. I guessed that callous on her hand wasn't strictly from twice-a-week sessions at some karate dojo, from the loose but controlled way she moved. She'd been in some action, for sure.

"You might want to carry small-of-the-back, 'cause you're too skinny for that FBI-style butt-forward paddle holster," I said as she sat down. "You're printing through the jacket. Maybe something smaller than a Glock 22, too. Which is what the print suggests."

"Aren't you clever," Francesca Russo said. "But guess what? The only people who could spot I'm carrying are types I want to know that. Since I'm not undercover at the moment. And I've got a solid long-term relationship with my Glock."

"You like what it does for you?"

"Love the .40 madly," she said. "Ask any woman, Luther. Size does matter. And by the way, you're printing, too."

"Sure."

"I didn't mean your pistol. Meant your attitude. Is it just me you don't like? Or Feds in general?" She ordered a pint of Guinness, drained a third of it in one go. "We're a lot alike, you and I."

"Doubt that very much."

"Try this: we're not exactly straight. We get pissed off at the rules. We bend them when we want to. We break them when we have to, to get a job done. Am I right?"

"Let's cut the shit," I said. "What's your real interest in Russians?"

"None. That's all Braunstein's business. He just thought it would be politic to have a local along when he came calling. I was supposed to be liaison. Poor choice on his part. I'm not much good at liaising. As you proved."

"What are you good at?"

"Cases. One or two little other things," she said. "That's why I'm so damned bored in Baltimore. On the DEA scale, it's the minors. The show's in Miami, Phoenix, L.A., New York."

"So why are you here?"

"I ran with the big boys in the high-intensity zones for a couple of years. Handled some major things better than most of those dicks could. Maybe they felt threatened. Maybe I didn't bother to kiss the right asses. So just about the time you were going round and round with your Russian friends, I got exiled here. They covered it with a promotion to bureau chief. But it's still exile."

"Yeah? And what do you want from a suburban narc like me? Shoulder to cry on?"

"Hey, Luther? First, get fucked." She smiled. "Second, since I have to be here, I figured I might try to find a local who was into some action, since my guys seem to prefer sitting on their cans. You seemed likely. Because you're in exile too."

"Wrong."

Russo unleashed that laugh once more. "Okay, first contact fails. Usually does with me, given my people skills. But I think I'll be seeing you around."

"Doubt that," I said, dropping a ten on the table to cover the drinks and leaving her sitting there, a third of her Guinness still in the pint.

6.

I'm a spectre. I'm a demon from hell, silent moving death. I garrote one of Vassily's heavies as soon as I slip into his house, snick three bullets from a silenced High Standard semi-auto into the ear of another. Then I'm upstairs in Vassily's bedroom. He's broken my arm before I put him down with three snicks of the pistol into his groin, sap him senseless, truss him immobile with duct tape. I have a scalpel in my hand. I'm about to cut his carotid, watch him pump his own life away with every beat of his heart. But it's all so slow, so very slow. And dim as a dream.

It is a dream.

The door buzzer and Helen's voice calling yank me out of it. I'm lying there on the futon in the living room, no clue at all how long I've slept. No clue, for an instant, why my left arm and shoulder are bandaged tight, or why I'm wearing a sweater about five sizes too large.

And shaken. I never dream of the things I've done, the lives I've taken.

"You look wasted, Luther," Helen says when I let her in. Then her clear laugh centers me perfectly in the now. "That sweater!

Were you on drugs when you got that thing? Of course! You are on drugs. Painkillers up to the eyeballs. Are you gonna be selfish and not share, babe?"

"Hello, pretty," I say. My grin couldn't be broader, or more genuine. I am so delighted to see this bright, perfect girl, sexy as hell in low-cut, steel-gray leather pants, a cropped olive top that reveals her navel, and a black duster so thin and drapey it's hard to believe it's leather too. Hard to believe she's been my lover so long, hard to believe how well I know her smell, the taste of every part of her, the feel of her young skin.

"How'd you know I'd be home?" I ask, grabbing a bag of Thai take-out from her and putting it on the kitchen counter, then kissing her.

"How else? IB tells MJ, MJ calls Helen. Luther made a promise to Helen when he was in the hospital. Helen comes over to see if he can keep it." She smiles. "But in case you can't, I've come prepared," she says. "Dinner, some new music, a DVD. And clean panties for tomorrow, since I'm staying overnight, like it or not."

"Like it lots. But given this and this," I say, pointing to my left shoulder and to the plastic container of Percoset tabs, "I'm afraid I can't guarantee much, even with you on top."

A little pout then, quickly replaced by the smile. "At least you remembered! I wasn't real sure how clear-minded you were when I came to the hospital. God, that was so scary, Luther. You're sure you're okay? No complications? No, I guess not, or they wouldn't have let you come home."

"I'm doing good. Just this bandage is a problem. Can't even take a shower."

"Got any Saran Wrap? We'll cover it up with that and I'll give you a bath and a shampoo. Decide. Eat first, then the bath? Or the other way around?"

Bath wins. Soon enough, shoulder wrapped and taped, I'm lying up to my chin in hot water made silky and smooth with lavender-scented oils. Helen's taken off her leathers; she's kneeling on a folded towel next to the tub. Her long fingers are spreading suds through my hair, then massaging my scalp. It's paradise. I'm just lying there, eyes closed, digging every sensation; first time since I was capped that I've gotten anything besides an in-bed cold sponging. I want it to last a long, long time.

It does. But it still feels too soon when Helen helps me, limp and weak, out of the tub, dries me off and wraps me in a terry robe. She microwaves a couple of the Thai dishes that have gone cold, then sets the food on the low maple table. "You gotta hear this, Luther," she says, putting a CD on. She sits on a floor cushion on the opposite side of the table from me. "Group called Reindeer Section. Just discovered them on the Net. Really fresh sound."

The music's lo-fi, very cool. The food's wonderful, or maybe it just seems so much better than usual because of what I've had to eat lately. We don't talk much for a while.

"So," she says, once she's finished the last of the lemongrass chicken. "What's it feel like?"

"Feels like heaven."

"That isn't where you would've gone, babe," she says with a grin. "I mean, getting shot. What's that feel like?"

A little bit of the contentment just slides away. I don't blame Helen, though. She's only twenty-one. How could she not have picked up some of my bad attitudes after all this time, how could she know what bullshit all that casual and careless talk about extreme violence is? I decide to drop the jive-ass warrior pose for once.

"You don't feel much at all physically, for a moment, except a big blunt impact. The adrenaline dump's too large. You can't believe you've been hit, for a moment. You feel really stupid, like you've fucked up bad. Then you feel scared, scared as hell. You piss yourself. You lose control of your bladder and you piss in your pants. Then, then an agony you cannot believe slams through you. Depending on where you've been hit, the pain can be so bad you might even wish you'd been killed instantly."

Helen pales. "Oh, God, Luther. I'm an idiot for asking a question like that. I am such an airhead. I can't even look at you, I'm so embarrassed. Shit, can't we erase this?"

She starts to cry. I take her hand.

"Hey, it's okay. Really," I say, kissing her fingertips one after the other. "It was a natural question, not a dumb one. Considering you know me the way you do, considering the way you've heard me talk. I just gave you a true answer this time. I'm so sorry if it's upset you. Come over here. Please?"

She slides around the table, snugs herself in under my good right arm. The tears have lessened, but she's shuddering. "You've always made it seem like some kind of game before. Lots of bang-bang, but nobody gets hurt," she says. "Now it suddenly seems too real. My God, you just went through it for real. Oh, Luther, this is so scary."

"Shhh. It's all okay. We're safe and sound," I whisper in her ear, holding her close. I kiss the top of her head. I stroke her for a long time, just her face and arm for a while, but moving eventually to a small, soft breast. I can feel her body untense. She says, "Love you forever," when I suggest we move to the bedroom futon and see if I can fulfill my promise.

We move. I fail.

. . .

Very late, Helen deep in dreams. I have to lie flat on my back—not my preferred sleep position. Sleep won't come, though I dropped four Percosets. It's recall mode again.

After Vassily, I'd had enough. I'd had too much, maybe. For the first time in my adult life I didn't want any more bang-bang. Just thinking about it made me feel sick, instead of giving me the rush it always had before. So, when I felt sure there was going to be no counterstroke, that the general threat level was low to moderate, I demilitarized myself altogether. Hell, I'd been acting like the county was a fucking war zone. No more. I'd greased and packed my twin Heckler & Koch MP5s, my HK SOCOM .45 pistol, my .50AE Desert Eagle. I'd wrapped up my stash of C4 explosive and detonators, a dozen grenades. Locked it all in a heavy-gauge steel case, drove it down to Tyding's Landing in the Virgina Tidewater country, where my father, Gunnery Sergeant Thomas "One-Way" Ewing, USMC (retired), lives with Momma in a neat white clapboard house on a creek. Gunny, in possession of some prohibited military souvenirs himself, has a steel-doored cinderblock strongroom in his basement. He didn't mind at all if I left my case there.

Now I'm just a regular cop, even if my equipment isn't standard BCPD issue. Now I carry a service-grade SIG 226 in .357SIG. My back-up piece is a Walther P5 in 9mm, old-tech but beautifully handcrafted and absolutely reliable; hell, maybe 40,000 European cops carry the P5 as their issue weapon. I'd had both my pistols trigger-jobbed, tuned, and accurized, but almost everyone who carries has that done.

Just a copper on the beat, as McKibbin liked to say. Anybody sniffs around—the DEA or the FBI or our Internal Affairs—I'm an ordinary plainclothes detective on the narcotics squad.

Could be much worse, I tell myself. I could still be the Virginia state trooper I was just after the army, cruising highways in a ridiculous Smokey uniform until a suit from the CIA invited me and a bunch of other disreputable but highly skilled special ops veterans to do a little work in the Balkans. Might still be, if that head shot hadn't put me in a Swiss hospital for ten months, and the Company hadn't been better than I expected about resettlement after I healed up.

Could be worse in all sorts of ways, I think, looking at Helen's peaceful face, so lovely on the pillow beside me. Sudden stab of regret in advance, now. The girl will be graduating in a couple of months. She'll probably go home to her rich family in Westport, Connecticut, for the summer, then on to graduate school, English Lit.

I'm going to lose her. I'd thought that was the way I wanted things. I explained it all once to Annie when she questioned me about my string of co-ed girlfriends. Told her it was deliberate, told her I didn't want a future with any one woman.

Now, looking at Helen, I wonder if that all wasn't just another lie. Wonder if my whole life hasn't been mainly a string of lies.

A good night turned bad, any way I look at it. And too long. I pretend to be asleep when Helen rises and gets dressed in the morning. Give her a sleepy "Uh huh" when she says "Call me later, babe? Maybe keep your promise one of these nights soon?" and leaves my apartment.

■ ■ ■

As the day goes on, I start to feel very clear about one thing. The worst part of getting hurt is not getting hurt. It's the tedious, boring, brain-numbing time it takes to get healed. It's being confined to quarters, no place you can go, nothing worthwhile you can do. It's the certainty that, for a while, when you do go back to work, you're going to be superglued to your fucking desk chair instead of running around chasing bad guys, having some fun on the streets.

It gets more depressing. I start thinking that apart from work, so much of what you do in your waking hours is pure maintainance: you wash yourself, you wash your clothes, you wash your car, you vacuum your crib, maybe change the sheets every so often, cook some meals, and wash up afterward.

And when you're not doing any of that you're most likely engaged in bullshit exchanges with people who pass like ghosts through your day: the fucking mailman, the girl who serves you coffee, the waitress at your regular lunch spot, the Korean behind the counter where you have some clothes dry-cleaned, the teller at your bank who, even if you've been greeting her by name for years, in truth isn't any more of a presence in your life than a fucking ATM machine. You wouldn't know if her dad had recently died, or if she'd had an abortion a few weeks ago, or if her boyfriend had just ditched her for a man. And if by some chance you did learn anything like that, you wouldn't care much.

And then there are those you do care about. Like poor fucking Dog. I want to weep for the man.

A down, down day. I'm feeling sad and foul when somebody leans on my buzzer at about seven that evening.

I go to the door. "What?" I snarl through it. I'm in no mood for visits by Jehovah's Witnesses or Roper pollsters or anybody at all.

"It's your friendly local Fed."

That TV voice jolts me. I open up and Francesca Russo's standing there. I haven't seen her since that night at Flannery's. This time, no gray suit. Navy cashmere V-neck, Levi's, styled hair destyled, pulled back into a pony tail. She vaguely waves a six-pack of Guinness Draft in cans as she walks right past me to the kitchen. I see her ass is high and tight, see she's carrying her Glock in the small of her back. She puts the six-pack on the counter, breaks one loose, pops it.

"Drink?" she says.

"I don't. Much."

"I do," she grins, taking a long pull. "Interrupting anything important, falling by like this? Disturbing you in any way? I heard you got popped. I was around this area, thought I'd see how you were making out. Hope you don't mind."

"Not much," I say.

"You're not still nursing some hostility or anything, then? No lingering anger? No 'who does this fucking DEA bitch think she is, showing up at my home' sort of feelings? After all these months?"

"Nah," I say. "And I won't even bother asking how you knew where I stay."

Then that laugh. But some of the edge seems absent. She looks around my apartment, looks back at me. I've got Reindeer Section on the Aiwa.

"Nice place. Very minimalist. My taste, too. Who's the band? Never heard them before. Cool sound," she says.

"Some new indie group a friend of mine heard on the Net," I say. I'm feeling a little revved, wanting to see how this plays out. "Have a seat."

Russo eases herself onto one of the floor cushions by the table. I sit on the futon. Only then do I notice she's barefooted. Quick glance: her ankle boots are parked right next to the door. Pretty slick, I think.

"So how are you doing, Luther?" she says. "You're looking pretty good for a guy who took a hit from a .45. Amazingly good, actually."

"I've been worse."

"Yeah, much worse. So I've been told."

"C'mon. You're too smart to credit rumors. And too clever to think you're going to get any confirmation, even if there was anything to them. Which there isn't."

The laugh once more. "You know, Braunstein actually bought your story about Vassily riding your buggy in Iraq. Sarajevo never even entered his bureaucratic little mind. Hey! I really like this tune. What's the name of the band again?"

"Reindeer Section," I say. I'm focused on her eyes now. I'm searching for how much she knows, how she knows it.

"Have to remember that, pick up the CD," she says, swaying a little to the music. "Quantum leap from sitting around drinking rakia, listening to Yugoslav disco, no?"

"You been dropping something illegal, or are you just naturally whacked, Francesca?" I say. "You seem to have some really strange obsessions."

"You mean about Bosnia in general, Sarajevo in particular, a merc sniper known as Shooter? Whose best buddy there was called Vassily? Same guy who was called the Comanche until he got kicked out of the Special Forces for wasting a whole bunch of Iraqis who'd surrendered?" She drains her Guinness, smiles, goes to the counter for another, and very gracefully assumes the lotus position on the cushion. "Just history, as you called it during that awful meeting in Dugal's office. But I'm an amateur historian. For the fun of it only, no purpose at all."

"And I have no idea what you're talking about. Even if I did, I'd have nothing to say."

"Perfect rulebook response, Luther. The trainers would be proud of you. By the way, your room number in that hospital in Lausanne was 57G."

Fuck. The bitch has me cold. And I know how. It's my turn to laugh, to act like I'm laughing it all off. Russo reads me anyway.

"Now you know my dark secret, don't you?" she says. "Yeah, you got it, all right. Now you know I used to work for the Company, that I've still got friends there who will slip me file data."

"This supposed to impress me or something? I'm supposed to feel nervous, edgy? A little off-balance at least?"

"I doubt anything I could say or do would achieve that," she says. "Hey! I'll even tell you my history. I was young, easily bored. You know how that is. So I left because I was stuck behind a desk at Langley and I wanted some action. The DEA seemed like the right place for that, not nearly so buttoned-up and stiff as the FBI. And so it was, 'til I got posted here.

"I'm telling you all this," she goes on, "because it looks like our paths are going to cross, like I said at Flannery's that night we got off to a bad start. And I want you to know who exactly you're going to be rubbing up against."

"Sorry, but I'm spoken for," I say.

"Okay, have your little flirty joke, if that sort of thing makes you happy. Here's what makes me happy: crystal meth. Lots of crystal meth. You've been taking a look yourself into that traffick in the north of the county."

"Yeah, and pretty soon I'll be back up there doing it again."

"I'm there already. Not real interested in a joint operation or anything. Sure you're not either. But I want you to know what I'm up to, because it would be a real shame if my team and you guys bumped, got confused, and started shooting at each other or something idiotic like that. Also thought it might be a good idea if we talked once in a while, traded some intelligence."

"I've got nothing to trade."

"But you will soon enough," Russo says. "Meanwhile, I'll give up what I've got. One of the hottest spots for meth cooking has been Grundy County, Tennessee. Redneck heaven, local cops as dumb as a box of rocks. The problem, for the bad guys, is distribution, Grundy being in the middle of fucking nowhere. Baltimore County, on the other hand? Interstate 83 makes easy hook-ups south to I-95 and the whole D.C.–to–New York corridor. And north to the Pennsylvania network, which means an east-west route. Short hauls to big markets."

"I didn't exactly see many signs of industrial-scale production, though," I say.

"It's early days yet," she says. "Let it alone, it'll be bigger than Grundy in six months, a year."

"Maybe you're right. I wouldn't know," I say. "But so what? Speed's still not major. I thought you were into cartel-scale action."

"You see any around here? No. If you did, you'd be all over it. And so would I. Meth's the only game playing at the moment. Since you guys fucked up the Russians, who fucked up the city gangstas. So I'll take on anything that'll get me unstuck from my desk."

She rises in one smooth motion, takes a card from the wallet that's been riding in her hip pocket—Russo doesn't have a thing for handbags, apparently—scribbles two numbers on it.

"Here's my cell number, and my home phone. Both clean. Give me a call sometime?" she says. Then she goes to the door, pulls on her boots.

"When you're better and back on the case," she smiles, "think twice up in the sticks. Literally. Twins, identical."

"Oh, sure. Twins. I'll make a note."

Russo laughs then. "Evil dwarf types. Short, stocky, beady little eyes, you know? Don't let that fool you. They're smart operators, very tough, and ruthless as hell."

As soon as Russo leaves, I go to my front window. Down below, idling at the building's entrance, is a huge and supremely ugly SUV, a Cadillac Escalade, black. A tall black dude in a black suit is flicking dust off the gleaming clear-coat with a piece of gray terry. Shaved head, a pointy goatee, and big challenges being inconspicuous, besides his taste in vehicles: there are dead-white splotches on his face and hands. He must have that disease that eliminates the melanin from your skin. He opens the front passenger door like a chauffeur when Russo lopes up, gently closes it when she's seated. She doesn't rate a driver, so the goatee must be one of her agents. Goatee walks around the bloated front of the Escalade, climbs carefully up into the driver's seat like he's worried about scuffing the upholstery, and pulls that monster away.

7. "Okay, okay. You're gonna love this," Ice Box says, huge hands white-knuckled on the steering wheel of a Ford pickup he's never driven before. Feels like the Ford would much rather drive itself—at least judging by the way we're cruising less than perfectly straight down a perfectly straight stretch of Bently Road between the nothing little towns of Five Forks and Bently Springs.

"Remember now, this is direct from the morning paper. Double murderer Thomas Grasso, on death row in the Oklahoma State Penitentiary, has ordered his last meal. You ready?" IB says. "A dozen steamed clams flavored with a wedge of lemon, two dozen steamed mussels, six barbecued spare ribs with sweet and sour sauce, a cheeseburger, a can of Spaghetti-Os, a strawberry milk shake, and half a pumpkin pie."

IB's shaking with laughter, the Ford's offside tires spray shoulder gravel until he jerks the truck back onto the asphalt.

"Hell, they can skip the lethal injection, just let him die of indigestion. Spaghetti-Os and a strawberry milk shake? Christ!" he says.

IB's immune to ptomaine, I'm thinking. The crap he eats has

just weirded out his brain. For months now, first thing he does every morning is scan the *Sun* for those strange little wire service stories they use to fill up columns that have run a paragraph or two short. He cuts out the most bizarre, keeps them in a folder. Sooner or later, he tells me.

"What? What? You don't think that's hilarious?" he says when he doesn't hear even a chuckle. He looks over at me. Another gravel spray, another lurch back onto the road.

"Right this minute, I'd love a lethal injection," I say. My stomach's churning. "It'd be the perfect antidote to those Whoppers with cheese and underdone fries you just made us scarf for lunch. And this seasickness I'm getting from the way you're driving."

"Aw, man, are you turning pussy on me or what?" he complains. "This fuckin' truck just won't go straight. Wheels gotta be out of alignment or some shit. And my Whopper was delicious."

The pickup—confiscated from a busted grass dealer—is my idea. I'd realized the first time I'd come up here in the sticks that there was an image problem. Driving my silver Audi and wearing baggy gangsta rapper gear flew real well with the overprivileged white kids on the Towson-Cockeysville axis I'd been working. Missed the irony completely, the stupid fucks, of dressing like city gang-bangers themselves. But I drew some hard looks up north.

So I switched my duty attire. To another total cliché. Bought a couple of pairs of Wal-Mart jeans, some plaid and some plain workshirts, a good pair of Red Wing steel-toed boots, a baseball-type cap with a John Deere logo up front. That's what I'm wearing now, a month since I got shot. Haven't had a haircut since I shaved my head for the Russian run last fall; don't plan on getting one anytime soon. Pay attention to the little details, too. Don't cut my fingernails very often, leave the thin crescents of dirt under them.

The pickup's perfect: clearly hard-used, but sporting fancy custom chromed wheels and fat tires. An NRA decal on the window, two bumper stickers: "Keep Honking, I'm Re-Loading" and "When in Doubt, EMPTY the Magazine." Even a gun rack. It's overkill, but sometimes I hang the cheapest Savage .30-06 wearing the cheapest BEC scope on it.

Not that any of this has done us good. We've been to every substation north of Cockeysville, all of them small, all of them all-uniform, no plainclothes guys at all. "People here, they like their police to look like police," was the explanation I got from the sergeant in charge of one. "Since most of what we get is domestic violence, bar fights, once in a while an armed robbery at a gas station or convenience store, it works out pretty well. Oh, yeah, traffic work, too. Lots of speeding tickets, DUIs."

These guys are supposed to know their turf, and the people who live there. They do. Problem is, they've got no idea what these folks get up to. When we've asked about possible drug dealers, all they've given us is some names of people it turned out they just didn't much like: a few bikers, a long-distance trucker with a nasty habit of punching out his wife once in a while, even a teenager whose only encounter with law enforcement came about because he got caught keying the paint on a brand-new BCPD cruiser. We tracked and talked to every name we got. Not one seemed likely. And not one cop ever heard of any identical twins who might be in the business. So much for Russo's evil dwarves.

I never told anyone about her visit. Never mentioned to Dugal that the DEA had some interest up here. Never called Russo either. Now I'm thinking I may have to.

"Should I be turning off around here anywhere?" IB asks. "I mean, you're supposed to be the navigator here, am I right? I'm right. So navigate, okay?"

We're on our way to see some farmer who's been complaining to the local cops that he thinks there's a bunch of people trespassing and messing around in his woods; he's got about 150 acres too hilly and rocky to go under the plow. A uniform drove around, found a track into the woods that only a four-wheel drive could handle. Brilliant fuck. He parks his cruiser right beside the track all day for two days, probably reading skin mags and jerking off, mostly. Sees nobody coming or going, tells his boss the old man must be dreaming. The farmer gets brushed off the next few times he phones.

The old man's name is Early. We're going to have a talk with Early. It'll probably yield dick. But we're gonna talk anyway.

I see the farm long before I see any turn-off, one of those classic two-story wood Victorian houses about a half-mile in from the road, a white island in a sea of low, fresh, green something or other, maybe soy beans or alfalfa. A couple of huge old oaks and beeches in early leaf near it, and beyond it the roof of a barn and the dome of a silo.

"Slow it down, IB," I say. "Think that's the place up ahead on the left. Supposed to be a cow skull on the mailbox at the entrance."

"Cow skull? Man, the taste level out here astonishes me. Lawn dwarves, that sort of thing, I can understand. Don't care for them myself, but I can see how some people would think they're cute. Skulls and shit? Forget about it."

I laugh then.

"Oh, so you finally got the thing about Grasso's last meal, huh?" IB says. "About fucking time."

"About a hundred meters along. On the left. That's the guy's driveway," I say.

IB makes the turn, sways the Ford along the gravel drive, sort of bucks to a stop near the house. I get out, rotate my left shoulder a few times. It stiffens up a little if I sit still too long. I scan the place. Very tidy. The little patch of lawn's been mowed, there are daffodils around the trees and some other spring flowers blooming in a mulched bed along the base of the porch. The paint on the house and the red barn off to the back a few hundred feet isn't faded or peeling. But it's dead quiet. There's nobody around.

IB thuds up the porch steps, me trailing, and knocks on the front door. Waits. Knocks again. Waits, tries once more.

"Nobody home, I guess," IB says. "Thought you called, told him we were coming?"

"I did."

Then I hear someone behind us rack a shell into the chamber of his shotgun. "Turn around, slow, you hear? And tell me what it is you think you're doing, besides trespassing on my property."

"Now, Mr. Early," I say, turning. There's a man in denim overalls at the foot of the porch steps, an old 12-gauge pump, looks like a classic Ithaca, shouldered and pointed at our stomachs.

"It's Mr. Wynn. Early's my Christian name, boy. And since your friends already dropped by a little while ago, what're you here for?"

"Aw, fuck," IB sighs.

"You watch your mouth, boy. I won't have that kind of talk. I'm church-going. Your friends were as foul as you. If I'd had my Ithaca then, I'd have taught them a thing or two."

"Mr. Wynn, we're police detectives. My name's Ewing and this is my partner. I phoned you earlier about your trespassing problem, remember?"

"Yeah, I remember a fella phoned. You don't look like the police to me, though. You look more like the fellas that came busting up here on motorcycles a little while ago, held a revolver to my head and told me I'd best not be calling the police about my woods ever again."

"We are plainclothes detectives from BCPD headquarters in Towson, Mr. Wynn," I say. "You spoke to me around ten this morning. I'm going to reach in my pocket, and throw you my badge."

"No, you are not going to throw anything. I'd have to take a hand off my shotgun then, wouldn't I? So you're just going to walk down here, nice and slow, and show me this badge you claim you got. And the fat boy there isn't going to even twitch while you do that."

"Yessir. Understood." I take the steps slowly, my right arm stretched out straight toward the man, badge wallet open in my hand so he can see the photo ID and the gold shield.

"You can stop right there," he says, when I'm about two feet from the shotgun's muzzle. "I can read fine at this distance."

He looks hard at the photo ID, looks at my face, looks hard at the shield, looks at my face again. Then he seems to consider whether face and photo are a close enough match. For a long time. I don't move, I don't say a thing. Finally, he unshoulders the Ithaca and points the barrel toward the sky.

"Suppose you must be who you say. But I still say you don't look like police. Driving a pickup too, not a police car," he says. "Your friend can come down now. We'll talk."

"Fine, Mr. Wynn. Like I said, I'm Detective Ewing and this is Detective Cutrone. We're very interested in what's going on in your woods. But I'd appreciate it if you'd shuck that chambered shell."

"Oh, that?" he says, looking at his shotgun. "Yes, I don't much like firearms with chambered rounds. Dangerous. Fools are always shootin' themselves or somebody else during hunting season, walking around chambered."

"Oh, God," IB says when he joins us.

"Watch your tone when you utter His name, boy. I've explained my feelings."

"Sorry, Mr. Wynn. Having a 12-gauge pointed at me generally makes me nervous," IB says.

"I guess it might. That revolver sure made me nervous. Call me Early, boys."

■ ■ ■

"Goddamn shit-kicking son of a bitch! The fuck might have shot us, Luther. You realize that? Son of a bitch, I hate shit like that," IB says as we're driving home. "We should have arrested him."

"Little tense these days, IB?" I say.

"Hell no. I'm cool, I'm cool."

"Like hell."

"Hey, man, geriatric fingers on shotgun triggers ain't funny. Suppose he had a spasm or something? Jesus! I got the twins to think about, all right? And MJ would kill me if I got killed."

"She would, absolutely." I grin. "But give the old man a break. By his lights, he'd have been right to shoot us. How'd you like to have some biker push the barrel of a .44 magnum against your temple?"

"I hate shit like that, too, now that you mention it." IB laughs suddenly. The Ford swerves about a yard over the white center line, swerves back into our lane.

"What we got from Early Wynn, besides a scary minute or two, is a possible break. No, make that a highly probable break," I say.

IB laughs again. "Nah, Early was a fastballer. No breaking stuff at all."

"What?"

"Early Wynn, man. Great fastball."

"You losing it or what?" I say.

"Your ignorance astounds me, Luther. I'm talking about one of the best pitchers ever, won three hundred games lifetime. He's a Hall of Famer, for Christ's sake."

"Baseball or something?"

"No, numbnuts, I'm talking about badminton." IB's chuckling. "Early Wynn pitched for the Senators, Indians, White Sox. It's really weird, this old coot having the same name as a baseball great, that's all."

"What is it with you and sports shit that happened before we were born?" I'm saying when IB's cell chirps. He takes a hand off the wheel, holds the phone to his ear. I reach over and put my left hand on the wheel, countering most of what IB's doing to it.

"Yeah? Oh, hey. What's happening man?" IB says. "Yeah? Yeah? No shit! Sure. Ahh, don't know. Hang on."

"Luther, are we anywhere near where some Rayville Road hits Armacost Road?"

I check my map. "Maybe five miles northeast."

"Luther says five miles. Right. Okay. Catch you later, dude."

IB pockets the phone, puts his right hand back on the wheel. I take mine off. "Well?" I say.

"Radik's got a multiple," IB says. Radik is chief of the homicide squad. "Like a multiple multiple down on . . . shit, you remember the names of those roads?"

"Rayville and Armacost."

"Anyway, somebody phoned it in to Towson; he's on his way from there. But he asked if we'd do him a favor, go there fast, make sure the dumb-ass local uniforms he called don't fuck up the scene too bad before he gets there. I told him okay."

"Aw, fuck me," I say. "I wanna get home. I've got a hot date tonight."

"Chill, birdbones. Your whole life's one great big hot date. The way you always tell it anyway." IB giggles. "If the fuckin' horny navigator would tell the fuckin' pilot where we're fuckin' going, we can get this over quick and the navigator can go get fucked. Am I fuckin' right, or am I right?"

In ten minutes, with maybe twenty swerves and shoulder sprays, we're there. Easy to spot. Two cruisers with all their lights flashing, four uniforms unrolling yellow tape. It's a ranch house with aluminum siding set on maybe a quarter-acre, surrounded by forest. There are two lawn dwarves by the front door, but some joker has painted them so it looks like they're wearing GI camo. A large patch of that quarter-acre is asphalt, and there's a huge custom-painted Peterbilt hulking on it, no trailor hitched on. Independent long-distance trucker between runs, I figure. Probably murdered his wife and kids, some shit like that.

IB and I gold-shield the uniforms, ask them very politely to stay at the perimeter, don't touch one single fucking thing, because the homicide chief is on his way and he hates, really hates, it when officers trample a scene. The uniforms look sulky and sullen, but they go sit on the hoods of their cruisers. We should probably just stand around, wait for Radik and the crime scene team. But I'm too curious.

"Let's check it out," I say to IB.

"Nah. You check it out if you want to. Murder scenes give me the creeps," he says.

So I move out, very carefully, on a wide circle around the house, scanning the ground, watching how and where I step. Looks clean. The house looks clean too, a fairly new prefab job. I'm just rounding the far rear corner when I hear a scream out front. I draw my SIG and move out.

One of the dickhead uniforms who must have a thing for

trucks decided to open the driver's side door of the Peterbilt. Because he's standing right there now, frozen. Staring at the body of a man fallen half out, with what is clearly a large-caliber pistol wound in his head, since the top of it's been blown off and gray brain jelly is showing through the blood.

"Get the fuck back to your cruiser. Now!" I shout. The screamer seems rooted. IB moves over, takes him by the arm, and practically carries him away from the truck and the body.

"Going inside now, IB," I call.

"Be my guest," he calls back. "Hope this dude doesn't puke all over me. He looks like he's gonna puke any second now, Luther."

I holster the SIG, put a surgical glove on my left hand, draw the SIG with my right. Then I try the front door. It swings open with a light push, no need to turn the knob. The place has wall-to-wall, some weird shade of pale blue polyester. The walls are painted dark blue, with white trim. Seems clean and tidy, no sign of any trouble or struggle in the living room, the dining L, the kitchen, the bathroom, and the three bedrooms. There's a water bed in the largest, maybe a dozen *Penthouse* centerfolds taped to the walls. The other two have no furniture at all.

I go back to the kitchen, lightly push on a door, find myself at the top of a steep wood staircase. I see two light switches. I flick them on. The basement gets real bright. I go down the stairs, noting cinderblock walls, a poured concrete floor. Scan the place when I hit the floor. There's a big workbench, home-built of two-by-fours and plywood. The top and the floor around it is heaped with shattered glass vials and chemistry-class beakers, twisted coils of clear plastic tubing, a few metal beaker stands, a couple of handheld propane torches, shit like that. Somebody was trying to cook something down here.

Then, maybe twenty paces to the left near where a hot-water

heater and a well-pump are grouped against a cinderblock wall, I see them.

Seven guys lying face down in a neat row, hands neatly duct-taped behind their backs, one neat hole in the back of each head. I don't feel like moving one to see the exit wound; I know what I'll find from the size of the blood pools. But I do touch the neck of one of the bodies with a fingertip. The skin's lukewarm. Shit, these fucks got capped no more than an hour or two ago.

Radik, the scene team, and a couple of meatwagons are crowded onto the asphalt when I step out the front door. Radik's talking with IB. He's what IB would be if IB was a cheap cotton T-shirt some fool put in a clothes dryer set extra-hot: about one size smaller. Which means he's a huge fuck too.

"Hey, Ewing!" he calls when he sees me. "I only asked you guys to contain the place, not piss all over it."

"I figured you'd have more fun figuring things out if I messed everything up for you. More of a challenge, you know?"

Radik laughs. "So what we got? Besides pretty boy dangling from the Peterbilt here?"

"Kind of boring. Nothing to get a hard-on over. Pretty boy didn't chop up his lovely wife and six adorable children with a sharpened lawn-mower blade, then get in his truck and suicide," I say.

"So, what then?"

I'm beside him now, well away from the local uniforms, who're still sulking on the hoods of their cruisers—except for the screamer, who seems to be lying down in the backseat of one.

"What we've got in this very neat and tastefully decorated place," I say, "is seven little shit-kickers all in a row down the basement. Very definitely executed. Still warm, too."

"Oh, yum," Radik says.

"Favor?"

"Sure."

"There's a lot of busted-up chemistry lab–type stuff down there, too. Your guys find and ID any trace of what they might have been cooking, let me know? I'm pretty sure it wasn't muffins or cherry pies."

"You thinking maybe something really nasty? Like, say, angel food cake?" Radik laughs. "We find any crumbs, you'll be the first to know, man."

IB and I aren't a hundred yards down the road in the Ford when I notice it.

"What the fuck is that awful smell in here?"

IB looks down at his jeans. The Ford swerves. I see some damp spots on the denim below his knees.

"I told you the uniform looked like he was gonna puke, didn't I?" IB says, a real aggrieved expression on his face, as if I'd accused him of letting off an atrocious fart. "Well, he did, the simple fuck. Real sudden. I couldn't get all the way clear."

"And so now I gotta smell vomit for thirty or forty miles? You slob."

"Hey, I wiped the stuff off best I could, man. What else can I do? Throw the jeans away and drive home in my fucking underpants?"

"What you can do," I laugh, "is have the decency to roll your fucking window down and keep it down."

8.

I shower long and slow, shampoo thoroughly, shave carefully. Then I study my wardrobe selection. There's not a lot to choose from, since all my clothes got shredded by the frags that destroyed my Cockeysville place and I'm not a big shopper. But I do want to look good.

That "hot date" I mentioned to IB is only dinner with Annie. Not a date at all, since she's got zero interest in anything but being pals. I've never sensed or seen even a hint of anything romantic from her. Yet, I wonder as I put on a pair of black lightweight wool trousers and a crisply starched collarless white shirt, why does it always feel like a date, like an encounter full of possibilities?

I know why. Momma put it perfectly last autumn, after I'd taken Annie one weekend and Helen another down to Tyding's Landing for a visit. "Helen, she too young, *n'est ce pas*? Nice girlfriend, but short-time only. Annie, she is the one for wife, Luther. *C'est vrai?*" Momma always liked to throw a little French in here and there, since she's from an old Cochin China family with a bit of French colonial blood mixed in, not just another Viet bar girl who hooked her GI. Often considered why she hadn't thrown

Gunny, a big, foul-mouthed spade in the best Corps tradition, back in the Mekong. Why in the world had she married him? Her family must have gone berserk when she did.

Strange match. Stranger issue: me.

I put on a Galco shoulder holster they call "The Executive" that rides high up near my left armpit and will hold only a small pistol like the Walther P5 I slide into it. I can't carry a full-sized semi shoulder-holstered; I'm too skinny—the pistol sticks out front and back. The big SIG never goes on dates anyway. I slip into a black Hugo Boss three-button jacket, pat myself down for wallet and keys, take a last check in the mirror. I guess I'm as good as I ever get, which means passable but not great. Then I lock up the apartment, get into the TT, and head downtown to pick up Annie at her old Federal Hill house, the one she's been personally restoring as long as I've known her.

Annie's great even when she doesn't make an effort. Feels good to be walking her into Bleibtreu, a nouvelle-German place that's supposed to be cool. It looks kind of cool, a sort of Cold War East Berlin style to it, though the shabby bits are artfully artificial. I scan the crowd as a white-aproned waiter leads us to our table. No surprises: prosperous yuppies from the hipper professions, judging by the clothes. No lawyers, no bankers.

"Isn't New York," Annie smiles, "but about as close as it gets in Baltimore."

"Girls are pretty. Most of them," I say.

"No super-Natashas, though."

"No what?"

Annie laughs. "Just something I read in a magazine. The story was about how all these tall gorgeous girls from the Ukraine, Russia, and Poland have flocked to New York. Supermodel ambitions that don't work out. So they've become status dates for the young guys who're hoovering up money. Not high-priced call girls. Technically, at least. But as close as it gets. Really expensive 'dates.'"

"Super-Natashas?" I'm laughing too. "That's perfect. Hey, with my Russian as good as it is, I bet I could get one at bargain rates. If New York wasn't one of my permanent no-go zones."

"You've collected quite a few of those, Luther. Hope you're not planning on adding any more."

"Nothing shaping up, except maybe the country near the Mason-Dixon line."

"Oh, huge loss. Imagine never again being able to revisit all those delightful little towns with strange names, like Shane, Gorsuch Mills, Wiseburg, Grimesville. And Yeoho. Especially Yeoho."

"No problem. Yeoho's too far south. The locals pronounce it Yo, Ho! Sounds exactly like a city pimp calling one of his working girls."

The menu's small but unusual. Annie orders a fish soup—cod-based with leeks and sorrel—followed by grilled Baltic herring. She accepts the waiter's recommendation of a half-bottle of a Moselle. I choose sliced breast of roast goose with string beans and pears, an old Hanseatic specialty, according to the menu, and a glass of red Kaltersee.

"So how's the meth thing going?" Annie asks.

"It goes. Some wicked stuff today that might take me somewhere. Including an eight-man execution scene."

"Jesus! That's more than wicked, I'd say."

"Yeah. But I'm having a hard time getting revved about this operation."

"I would have thought today was enough of a jump-start."

"Didn't do it for me. You know, when I came here after—well, you know what after—it suited me. Kids getting high on Ecstasy, about as low-intensity bad stuff as it gets. But it got too easy pretty fast. So that Russian thing comes along, all of a sudden I'm really digging it. Hi-rez, high intensity, everything I was trained for. Felt like I was working at my real level again. After it was over, though, I felt like I was finished with that warrior shit. For good."

"That would be a good thing to put behind you, Luther."

"Thought it would happen. For a while. But this meth stuff, I don't know. I'm starting to feel like I'm playing in the minor leagues, when I should be in the majors."

"Baseball analogies, Luther?" she says with a grin. "You hate baseball."

"Yeah." I feel sheepish under her gaze. "It's hard to explain. Maybe I'm just wired a certain way. I'm feeling underutilized or something. I'm finding it hard to care if some assholes are making and selling a dumb drug like crystal meth to assholes dumb enough to use it. I feel like I'm wasting my talents on petty shit anybody could handle."

"Ego's getting larger by the minute," Annie says lightly. Then she goes serious on me. "You're starting to worry me here, Luther. Are you paying attention or sleepwalking? A month ago you took a bullet. Somebody tried to kill you. A few hours ago you saw the bodies of eight men, murdered. Probable cause: this meth business you're saying is minor-league. Eight guys dead? What would it take to make it major in your book? Eighty? Eight hundred? A whole battlefield littered with bodies?"

"That's what scares me a little, Annie. It might take eighty or eight hundred on a battlefield. And that's insane. Which makes me insane, doesn't it?"

"I don't think you're insane," she says, taking my hand across the table. "I think by nature and nurture and too much experience you've got a higher threshold of horror than ordinary people. You've built up a tolerance, like a junkie does. You need rehab. I think you were well along detoxing yourself until the Russian thing came along. That episode was like a free double speedball injection to an ex-addict who's been clean for a long time. Then another, and another. When it stopped, the addict wasn't ex-anything."

"But I tried, Annie. Yeah, I dug the Rattle. Lots. But I was glad when it was over. I really chilled. You saw that. I was sure I'd never want to go anywhere like that again."

"But now, for some reason, you *do* want to go somewhere like that again," she says. "There has to have been a trigger. Can you think of anything, anything at all in the past few months, that might have triggered you?"

Somebody has moved up pretty close behind me, slightly to the right. I can feel the presence. I catch Annie's eye and we both shut up. Then I hear, "Hello, Luther" in that TV talking-head voice.

As I half turn, Russo moves around toward my front. For some reason I don't feel at all surprised.

"Hey, Francesca. What're you up to?"

"Same as you, eating unusual German food," she smiles, gesturing across the room. I see a table with one empty chair, and two male faces and one female face vaguely smiling at us. They don't look like Feds, their clothes are too nice, too stylish. But then Russo doesn't look much like my friendly local Fed tonight either. She's ditched the anchorwoman do, had her hair cut blunt around the line of her jaw, with bangs ending just above her eyebrows. Nicer cheekbones than I'd remembered. Nicer mouth, too. She's wearing a short black dress, sleeveless, with a fitted waist and princess seams down the front.

"Friends, not business," she smiles, waving toward her table again. "Did you lose my numbers, Luther? Because I was feeling fairly confident you'd call. It's been more than a month."

"Annie, this is Francesca Russo. Francesca, Annie Mason," I say. They exchange those fake-friendly smiles women sometimes do when they're curious about who may be sleeping with who, or whatever connection there might be. "Matter of fact, Francesca, I was going to call you in a few days."

"I'll look forward to it, Luther," she says, then addresses Annie. "Sorry for the intrusion. Hope I haven't interrupted anything."

"Not at all," Annie says evenly.

"So long, then," Russo says. "Oh, Luther. Watch me going away, see if I'm printing tonight."

The only thing printing as she walks off is that tight, high butt.

"Well?" Annie says. "Who's that babe? You test-driving possible replacements for Helen already? Understandable, I guess, since she'll be graduating in, what, maybe six weeks or so? But I'm a little surprised here. This one's a bit outside your usual age preference."

"Wrong, wrong, and wrong, Detective." I grin. "She's DEA, chief of bureau here. The one I told you tagged along with the big DEA dick from New York who came to talk to Dugal and me after the Russian thing. She got in touch again a few days after I got shot."

"None of that negates what I suggested, Luther."

"It does absolutely. She's a sly, tough, manipulative bitch, and I'd be very reluctant to be alone with her in a closed room anywhere, even Dugal's office, for more than ten seconds," I say. "Plus, she's so old."

Annie laughs and laughs. I always love it when she does that. I'm loving it now. Until she points her fist at me, forefinger extended, squeezes that finger back. And says "Trigger!"

■ ■ ■

First thing next morning, spring sun bright and promising a pretty day, I park behind Early Wynn's barn. Early's decided he digs IB and me. He won't hear no to cups of coffee in his kitchen before we go bird-dogging into his woods. Just a little recon trip, no special equipment beyond nice Steiner binoculars. And my SEAL knife, to make discreet blaze marks that'll help out if we ever want to go back in.

According to Early, there are three ways into those hundred and fifty acres of oaks, maples, and hickories without busting bush, one which he uses himself when he wants to collect a cord or two of firewood. That's the track passable only to four-wheel-drive vehicles that starts off the asphalt road about a half-mile from his farm drive. There's another slightly rougher track that goes in from a little-used country road on the opposite side of the woods. And, straight across his fields from the house, there's a path you can only walk. They all move toward a little area in the center of the woods, where his years of gathering firewood have cut out a stumpy clearing of maybe a half-acre.

"I mostly just chainsaw fallen timber," he says. "Hate to cut a standing tree, if it's healthy."

"Yessir," IB says, though he's a city boy who only moved to the suburbs as an adult and probably couldn't tell the difference between an ornamental blue spruce and a wild white pine. "Seems a real shame to cut something down that took maybe a hundred, maybe two hundred, years to grow."

"More than a shame," Early says. "It's a crime, in my view."

What got Early calling the cops was this: starting two months ago, late at night he'd sometimes hear what sounded like a truck laboring up that main track, or at least somewhere over in that direction. It was dead quiet in these parts late at night, and he was a light sleeper, he said. After a few such incidents, he'd driven up himself in daylight, saw tire tracks but couldn't be certain they weren't his own from previous trips, and saw nothing out of the ordinary in the clearing.

Then he'd stopped hearing anything at night, except once just about three weeks previously. He figured people might be going in after that during the day; he'd never hear anything then, what with the noise of the farm machinery, and he'd been so busy plowing and planting he had no time to go poking over there. So he'd called the police. They told him nothing was going on.

"But there is, isn't there," he says as we're walking through his field toward the footpath. "Otherwise those fellas on the big motorcycles wouldn't have come by and put a pistol to my head."

"No, sir," IB says. "Putting pistols to peoples' heads is not normal."

That's why I'm a little worried about what our presence might mean for Early. Especially after that execution yesterday. That's why I've told the boss at the local police substation that Early's just a crank and we have no further interest in him or his complaints. That's why we've come out here carefully, not in the pickup but in a crappy old Chevy sedan. And that's why, when we hit the trailhead, I ask Early to wait.

"Why?" he asks. He's toting his Ithaca—unchambered, but with a full tube of buckshot shells.

"It'd help if you kept an eye on your house, on the road, see if anyone comes along," I say. "If you do, come after us."

"We don't like the idea of people maybe coming up on our backs, Mr. Wynn," IB says. "You get the idea."

"I do," Early says. "I was in Vietnam in '63, '64. Getting on to forty years ago, imagine that. I was younger than you boys then. And look at me now. Anyway, I'll squat here just inside the tree line and do like you said. You hear anybody coming up behind

you, don't get nervous. It'll only be me, and I'll have seen something I figure you'd want to be warned about."

We move into the forest. I take point. You look at IB, you figure
he's going to sound like a herd of elephants stomping through the
bush. But the big man moves silent as a fucking jungle cat, a tiger
or something, very light on his feet. It's a good woods, not first-
growth of course, but very mature second or third. From the size
of the oaks, slow-growing as they are, my guess is this place was
last clear-cut and logged off well over a century ago. The path follows terrain contours, twisting, dipping down, rising. There isn't a
straight, flat stretch more than fifteen meters long. Until about a
thousand meters in. That's when I get a direct sight on the clearing, maybe seventy-five meters off. That's when I also see a trip
wire. It's OD, looks military; any fool can buy spools of the stuff
from any surplus catalogue. But it's well-placed. I wave IB up,
point it out to him.

"Somebody's not too stupid," I whisper. He nods.

"And somebody must have a reason," he says.

I scan the clearing with my Steiners. The field of view is narrow,
but it looks just as Early had said. A bunch of big stumps, lots of
seedlings and young trees coming up, lots of undergrowth that
seems undisturbed.

We go off the trail to the right, following the trip wire. It zigs
and it zags, but by the time we can see that second track back into
the woods I know the whole site's been more or less circled by
the wire. We cross the track. It's narrow and deeply rutted, but a
medium-sized SUV, say a Toyota 4-Runner, wouldn't have any
problems. It's been a dry spring, the snow melt-off was long ago,
so the track's firm, no obvious tire traces in mud or anything. I
raise the Steiners and get almost exactly the same view I got from
the footpath, except I can see an opening in the trees directly

across the clearing and the main track that goes to the same asphalt road that fronts Early's farm. We follow the wire maybe another hundred meters. You'd never know there was a clearing, the
forest is that thick. I step over the trip, IB follows, and we move in.

Fuck me! I don't need the Steiners. I almost bump into the
thing. I point it out to IB. He looks hard, shakes his head. His face
tells me he can't see anything but trees and brush. The camo is
that good. Maybe twenty meters in front of me there's a small
house trailer. It's obscured by ghillie netting, the kind snipers
build their stalking suits with. Woven into the netting are fresh-
cut saplings and branches, their leaves still new green. It gets better. Instead of just draping the netting over the trailer, which
would have left an unnatural rectangular outline, whoever got
this trailer in here and hid it has hung the camo at varied heights
on trees all around the thing. A textbook-perfect breakup—not a
single straight line or corner, or anything you wouldn't see in nature, visible.

I explain all this to IB when he squats beside me. I try the Steiners. I can just make out bits of the trailer through the thickly
leafed netting, though it isn't easy even so close, and with binoculars. The aluminum trailer itself has been given a damn good
camo paint job.

IB still can't see it, even through the binoculars, until I point
out a couple of almost unnoticeable telltales.

"Jesus," he whispers when he finally gets the picture. "How in
hell do you make a fucking trailer just disappear in the fucking
woods?"

I leave IB, move in real close, move around it until I'm at the
edge of the clearing and can scan the whole site. It's as good as
anything I ever saw when my team did its jungle training.

We go back the way we came in. There's only one reason for

anybody to take so much trouble over a trailer in the woods, and only one way to do anything about it—if we want to actually catch the meth-cooking fucks and seize a lot of product, not just go in there with a bulldozer and destroy the site.

"Fuck that," IB says when I tell him my conclusions. "Bring on the bulldozer, man."

"Hey, these guys'll just put another trailer in another woods. We're supposed to catch 'em and send 'em to prison, not just make 'em move their little factories around, right?"

"Yeah. I guess." IB sounds very unenthusiastic.

"Think about this then, IB. We do the bulldozer thing, we're gonna be spending the rest of our careers up here, humping through woods every fucking day. Won't matter if it's zero degrees in a blizzard, or raining like a monsoon, or so hot we get fucking heatstroke and die. We're just gonna be humping through the woods until we're as old as Early. Sound like fun to you?"

"Sounds like shit to me. I wanna go back to the mall beat, checking out all those cute young girls, maybe making an Ecstasy bust once in a while."

"First this, then that," I say. "And it's time we cut Early loose. Don't want him to wind up like that asshole hanging out of the Peterbilt, do we?"

"I'll handle it," IB says.

And there's Early, still at the tree line with his Ithaca. "You boys find anything?" he calls as we approach.

"Sure did, sir," IB says. "Looks like some of the local teenagers are using that clearing as a party spot. Drinking beer, that kind of thing. Not such a big deal."

"Well, I won't have it," Early says. "And what about those boys with the revolver? What about that, hey?"

"We figure they're probably local bikers. Probably they get the beer for the kids. Maybe they sell the kids some marijuana. We'll catch them pretty quick," IB says.

"Huh," Early snorts. "And what about those kids? If you aren't going to go in there, I'm going in with my shotgun and give them a little scare, so they'll stay off my property."

"You know, Early, you could help us out a lot by not doing anything like that," IB says. "They're probably not bad kids. I'd bet you drank some beer with your buddies before you were twenty-one, and never caused anybody any real harm."

"Yes, I did do that." Early smiles.

"You ever hear any gunfire? No? Well, you probably wouldn't because it's just twenty-twos," I say. "Looks like one or two of those kids must have himself a little twenty-two, likes to set up beer cans and do a little target practice. I'd bet you did that, too."

"'Course I did, it's part of growing up." Early grins.

"Now if you go in there and the kids just happen to be there, and you've got your Ithaca and a boy's got his twenty-two . . . ," IB says. "What was that you were telling us about hunters accidentally shooting other hunters? Now I know you'd never make any mistake, but you know guns and beer are not a good combination, especially with kids. Some terrible accident might happen."

"I take your point," Early said.

"So it would help us if you'd just keep clear of the woods for a while," I say. "It would help if you just let things be, didn't call the police if you hear a vehicle at night. My guess is the kids won't be going back there much anymore, since word has surely got around that the police are watching those woods."

"Okay," Early says. We're almost up behind his house now. "But you boys are gonna arrest the ones who came here and threatened me, right?"

"Just as soon as we can track 'em down, they'll be thrown in jail," IB says.

"Meanwhile, Early," I say, "you call us, not the local station, if anybody gives you any trouble at all, or if you hear a real ruckus in the woods, like lots of vehicles, not just one, and a lot of loud music or anything. And since we're plainclothes, it'd be best, as I mentioned, for you to say you never heard of us, if anyone at all asks. Which no one will, most likely."

"All right boys, I'll do like you say." Early shakes IB's hand, then pumps mine. "I appreciate you taking so much interest in my problem."

9.

Dugal thinks I'm nuts. He's tilting toward a bulldozer-type solution. My fault.

"Are you falling back into that military daydream you arrived here in three years ago, Luther?" he says sharply. "That *warrior* mode? This surprises me very much."

I should have choosen a softer analogy than an SAS shoot-to-kill, Ulster-style ambush to describe my plan. Certain words push certain buttons in Dugal's brain, causing most of the other words before and after not to register. He'd demonstrated a clear understanding as IB and I described what we'd found, what we suspected, the difficulties the site presented to any ordinary surveillance and any ordinary raid tactics.

Then I'd suggested a way. Buttons got pushed. Dugal got crazed.

I try again.

"I think I misspoke myself, Captain," I say. Dugal's a formal guy, big on hierarchal deference and shit like that, but in a good mood he digs being called "Cap" like he dug being called "LT" when he was a lieutenant. He thinks it indicates a respectful admiration mixed with an allowable personal affection by the troops for an outstanding leader of men. In a bad mood? By the book, strictly. "This hidey-hole thing is absolutely for observation only. I'll have no weapons except my carry pistol. Under no circumstances will I confront and engage the suspects. I'm only there to record and report any activity."

"Yes? Go on," Dugal says.

"If I observe a pick-up of the product being cooked in that trailer, I'll radio in the license number of the vehicle. You send out an all-points, and if we're lucky we'll make a stop of a car or truck with a very nice load of meth aboard. We'll need just one stop, just one vehicle pulled over before the perps can cache the drugs. Then we'll have probable cause for a planned, coordinated raid. And enough information to carry it out at the right time to ensure we bag the cookers, not just hit an empty lab."

"This makes a great deal more sense than that Ulster nonsense you spoke of, Luther," Dugal says, calming now. "It seems like an intelligent way to approach the problem. Are you fit enough for it?"

By that he means is my shoulder up to humping a full ALICE pack into the woods, digging a hole long enough to lie down in, deep enough to sit up in, camouflaging it. And, once I'm tucked into the hole, staying in it for a minimum of forty-eight hours.

"Good to go, Captain," I say.

"You're certain of this?"

"Absolutely. I won't say I'll enjoy it. But I can do it."

"All right." Dugal actually laughs. "When do we go?"

He loves that "we" shit.

"The place looked to us like it'd just barely gone operational, right, IB?" I say.

IB nods. "I think we ought to wait at least two weeks. They might be extra cautious at start-up. Let's give them time to get comfortable, to crank up their production," he says.

"So I'll go in maybe two weeks, three weeks tops, from today. Depending on how they're running things, I may have to go in and out a couple of times, minimum stay of forty-eight each time. Until I see a pickup."

"Right. Do it," Dugal says. "And in the meantime?"

"We'll be going out pretty much as we've been doing," IB says. "See what else we can see, talk to whoever we can talk to."

"But we'll stay well clear of Wynn's woods," I say. "And the local substation. Those uniforms there are dangerous, Captain, they're so fucking dumb. We'll do our look-sees and talking everywhere else in the north county but the district Wynn's place is in."

"Yeah," IB says. "We don't want to rattle any chains in that district. Plus I'm sure, if this is major, the bad guys have other factories scattered around. Maybe we'll find another few Wynn-type places."

"That would be outstanding. We could roll up the entire enterprise in a coordinated series of raids," Dugal says. We've made him happy. He's already dreaming of his face on TV and in the newspapers, like it was after the Russian Rattle. "Would you like some other squad members to give you a hand?"

"Ah, no. Not really," IB says. "These people out there, they're real suspicious types. Too many new faces, they'll notice. Better if it stays just me and Luther."

I buy IB lunch for helping save our asses. It's well past his usual eating hour when we leave Dugal's office, and IB wants to just hit the Mickey D's across the street and shovel down some Big Macs, but I take him to this little Italian place a five-minute drive from HQ where they have great pastas. Pretty soon he's happy too.

Which leaves me. I'm not happy yet. I like the idea there may be some action coming. But I hate that "may be," and the waiting. And part of me is wishing this was going to be SAS-style, wishing

I could take an MP5 out to Wynn's woods, wait for a crowd of meth-heads to gather, and hose all the fucks.

But that would be illegal, Luther, I hear in my head. I laugh.

After lunch I go down to the basement range at HQ to practice shooting left-handed. Weak-side accuracy had fallen off a lot after I got shot. Got to bring it back. So I put about ten magazines through the SIG. Getting better. The holed targets say so.

I'm chatting with McKibbin about this when Radik approaches, carrying something heavy in a big plastic evidence baggie. "Hey, Luther, look what we found in that trucker's house," he says, holding up the bag. Inside there's a well-worn 1911-type .45 pistol. "Auto-Ordnance, made in the sixties, cheap clone of the military-issue Colts, all parts interchangeable. May be the piece the guy who hit you used. Thought I'd have ballistics look it over, put a few rounds through it, see if it marks up the brass the same way as the brass found at your parking lot."

"Cool," I say. Then I realize something's real wrong with me. I haven't given a single thought to my shooter since I got out of the hospital. Felt no urge to hunt the fuck down and kill him. Totally out of character. I feel weird all of a sudden.

"So what's the story?"

"So far, just what you saw," Radik says. "Execution. All eight guys domed with single .44 Special wadcutters. Which means, of course, if it was one shooter he'd have to stop to reload, maybe admire his artistry. But then there's the guy in the truck. If he was capped first, the guys inside would have heard it, run like hell or something. So probably he was capped last. The scenario that's crossing my mind is the dumb fuck thought he was partners with the shooter, was set to drive away in that rig after the business in the basement was finished, was surprised as hell when the shooter domed him too."

"Sounds good. Drug traces, IDs?"

"Yeah. The lab says there was some meth chemical residue in the busted up glass. We got IDs on all eight. Three of 'em have minor drug jackets, did minor time in jail. The rest? A couple arrests, no convictions. I'll send all the ID shit to your e-mail."

"Thanks, man."

"No problem. One strange thing. The scene guys dusted the house from top to bottom, and the truck, and didn't turn up a single fingerprint anywhere. Except one set on the back doorknob of the house, the truck door handle, and the steering wheel. Belonging, you guessed it, to the dead guy in the truck."

"Kind of spooky."

"Yeah, imagine a shooter, who's probably wearing gloves anyway, taking the time to wipe down an entire house when anybody whose prints would be there is already dead in the basement. Some kind of obsessive-compulsive, man. Very weird."

Radik starts to leave. "Oh," he says. "No prints on this .45, either. One bullet shy of a full mag, though. Federal FMJs. Same brand that hit you."

■ ■ ■

I meet Annie for a drink at Flannery's after work. Usually we try to keep shoptalk to a minimum. I'll ask about what particular renovation job she's in the middle of, for instance, and she'll tell me she's stripping paint from the door and window frames of one of the top-floor bedrooms or whatever. She'll generally have a shot of tequila and one or two Dos Equis for chasers. One beer is my usual portion; the medication I have to take every day for the brain damage that's my Bosnian souvenir, a nice number called Klonopin, supercharges alcohol as a side effect.

When it gets more personal, it also gets pretty much one-sided.

Annie hears all about how things are going with Helen and me, but gives nothing back about her own romantic life. I don't think she has one, hasn't had one for a long time, maybe the entire time I've known her. Which is the biggest waste I can think of. She's got so much to offer: great mind, great heart, great body. If she ever crooked her little finger at me, I'd come running to her fast as I could. I'm sure she must sense this, but she never lets on, never gives away that she knows I've always been a little in love with her and would be totally in love with her if she wanted me.

In my less selfish moods, I find myself wishing she had a good man, any good man, who made her happy. Maybe that's pure projection. She seems content enough being alone, happy enough on her own.

But tonight, shop crops up, not in a specific way, but just chat about the north part of the county.

"It's the biggest cliché in the world, but you know what kinds of cases I get out there?" she says. "Fathers, even grandfathers, screwing their thirteen-year-old daughters or granddaughters. I mean, they're raping the kids, but it's not like a onetime thing. These dirtbags come creeping into the kids' rooms night after night. It's like they train the kids into almost believing there's nothing wrong with it. By the time I get involved, the psychological damage is tremendous. Probably permanent, for some of the girls. And I estimate that for every instance we do get involved in, there are four or five that're going to stay some family's dirty little secret forever."

"That turns my stomach," I say.

"Sick beyond belief. So it's that, or date rape. I don't think I've ever had a standard rape, a stranger forcing himself on a girl or woman by violence or threat of violence," she goes on. "The funny thing is—if you can find any black humor in it at all—it's only rural up north in the broadest definition. It sure as hell isn't some isolated part of Appalachia, some weird hillbilly country where everybody still marries first cousins and stuff."

"No, it isn't," I say. "But some of the folks I've run into out there make me wonder if there hasn't been generations of inbreeding or something. Seems like a pretty high proportion of dolts and retards."

Annie laughs. "I think the operative word is 'seems,' Luther. We've got plenty of those down here in our nice rich suburbs, too. Every once in a while I get a successful lawyer or business guy, university degree, pillar of the community, messing around with his own little pubescent darling, too. What the hell is it with men?"

"You've got that master's in psychology. You tell me," I say.

"The standard answer—that everybody's got these atavistic, stone-age impulses, but ninety-nine point nine percent are successfully socialized into permanently suppressing them—seems too pat to me, too simple. Not just the sex thing. The violence thing, too. So then you get into that whole nature or nurture debate. You've been in the middle of it. Drug dealers who are stone-cold killers, some people claiming it isn't the killers' personal fault, it's society's fault, it's the environment they were raised in."

"And since nobody knows for certain," I say, "you get intelligent people on both sides of the issue."

"Yeah, all passionately sure they're right and the other side's wrong," Annie says. "I don't believe either side. It's some mixture of both, with a wild card somewhere in the deck. At least aside from certifiable psychos, who are very rare, actually. The more I work cases, the more I'm convinced nobody has a clue why some people go bad. They just do."

"And we get the privilege of cleaning up the mess. We lock 'em up when we can, waste the fucks when we have to."

"Guess that's about it," Annie says.

"Much darker view than usual for you, Annie," I say. "You're sounding a lot like me, in fact. And as you've pointed out on occasion, I'm the classic borderline case between civilized man and savage."

That brings a smile. "Maybe you're a carrier. Maybe I'm catching what you've got."

"Oh no! Get some professional help, quick."

"I am a professional," she says. "So who knows better that professionals are useless?"

One of those nights. Law enforcement, military service, even ER medicine—it doesn't matter which you work. Every once in a while you're going to have one of those nights that get you feeling it might not have been a bad thing if the Cold War had turned hot, and Mutual Assured Destruction had wiped the planet clean of the human race.

■ ■ ■

All it takes is a fine, fun Saturday night with someone like Helen to brighten me up, and that's just what I get. I know how lucky I am. Got lots of faults, but not the one that'd let me take that girl's presence in my life for granted. Ever.

She likes to sleep in on Sundays. Which is good. Sunday's the day I generally go visit Dog. I sometimes wish that day would disappear from the week, that I could jump straight from Saturday nights to Monday mornings. In no way was what happened to him my fault. I've got no guilt about it. But I do feel shitty about how much I hate having to see him, the way he is.

I don't wake Helen when I leave my crib, jump in the TT, drive to Towson, and then head down Greenmount Avenue into the Waverly section of the city. I turn left off Greenmount at 30th Street, turn left again to go north on Old York Road, which is a one-way. Dog never married, had a family, or anything, though he used to have his own place and a string of girlfriends. Now he stays at his mother's, the row house where he grew up. I'd had some fine meals with him there before he got capped. I pass some black kids hanging on corners, most of them too young to be gang-bangers but trying real hard to look like they bang. It's a style. It's a fucking shame.

"Good morning, Luther," Dog's mother smiles at me as she lets me in. "I do hope you're staying for lunch. Crab cakes today."

She says this every Sunday. I always stay. Only thing that changes is what we eat for lunch.

It's a nice place, spotless, well maintained. But not ideal for a man in Dog's condition. It's like two shotgun shacks, stacked. The front door opens straight into the living room, which opens straight into the dining room, which opens straight into the kitchen. The problem's those steep stairs near the front door. You have to climb them to get to the bedrooms and the one bathroom. Dog has to pull himself up the stairs with his arms, his legs dragging useless behind.

"Hey, man, what you know good?" I say as we tap fists and his momma moves on back to the kitchen.

"Nothin' good, nigger," he grins. He's sitting in his wheelchair. There's a pair of crutches—the short aluminum kind with sort of half collars that fit behind your upper arms and rubber-covered handles, not the long type that fit under your armpits—propped against the chair. "Hit a plateau, man. I'm walking pretty good with my sticks from here to the kitchen and back, but I still got to baby-crawl upstairs."

"Just a plateau, home," I say. "Been there. Then one day you're off that plateau. The Dog'll be climbing those stairs on his feet then."

"Oh yeah, and the day after that I'll be sprinting down alleys chasing dealers again."

"Catch the motherfuckers, too."

"Frontin' hard today, Luther."

Dog is the only live body in the world who knows what I did to Vassily. I told him every move, every little detail of how I took the big Russian down. Whispered it in his ear, gripping one of his hands, as soon as he was far enough out of a three-week coma that I felt sure he was clearheaded and would register and re-member those details. He'd grinned. He'd dug it. "Treated him like a bitch," he'd said and then laughed.

"You know that old high school physics thing," I'd said. "For every action there is an equal and opposite reaction. Don't know about that equal shit, though."

Dog had laughed harder.

"You still doin' rehab, right?" I ask him now.

"Oh yeah. That physical therapist, she some kind of torture freak, man. She loves bending my legs 'til they almost break. Loves dissin' me, callin' me a pussy when I can't step along fast enough or far enough on that fuckin' walker thing. But what she digs most is taping on those wires, jackin' up the transformer 'til she sees pain on my face and the legs jerkin' like a fucking frog's. Then turning the voltage way down, waiting til I relax, then hittin' me with the full juice again. Over and over. She gets off on inflict-ing pain, man."

"That electric stuff helps the nerves regenerate, get back in busi-ness."

"That's what she say. I ain't seein' it happen yet."

"Takes months. You forgetting there was a time you couldn't even stand with the crutches, never mind walk with them?" I say. "Been there. I know."

"Fuck that." Dog laughs. "You always tellin' me you been there, nigger. I think you just imagine you been there."

"And I think you dig your therapist. Think you got a secret

thing for her, some kinky sex thing, her giving you jolts while you're fuckin'. You're just dying to do her in the back seat of your Jeep."

"I'm just plain dying."

"Now you sound like a bitch," I say.

Dog laughs himself out of feeling sorry for himself. Never stays in that place long. Too strong. Too much pride.

Then it's story time, while his momma's still fixing lunch. I tell him everything I know about what's going down on the streets. Who got capped, who's busting caps, who got arrested, all the true crime you never get in the newspapers. On slow weeks I have to make some shit up. But today, no problem. I give him a hi-rez, surround-sound home theater of seven rednecks domed on a basement floor, another head-shot and hanging upside down out of the cab of his truck. He likes it.

"About time whiteys started banging hard. I do love trash poppin' each other," he says. "Hope it's a trend."

We chill, keep it very clean and decent when we join his mother for lunch. It's hard to watch him wobble back to the kitchen on those crutches. But I learned early that Dog hates it if I take his hand or grab his arm, try to help him any way at all.

"Now these are some tasty crab cakes, aren't they, Lincoln?" Mrs. Lewis says to her son.

"Delicious," Dog replies.

"Lunch here is always the finest meal I get all week, Mrs. Lewis," I say. It's the truth, actually.

She laughs. "Luther, I know very well you are just a polite young man, brought up right. Taught to be nice to an old woman," she says. But I know she likes it whenever I say stuff like this.

"Old? Old? No disrespect, Mrs. Lewis, but I'd be asking you to go out with me, if I wasn't afraid your son might take it wrong," I grin. "I don't want to get on the wrong side of the police, you understand."

Both of them are relaxed. We have a fine time for an hour.

But I only untense when good-byes have been said and I'm in the TT, heading back to the county. Where, if I'm lucky, Helen might still be hanging in my place.

■ ■ ■

Very slow week. IB and I waste a lot of time and put a lot of mileage on that shitty red Ford up north. We get a few names, we find them and talk to them. They're dumb or sullen or got chips on their shoulders the size of six-by-sixes. We come away with nothing but the bad taste of having to be reasonably polite to bad-mouthed shit-kickers who I'd rather just kick the shit out of. IB has to actually stop me—only with a word, but still stop me—from doing just that to one especially irritating scumbag. A big guy about six feet two, two-hundred-twenty pounds, lots of that weight in a beer gut, who thinks he's real bad and keeps calling me "boy."

We go back to the Towson station early Friday afternoon, do some paperwork. Not on paper, of course. On our iMacs. I hate that machine. I feel like smashing the fucking mouse to shards of plastic when the thing keeps going wherever it wants on the screen instead of where I want it to go.

"What?" I snap when my phone rings and I pick up.

"'What?'" I hear Francesca Russo say. "You must have had a very productive and satisfying day, Luther."

"And this call is supposed to be the perfect end to my perfect day?"

"I wouldn't go that far," she laughs, ignoring the heavy-handed sarcasm. "I am extending an invitation for tonight, though. If you're free."

"To go where and do what?"

"With me, to a place up north I'm sure you'll dig, and watch the beautiful people while we drink a beer. There might even be a couple you'll be very glad to meet."

"Maybe another time."

"But there might not be another time. And I promise I'll have you home early. You really will like this place."

"Okay," I say. "What time?"

"Nine sharp. I'll pick you up at your place."

I'm standing outside my building just at nine when a jet-black Corvette with brilliant, expertly-painted red and orange flames streaming up from the grill and back along the hood growls up and halts. The passenger-side door opens. I look in. Russo's at the wheel, but not looking like the Russo I know. I slide in. She pops the clutch and the 'vette does a neat, controlled slide onto the road before I even get my seat belt fastened.

10. Damn. I haven't been near a place like this since I finished basic training, but I do know the type, the style. Same in Maryland as it is in Carolina. It looks like a long, low barn with a sagging roof, strung all over with white Christmas lights, off the junction of two country roads near Grimesville. No sign, no name. A potholed dirt and gravel parking lot half filled with Broncos and Blazers and pickups with oversized tires, plus a dozen or more black Harley hogs all in one row close to the building.

"The roadhouse," Russo says, finding a slot for her ride.

"No shit," I say.

Quick scan from the bouncers as we enter; no further interest. We look like we fit. I'm in denim, with a black leather vest covering my SIG, and my Deere cap. Russo's wearing cowboy boots, acid-washed jeans, and one of those sweaters of fluffy synthetic bunny fur with some kinked design in little sparkly spangles across the tits. She's gelled her hair kind of pouffy, too. We annex two empty stools at the long bar. My ears are ringing from the high-decibel assault by Metallica or Megadeath or some heavy metal shit like that on the sound system.

"Sawdust on the floor, even," I say after we've ordered bottles of beer. Not Grolsch or even Coors.

"Hey. The Roadhouse," Russo shrugs.

Seem to be very limited style idioms in this crowd. Which is normal. Guys have either shoulder-length hair hanging lank from under baseball caps, or else they're skinheads, most of those also sporting short beards. They're wearing denim jackets with the sleeves ripped off at the shoulder, to show off gaudy tattoos and pumped arm muscles. Or plaid workshirts. The women are still into that big-hair thing, bleached dead and dry as straw with dark roots, and jeans so tight they probably have to lie flat and suck in the gut to close the zipper. Some acid-washed denim, some weird shades of green and purple. And whatever kinds of tops make their tits look biggest.

Russo and I finish our first bottles of Rolling Rock, signal for seconds. I'm aware some ape of the skinhead sleeveless type's been staring crossed-eyed at Russo ever since we sat down. I can smell the fuck while he's still three struts off from getting close to her.

"Let's dance, baby," he says from maybe a foot away.

"No," Francesca says, smiling at him. "I'm busy."

"You ain't busy at nothin' I can see. Let's dance," he says.

"Walk away," she says.

"Fuck that," he says. "You're tired of sitting here with this Indian. You're gonna dance with me."

"Walk away," she says, still smiling.

"I'm walking away with you, bitch," he says, grasping her arm.

"Great tats, brother. For jailhouse tats," I say. "How many times you have to take it up the ass to pay for that work, punk?"

The asshole's punch is telegraphed so far in advance it's a joke. I just tilt my head a few inches to the left and all his fist hits is air.

"You're gone, faggot," he grunts, bunching his shoulder for another swing.

Out of nowhere, and very, very fast, Russo's elbow slams hard into the center of his windpipe. He goes down like he's been dome-shot, lies flat on his back in the sawdust, both hands at his throat. His eyes start to roll back, he's gasping so desperately. Russo doesn't bother herself looking at him, just sips her beer. Two bouncers appear, one on her side, one on mine.

"Let 'em alone," the guy behind the bar says to them, nodding at me and Russo. "Fuckin' Smitty started it. Just drag his dumb ass outside, leave him up against the dumpster. The fuck'll feel right at home there, he ever wakes up."

The bouncers each take an arm and start pulling Smitty toward the door. He's rattling and gasping. The bar dude moves away.

"So much for fitting in, being discreet, all that stuff," I mutter.

"Hey, I want to be noticed here, Luther," Russo says, low. "We've got just the right attention from just the right people."

She flicks her eyes toward a table near the far end of the bar. I give it a beat or two. Then I casually scan the room, the way anybody does when they're sitting at the bar after they've just put down a Smitty and are considering maybe he might have a friend or two coming on with pool cues in hand. Five guys at the table, three of them looking like every other piece of trash in this place. The other two, fuck me! Very short, very broad, little snub noses, oversized jaws, bald as eggs. Identical twins. And clearly the men to see around here. It's in the body language of the other three at the table, in that of everyone anywhere near them. No sleeveless denim jackets and tattoos. They're wearing sports jackets and open-neck dress shirts. One's blue, one's white.

"Check Bobbie and Butch Winneberger," Russo says. "I figure they're kind of interested in us now. Remember I told you to think twins when you think about crystal meth? Those're the ones I was referring to."

"So you want to get better acquainted with them. Okay," I say. "But why bring me along?"

"Because the only guys I got working for me who are nice with their hands happen to be black. Never gotten past the door." She laughs. "A girl can't come to a place like this all on her own, can she? She needs a guy who can handle any little thing that pops up. Like that stinking ex-con who wanted to dance."

"Looked to me like you handled him just fine yourself. Don't think he'll want to be dancing anytime soon," I say. "And, case it's slipped your mind, I don't work for you."

"No. But we do have mutual interests. Compatible couple, that makes us, wouldn't you say?"

"Don't think I'll say much 'til I see how you play this."

"Almost showtime," she says.

The bartender comes over. "Bobbie and Butch wanna buy you a beer."

"Who and who? We're just fine right here," Russo says.

"Whatever, lady," the bartender says. "'Cept Bobbie and Butch, they own this place. They like to be hospitable once in a while."

"Give us a welcome? Sort of like the fuck just got dragged out of here?" I say.

"Got it all wrong, bro," the bartender nods toward the table where the evil dwarves are sitting. The blue shirt catches my glance, smiles, raises a bottle. I can see a lot of muscle bunch up under his sports jacket. "But if you wanna blow 'em off, hey, I'll pass that on to them."

"What the fuck," Russo says, rising from her stool. "This bottle's empty. I'd just have to order another anyway."

Lots of heads swivel to check us out as we thread our way

through the crowd along the bar toward the freak table. Two of the biker-types get up and fade off toward the pool tables as we get close. Blue Shirt smiles, motions us to sit, tells the waitress to bring a round of Rolling Rocks.

"Fresh faces!" Blue Shirt says. "Nice. We get so tired of only ever seeing the same damn butt-uglies here night after night."

"I'm Butch," the other one says. "In white. Always in white."

"I'm Bobbie. In blue, always in blue. It helps people like this," he says, swinging his thick arm at the room. "As dumb as they are ugly, most of 'em. Always calling me Butch or Butch Bobbie."

"'Til I started wearing white shirts all the time and Bobbie started wearing blue," Butch says. He's as powerfully built as his brother. "Took some months, but most folks finally figured out how to tell who was who. Except the fucking color-blind ones."

They laugh in unison. The beer arrives. They take a swig. In unison.

"Never seen you two here before," Butch says.

"Never been," I say.

"Though we have heard there been a couple of fresh faces in the area. Talking to people," Bobbie says.

"Guess that's us. 'Cause that's what we've been doing," Russo says. "Seems most folks around here aren't real verbal, though. Getting mostly grunts, instead of conversation."

Bobbie and Butch laugh. In unison.

"Sounds about right. We don't run into a whole lot of avid conversationalists these days, either," Bobbie says. "Not verbal, or just not too bright, a lot of 'em. Now you two seem bright."

"Oh, we are. I'm a rocket scientist myself, and my man here, he's a physics professor." Russo grins. "We're investigating UFO reports. Haven't found any UFOs, but we've sure found some creatures who might be aliens. Though they'd only prove there is no intelligent life on other planets. So we figure alien civilizations are using Earth as a kind of asylum for their retards and psychos."

Butch and Bobbie seem to think this is the funniest thing they've heard in months. They're guffawing and nudging each other with their elbows. The biker-type still at the table looks like we're all speaking Chinese or something.

"We have heard, though, there's twin brothers around here who are real, real smart. Name of Winneberger," Russo says. "That wouldn't be your name, would it?"

The twins are still smiling and chuckling, but I feel the temperature fall a few degrees, fast.

"Certainly is, certainly is," Bobbie says. "We've got some cousins who might be aliens like you described, but we're the only twins, and the only businessmen."

"Well, I lied just now about us being scientists, but you knew that. I'm Di, really it's Diana but everyone calls me Di, and my partner here is Charlie. We're business people, too. Retail business."

"No last names, huh," Butch says.

"Stadtler," Russo says. "Married, what, five years now, Charlie?"

"Got yourselves a string of 7-11 franchises or something, Di and Charlie? Thinking of opening up in this area?" Bobbie asks.

"Franchises? Yeah, you might call it that," I say. "Convenience stores? Well, you might call it that too. We're certainly convenient for our customers, but we don't have any stores."

"So, are you planning to be convenient here?" Bobbie says.

"I don't think so." Russo laughs. "You see, we only sell one product, and our problem is our customer base in the D.C.–Baltimore corridor has grown so much our manufacturer is having trouble keeping us in stock."

"Never heard of having too many customers in business, have you, Butch?" Bobbie says.

"No, Bobbie. I never heard nothing like that."

"Well, it can happen when you depend on one manufacturer," Russo says.

"I see how that could be a problem. That's why we stock from six or eight at our seed and fertilizer place," Bobbie says.

"Our *particular* problem is there aren't six or eight manufacturers of our product," Russo says.

"Just one bunch of peckerheads in Grundy County, Tennessee, that makes this crowd seem like space shuttle technicians," I say.

"Sounds like the kind of place where people call themselves 'bidnessmen,' right?" Bobbie says.

"Oh yeah. Down south, they're all bidnessmen," Butch laughs.

"Grundy's so far south it's about to fall off the planet," Russo says. "About eighteen hours by car or truck from here, but the way these guys deliver, it might as well be eighteen hundred. Slow as molasses. And seems like they still count with their fingers."

"Depressing," I say.

"Yeah, Charlie and I are getting real depressed. Of course we could start manufacturing ourselves. Our product isn't real hard to make, doesn't require much capital investment," Russo says. "But we're not cut out for that. We're retailers. I mean, would you guys want to start your own fertilzer plant?"

"Hell, no," Bobbie snorts. "Too much trouble. You'd have to be thinking about all sorts of useless shit, from EPA regulations to the Teamsters coming in to organize your workforce."

"None of that would be a problem with our product. But making just isn't for us. Selling is what we're good at. Really good. You wouldn't believe our profit margin," Russo says.

"I'd believe anything you'd care to tell me, Diana," Butch grins. "I may call you Diana, may I not?"

Russo giggles, takes a long pull on her Rolling Rock, then looks at her wristwatch. "Well, I could just talk all night with you boys, but we've got a pretty long drive home, and things to take care of. Hey, if I give you my number, maybe you'd call me if you hear of any good manufacturers?"

"That'd be very unlikely, Di, since you haven't told us what product you're interested in," Bobbie says.

"Don't think now's the time and place to discuss it," Russo says. "But my instincts tell me a couple of very, very smart businessmen like yourselves have already figured that out. If not, maybe we should meet sometime."

"Sure," Bobbie says. "Next time you're in Westminster, drop by our seed and fertilizer outlet. We're usually there during the days. Big, ugly warehouse-type place. You can't miss it."

"Pleasure meeting you, gentlemen," I say, shaking Bobbie's hand first, then Butch's.

"See ya," Russo says. "Maybe here, even. Had such a good time tonight. Maybe next time some other dumb-ass like the one who got dragged out earlier will ask me to dance, too."

Bobbie and Butch laugh. In unison.

■ ■ ■

"What'd you think? Very cool, right?" Russo asks me after we've snaked down a few country roads and pulled onto I-83 South. She's opened up her Corvette all the way, and the fucking g-forces are pushing me back in my seat.

"You buy this thing, or is it a DEA confiscation?" I ask as the 'vette's speedometer needle passes 100 and keeps on going.

"You actually buy that punky little TT?" she laughs. "Cancel that. What did you think of the connection we made?"

"You made," I say. "They're your boys. It went pretty slick. But let me ask you something. Under what rock exactly did you find those mutant reptiles?"

"The usual. Got hold of a local just out on parole. Twisted his arm a little. He gave up the Winnebergers pronto," Russo says. "So easy, in fact, that I knew the little shit would rat us out back to them if anyone so much as stared hard at him. So I iced him."

"You what?"

"Told him word was the Winnebergers had made him for a snitch. Told him we had a nice safe place in Virginia he'd like much better than Baltimore County. He had his bag packed in about thirty seconds." Russo laughs, the exact tone of that laugh in Dugal's office. "Also told him we'd better not hear of him contacting any old friends. Or he'd be back doing hard time in lockdown at a federal pen for parole violation.

"Then we just put a paper mole to work," she goes on, letting the 'vette ease down to around ninety and keeping it purring there. "Solid citizens, those twins. The family's been the trashiest of white trash out here for five generations. Bobbie and Butch are the first to break the mold. Live on a sort of gentleman's farm in Carroll County, just north of Westminster. Started small, selling fertilzer and seed. Oh, but they grew fast. On paper, it's now a very big farm supply firm, one Chevy dealership, a brokerage agency that matches indie truckers who own their own rigs with businesses that need trailers long-hauled, and two or three great nightspots like the roadhouse."

"And off the books?" I ask.

"Using their truckers as drug mules, what else? Cooking crystal meth, what else? Maybe a little arson for hire, other insurance fraud stuff. Mean reputation. Butch is known as a never-miss pistolero. Bobbie gets the urge every now and then to stomp the biggest chump in his range of vision. Nearly kills the fucks. Nobody ever presses charges, though. And local legend credits them with giving the orders for at least six very nasty torture-type homicides. None solved."

"Oh, real sweethearts, these guys," I say.

"A lot of bikers gravitate toward them," Russo says. "I believe they use the bikers as short-haul mules and street dealers in three or four adjoining states. First step, as I saw it, was to locate all their little meth factories. Easiest way seemed to catch and turn one of the bikers or truckers. And we did. Had him deep in our pocket."

"Then why in the hell are you trying to get close to Bobbie and Butch yourself? That's a sting move."

"Because the guy we nailed and turned became one of those seven corpses the BCPD found in a basement recently," Russo says. "Before he could give us what we needed."

"You heard about that, did you?" I say, trying to mask the hit. Who gave her the IDs? Radik? No way. We've got a leak somewhere. "Three of them were ex-cons."

"Our guy wasn't. When we took him down, it was his first arrest."

Neat dodge, bitch, I'm thinking. If, that is, she really believes I'm not still wondering why she's moving into this action personally instead of simply nailing another biker. But she's too smart to think that. She wants more questions, wants to give me some more disinformation. Why? I'm not sure yet. So I decide I'll just shut up for a while.

She slips a CD into the 'vette's player, a Nakamichi. Some pretty fresh sounds, a mix of reggae and rap I've never heard. She's practically dancing in her seat. "New group," she says. "Long Beach Dub All-Stars."

I just listen to the music. After four tracks, Russo can't stand that anymore.

"Come on, Luther," she says. "Admit it."

"Admit what?"

"First, that you had fun tonight. Second, that we made a great team."

"If you say so."

"If I say so? You know we were smooth, we were slick together," she says. "No dissonance, no descrepancies, identical attitudes. We played those boys really well. Right now they're convinced you and I are long-time partners. One more meeting, they'll take the bait."

"You meet them. If you hook them, let me know and I'll congratulate you. Meanwhile, I've got my own moves to make."

"Have I offended you in some way? Have I failed to rise to your standards or something?" Russo says. "Because I can't think of any other reason you seem so fucking averse to a little cooperation that would be good for both of us."

"Hey, you're terrific at your job. Admire your many skills," I say. "But it's your job, all the way."

"Okay. Damn shame, though," Russo says as she drops me at my apartment. She smiles at me. "But if that's the way you intend to keep it, please make real sure you don't get in my way. Because that would be a bigger shame, Luther."

. . .

The only wrong move—that implied threat—I've seen the woman make so far, I'm thinking as I unlock the door and walk into my place. A second's jolt. Some mainly acoustic indie music's playing very loud, there are clothes tossed here and there. Then I see Helen's bag hanging from the bedroom doorknob. That door's open, but she's not on the futon. I'd almost forgotten I'd given the girl a key when I moved in, maybe a month after the Russian Rattle when I was going through my de-mil phase. I see that Helen's left on the low maple table one of those little plastic Zip-locs in which she used to carry her Ecstasy. There's one pill inside. Shit. I thought she was finished with that stuff.

I'm coming down from a rev. Russo was right about one thing:

I did dig the action at the roadhouse. Maybe best if I get all the way down from the rev. I go take a beer from the fridge, open it, drop the tab, and wash it down. I know Helen loved it when we did this together a few times last autumn. It was nice for me too, then. I feel now how short our time together is getting. I feel like making the most of it.

My boots are by the front door. So I take off my socks, take off my SIG, empty my jeans of wallet, cash, and keys. Then I open the closed door to the bathroom, slip in fast but quiet. She doesn't hear me; music's too loud. She's lying there with her eyes closed, water up to her chin. I just stand there a while, looking at her long toned body, her so-pretty, so-young face. After I've admired every inch of her, I step into the tub, all my clothes still on.

She sits up suddenly then, startled. Then she starts laughing.

"Ewing, you pig!" she says. I sit down, feeling the hot water saturate my jeans. Strange sensation, at first. She lies back, her knees raised slightly near my waist. I'm between them. She's looking at my face in that dreamy-eyed way she does when she's dropped Ecstasy.

"Leave that tab for me, or did you just get careless?" I grin.

"Are you gonna act like a cop again?" she says.

"Don't think so. Not tonight. I dropped."

"Pig," she laughs. "That was my last one. So if you're not gonna play cop, what are you going to play, babe?"

"Little of this, little of that." I slip my palms under her ass, raise her slightly so what I'm interested in is just above the waterline. I bend at the waist.

"How about a lot of that, if it's the nice thing I'm thinking?" she says, closing her eyes.

I go down on her. She doesn't say a thing once my mouth and tongue are on the right spot. Just sort of mews like a happy kitten.

11.

"Oh man, that conniving bitch. Out to scam your butt, Luther," IB says when I tell him about my roadhouse date with Russo. We're cruising up north in that Ford, no appointments, really pretty much a waste of time. Great day, though. The air's fresh, springy. No day to spend in front of our fucking computers. "She tried to set you up so you'd be trapped in a joint op with DEA, like it or fucking not. You conscious of that?"

"No!" I say. "Thought she was just showing me a good time, flirting with me. Jesus, you really think it was only a set?"

"Get bent, birdbones." IB laughs. The pickup isn't swerving as erratically as usual. "Somebody tell me why I bother talking with this spook beside me, please? Somebody clue me why he bothers telling me shit like he wants some kind of answer, when he's got all the answers. Or acts like he does. Glad you blew her off, though."

"I didn't, IB," I say.

"Tastes like a blow-off. Smells like a blow-off. Sounds like a blow-off. Ergo, blow-off."

"No, part of the game. I was flirting back. The hard-to-get act.

Russo wants something. Not a joint operation. I'm very sure she doesn't need any help from me to do a Winneberger sting. But she wants something pretty bad. Haven't figured out exactly what yet. She'll be trying again, though. I'm counting on it."

"The persistent type. Nag, nag, nag until you give, that what you're saying?"

"Oh, say determined. Say superambitious. Girl with a big agenda. A big secret agenda."

"I hate people like that. I keep thinking what the hell possesses them, makes 'em certain whatever they've got in mind is so important, so fucking superior to what anybody else's got in mind."

"That, IB, is why you're still a detective, not an LT or a captain like Dugal."

"Then I consider myself blessed, okay? Because I wouldn't sleep well at night, couldn't stand my face in the mirror every morning when I shave, if I had an agenda like that."

"Funny thing is," I say, "people who do, they usually sleep great and just love seeing their faces in the morning. Gives them a chance to congratulate their beautiful selves for being so smart, you know?"

■ ■ ■

We break for lunch at a truck-stop cafe just off I-83. The usual mix of long-haulers and locals, shoveling down burgers or minute steaks, chicken-in-a-basket or big bowls of chili. A few gourmets look pleased enough with the day's special: cup of navy bean soup, followed by meat loaf, mashed potatoes with brown gravy, green beans. Canned greens, by the washed-out color and even cut, not fresh.

The booths are all full. The waitresses, not one younger than forty-five, are rushing around in apricot-colored waitress dresses.

Classic. IB and I belly up to the Formica counter. It's a squeeze for IB, but he manages without too much complaint. We both order the special, a bargain at $5.95. While we wait, I'm scanning. Just an old habit, not because I think I'll see anything interesting.

Then I do see something that stirs an instinct. A beat-up Dodge van, white under the dirt, with copper piping lashed to the roof rack and SONNENBERG PLUMBING painted on the side, pulls in to a just vacated parking spot right in front of the diner. Guy gets out, stretches, takes a last drag on his cigarette, and heads inside. I make him in his early thirties, a local. Usual work clothes, hair Marine Corps buzzed, and a scraggy beard. He stands just inside the door, looks around. There's only one spot open: at the counter between me and some old fart in his sixties wearing a white shirt with a bow tie who's slurping soup. I see the plumber mouth "Fuck," but he walks over and takes the stool anyway.

Our food arrives. IB makes a few fussy passes over his plate with his fork, decides to spear a chunk of that meat loaf. He chews reflectively. "Not too bad," he says.

"Could be lots worse," I say, taking a bite myself.

"Hey, you see that great one in the paper this morning? Nah, you never read the papers. Get this one," IB says. "Dude flys in from Bogotá to San Juan. Now any dumb-ass knows you don't fly commercial from Bogotá unless your conscience is clean as a saint's, right? Anyway, dude comes up to Customs walking real funny, like he's got bad cramps or something. So, big surprise, Customs agents give him a pat-down. Feel something funny on his legs. They take him into the strip-search room, make him pull down his pants. Guess what they see? On each thigh, there's a fucking incision a foot long, stitches still in. Dude looks real surprised, like 'How the fuck did I get these?' When they get a doc in, open him up, fuck if they don't find a half-pound packet of the purest coke surgically implanted in each thigh. That gross or what? Anyhow, dude stays real surprised. Claims he has no idea how that shit got into his legs!"

IB starts laughing so hard the counter almost shakes. "Guess that's why they call these fucks mules. They gotta have about the same IQ."

I laugh too. I know the plumber next to me's heard every word. Impulse: play out that first instinct. 'Cause you just never know. And there's nothing to lose anyway.

"I'm gonna surgically implant shit in that fuckin' Randy's head, next time I see him," I say. Randy Schmidt's the name of one of the stiffs I found capped in the basement. "Except Schmidt's already got shit for brains, so it'd only make things worse. Like he had a real hard job, right? Meeting us here at ten this morning. Now it's past noon. He's burning us, man."

IB picks up instantly where I'm going, I know he's checked out the guy on my right. "Aw, Randy wouldn't do that. Most likely he ran into some little problem that's making him late. Give him another half-hour or so."

"Fuck that," I say, lowering my voice, but not so low the plumber can't hear. "It's a burn. I wanna find his ass. And I ain't going to surgically implant nothing. I'm gonna let my tool do an implant. Maybe two or three hollow-points. In his gut."

"Hey, cool off, man," IB says. "I say wait a half-hour. He still doesn't show, then we go over to his house and wait there all fucking day and all fucking night if we have to."

"I put down the fucking desposit. Nobody walks with my deposit."

"You friends of Randy's?" the plumber butts in, pretty belligerent. All right. "'Cause I am, and I never seen you before."

"Was I talking to you?" I say. "I don't think I was talking to you.

So why the fuck are you jumpin' in here on something that's none of your fucking business?"

"'Cause I don't like what I heard. Nobody's going over to Randy's house and bothering Angie and the kids." This plumber's either stand-up or truly stupid.

"We don't bother a man's woman and kids. We had a business deal with Randy, and he's punkin' out on us. So maybe we bother him some."

"Randy's out of business," the plumber says.

"You got no idea what kind of deal we had with him," I say.

"He's out of every kind of business," the plumber says. "He's dead. Some shit shot him in the head."

"Fuck if I believe that, pal. Randy's got my money. A lot of my money. And he better give up what I paid for."

"Randy ain't got nothing but a marker in the graveyard. You want me to show you that?"

"Nah. Since you're so smart and know so much, why don't you just tell me who got Randy's money and the product he was supposed to deliver to me?"

"Fuck you, man. I got no idea what you're talkin' about."

"A second ago you know everything, suddenly you don't know dick?" I say. "Touch the side of my jacket."

"What?"

"Touch the side of my jacket. I ain't going to repeat myself again."

The plumber looks a little rattled. Whole lot less belligerent, too. He pats the side of my jacket. His hand recoils. He looks real rattled now. He's felt the SIG.

"Listen, mister. I got no answers for you. I know Randy was into some shit on the side, okay? But he never offered no details. And I never asked. Swear to God."

"Then who did Randy tell details to? Who were his buddies in that shit on the side?"

"I don't know, mister."

"You better think real hard, and start knowing."

"Aw, shit, man. They shot Randy. They might shoot me."

"Never have the chance," I say, looking at him as evil as I can, almost hissing the words. "Because this is shaping up as your real unlucky day. If I don't get a name or two pretty soon, you and me and my big friend here are gonna leave this place very quietly, take a little ride together to some place very quiet. And I'm gonna shoot you."

"Man, please. You don't wanna do that."

"I do. I really do. I like doing it."

"Oh God. Oh God."

"You better chill, brother," I whisper. "Or we're leaving for that ride right now."

The plumber caves, big time.

"Randy hung with a guy named Eddie Blizzard. And a biker called Angel Dust. I never met 'em or nothing. Randy just mentioned them. Said he was making some easy extra cash from them."

"And where would I find Eddie B. and an asshole who'd call himself Angel Dust?"

"I got no idea where they live. Never met 'em. But maybe that roadhouse. The one over near Grimesville? They probably hang there."

"Place with no name? Owned by Butch and Bobbie Winneberger?"

"I guess. I don't know who owns it. It's big, it's right on a junction, near Grimesville."

I stare him down. Then I stare out at his van. "Sonnenberg Plumbing. You Sonnenberg?"

"Yeah, mister. Christ."

"I just forgot that name. I'm gonna keep forgetting it. Unless this Eddie Blizzard and this biker fuck Angel Dust turn out to be imaginary friends or some shit like that. Then I'm suddenly gonna have perfect recall. Got a problem with my septic system? Oh yeah, guess I better get Sonnenberg over. Stuff him in that septic tank. Permanently."

The plumber's hunched over his burger like a man deep in prayer when IB ponies up for our lunch and we leave. Once we're in the Ford and cruising, he starts laughing.

"Jesus, Luther. You are right up there with the best loonies Hollywood's got. I'm talking Harvey Keitel, Christopher Walken, maybe even De Niro. Or that crazy fuck, what's his name. Olham? No, Oldman, Gary Oldman. You evil sack of shit, terrorizing that poor man the way you did."

"Hell, I just played a hunch, and he played right into it, man. I mean, tossing out a dead man's name into thin air. Pure luck, a friend of the dead guy sitting next to me, knowing what he knows. And letting us know that. Doesn't come so easy very often," I say.

"Almost never, that's sure," IB says. "Hey! Brain wave. He said roadhouse. Big bells going off. That Russo lady's on the track, right?"

"That just occur to you? Little lag in your uptake here, IB. Told you she was smart, ambitious. But now maybe we're a step ahead of her, thanks to Sonnenberg."

Then I get on my cell, reach Tommy Weinberg in the narc squad room. Ask him to check if there's an Eddie Blizzard from the north county with a drug record, or any sort of jacket. Ask him to do a computer search of arrest files for anybody with the alias Angel Dust. Tommy says no problem, he's on it.

"One step at a time, we'll get there, IB."

"So what's the next step?"

"How long's it been since we went walking in the woods with Early?"

"Just over two weeks, I think."

"Long enough, then. It's about time I went in."

. . .

First move is to have a little chat with our Mr. McKibbin. I know the Special Forces way, but I want to know about SAS style. McKibbin humors me, as always. Doesn't matter how I probe or provoke. I only ever get that sly Irish grin, that "just a copper on the beat, in Belfast" response. It's a game he likes.

But this time McKibbin chooses to toss the puppy a small bone.

"Now mind you, lad, this is merely hearsay. I've no actual knowledge, do I?" he says. "First, hard intelligence of the exact location of an IRA arms cache. Almost always an abandoned farmhouse or outbuilding, quite isolated. The SAS sends in a two-man team. Two. Never more, never less. They do a quick but thorough reconnaissance, absolutely covert. Ah, the blessing of night-vision scopes, eh, lad?

"The boyos note all entrances, all exits, all avenues of approach. They pick spots, never more than a hundred meters off but much nearer if possible, that give clear fields of observation and fire. Then, together or separately depending on the number of access points, they bury themselves," McKibbin says.

"Bury themselves so neatly a man could stroll right over the top of the hole and never know it. Never spot the one small peep slit. Down there in the damp dark earth beneath the sod, with rations and a pot to piss in, the boyos wait. Night-scoped weapons, naturally. They wait. They watch. Never stir. Very patient lads, they are.

"Ah, but sooner or later a Provo or two or three is bound to visit the precious cache, aren't they?" he goes on. "Very likely the Provos do not linger. They fetch what they've come for and scurry out of the farmhouse. The moment they appear, man or woman or some of each, the young SAS gentlemen instantly shoot them dead. None of your shouting 'hands up, you are under arrest.' Not the point, is it? Shoot 'em dead. Simple as that."

Simple as that.

"So the little birds say, anyway," McKibbin smiles. "Quite illegal of course, that sort of thing. Even in Ulster. Rules of war and so forth. Then again, what no one knows, no one knows. The dead tell no tales, do they, lad? Personally I think it's all a wild invention, Provo propaganda. If you take my meaning."

I do. I know it goes down exactly as McKibbin described. Had to be the IRA's worst fucking nightmare, before the truce and the cease-fire agreement.

Second move: silent good-byes. Just habit, not necessary this time because my op is totally no-risk. But something I always do. Helps me go into action cool and clear. Dinner with Annie Friday night, light and cheery as I can make it. Fairly early Saturday morning, I ignore Helen's slurred, sleepy protests, roust her out of bed, help her dress. Then we take the TT over to a place called The Baker Man for brunch: buttermilk pancakes, eggs over easy, thick-sliced bacon, sausages, fresh-squeezed orange juice, a pot of coffee. It's half past noon before we pull away from the place. I wait 'til we're halfway home before I tell Helen she's going to have plenty of time to do her homework, because I'm going to disappear for a while.

"Oooh. Undercover stuff. Is it cool, being somebody else for while?" she says.

"Like being Russell Crowe in a wild film. You can get away with murder." I laugh.

She doesn't. She stops smiling, too. "Don't make it long, okay?" she says very quietly. "I'll be missing you."

She's silent for a while. "And please don't, don't let it turn into your kind of movie. I'm scared about this."

"Promise you one thing," I say. "This particular role is a walk-on. I don't even have any lines. And I will be safer in it than I turned out to be in my own parking lot that time. Remember that time?"

"I try hard not to remember," she says. "That was too awful. Every time I see that scar on your shoulder . . . fuck you, Luther! I had nightmares for weeks. I still have nightmares sometimes."

I lean over, kiss her cheek. A little surprised to taste tears there. "Don't worry. Please. This is a walk-on. Guarantee there's zero danger. Believe me?"

"Sure. Except your definition of danger, Luther, is a bit too loose for me. Zero to you doesn't mean nil. Not like it does to regular people, anyway."

■ ■ ■

Just before dawn, first Monday of May. Low ground mist. We cruise three miles up the little country road that borders the back of Early Wynn's property, make a U, cruise three miles down. Don't see a single vehicle either way. Make another U, drive back up. I roll out of the Ford maybe a hundred meters past that rough rear track into Early's woods before IB even comes to a full stop. I hoist my ALICE pack out of the pickup's bed, shoulder it, move fast to the trees. Don't hang to exchange a few words, or watch IB start heading down the road again, on his way back to Towson.

No need to. The plan's clear. I'll have cell communication, but I won't use it unless there's a damn good reason. Nobody's to call me under any circumstances. I've extended the timing. IB will come back to this spot exactly seventy-two hours from now. If I haven't called.

And if I haven't, nothing's happened. So I'll leave with IB, take a few days R&R, then go back for another seventy-two hours.

"Man, better you than me. I'd go crazy, buried alive," I hear IB say, just before he pulls off. I'm only a few paces into the forest, but I can't see the red Ford and IB sure as shit can't see me.

12. A nice walk in the woods. Feels great, even though I'm humping maybe sixty pounds of gear and stepping carefully, quietly as I can manage. Reminds me of going camping in Carolina with Gunny, when I was a boy. Reminds me of dozens of SF training humps, except I'm all alone, not with my team. I'm alert to the plays of early light through the leaf canopy, the gradual brightening of sunrise, the gnarly bark of old trees, the whippy saplings, the undergrowth of ferns and moss, the sweetish scent of last year's dead leaves moldering into loam on the forest floor.

It's thicker in there, more jungly than I remembered. I have to check my compass a couple of times. Have to start counting paces. Watch carefully for the trip wire, spot it, step over it. Even so, I almost blunder right into the clearing, have to backtrack a few meters fast. I squat, scan. Nobody around.

I see the camouflaged feature that's the trailer, the footpath that leads to Early's, the opening in the tree line where the main track from the road that fronts Early's farm debouches. My position's not the best. I slide thirty meters south, scan again. Perfect. Good sight lines to the trailer and the main track. I look around for a spot to site my hide. Great fucking luck: a natural hummock. I take off my pack, unsnap the small but efficient German military tool that's both shovel and pick. Scrape an outline on the forward slope. Absolutely wrong if this was a combat hole; I'd want to be on the far side, the hummock between me and where hostile fire would be coming from. But I'm here to watch, not get into a firefight.

Takes me two fucking hours to hack and hew a trench two and a half meters long by a meter and a half wide, and almost a meter deep, even though I'm lucky again; the hummock's not too badly veined with roots and rocks. I have to carry the dirt back in a five-gallon collapsible canvas water bucket, spread it around thinly well away from the hole, brush dead leaves over fresh soil. Always listening, always alert for anybody coming in.

When the trench is right, I drill a bunch of drainage holes in the bottom with a fat, foot-long hand auger. Spread a rubberized groundsheet down. Then I spend almost an hour building a grid of fresh-cut branches tied together with green garden twine. I weave more fresh branches into the grid, place it over my hole, leaving just enough space at one end for me to slither in. I spread a bucket of dirt on top, actually plant some ferns and small saplings, cover any visible dirt with handfuls of dead leaves.

Then I stop, listen a while. Step five paces into the clearing and look back. I look hard. Can't see a single unnatural shape or mark. Go back, shove my gear into the trench, snake in after it. Very carefully ease the camo'd grid closed. Check my peep slit. Perfect.

Arrange my gear: pack and a light down sleeping bag at the far end, cased Steiners and mil-spec night-vision goggles in a niche I cut into the wall of the trench just below the spy slit, rations up against the near end. I test. I can just lie down full length, just sit up in a semilotus.

Then I wait. I will not look at my watch. Hard evidence of how slow time can pass is exactly what you do not need in a situation like this.

I'm sure I'm good, physically, for the full seventy-two. I won't have to miss any sleep. Anybody comes to take care of business won't be walking; I'll hear their vehicle. Rations are light: high protein, just enough sugar to keep blood levels even, very low on carbs and bulk. And I've got Immodium tabs so I won't have to shit. Water's heavy—three gallons—because dehydration is the worst enemy. I've got a medical piss bladder I can empty each night. I know isometrics and relaxation techniques I can use to combat muscle stiffening and cramping.

Mentally? You can't know what being buried for three days and nights will do to your head. Even if you've done this before. The effect's different each time. Just have to deal with whatever comes.

Nothing comes, that first day. See a few does trailed by fawns that still wobble and stumble, they're that new in the world. Squirrels rustling around, then screeching complaints about whatever the hell irritates them up in branches. One bunny rabbit. A rabble of crows, rowdy and raucous. Only a few tuneful birds drop by; I make one for a cardinal by its song, another for a warbler. I stay awake for a while after sunset, listen to the night creatures on the prowl. Raccoons, skunks, possums. One possum tries digging through my roof. I hiss the nosey fuck away.

I sleep fine, wake around sunrise with a hard-on, to bird racket. Piss into the bladder, munch a couple of energy bars, take a No-Doz tab with a cup of water against a mean little caffeine-withdrawal headache. Wishing very badly for a big cup of fresh-ground, fresh-brewed coffee, with half-and-half, a spoon of sugar. Far off, I just catch what has to be Early tooling around on his tractor. The sound fades fast; he must be heading for fields away from his woods. I do some isometrics, tighten muscles and relax them, group by group.

I wait.

I'm rerunning my last night with Helen in my head when I hear them coming. They're coming slow, careful of engine noise. A Jeep, not a Cherokee SUV but the small Sahara model, sticks its snout out from the track, pauses, then pulls in a few meters, hugging the tree line instead of heading directly into the clearing. Before it stops, I've got my little digital camcorder, lens zoomed to the max, at the spy slit. Two guys get out, look around pretty casually, then take a big hard-sided suitcase each out of the Jeep. They look like regular citizens. Boots and jeans, but no sleeveless denim jackets, no tats, no caps, standard barbershop haircuts. One guy's wearing glasses with black plastic frames, kind of Buddy Holly style. All right!

Chemists. Cookers.

They walk, listing to the suitcase side, sticking to the tree line, to where the trailer's hidden. They stoop, lift the ghillie netting, and vanish. A few minutes later, I hear the low whirr of a well-muffled gasoline-powered generator. They've got electricity in the trailer.

That's it. Check my watch: 8:45 A.M. They're cooking in there all fucking day. Check my watch when the generator cuts off and I see them slip out from under the netting. No suitcases now. It's just past four in the afternoon. The Jeep backs and turns and heads down that main track, slow and careful.

By sundown my brain's starting to chafe. It wants action, it wants to go places I'd like to avoid, very particular places I've been. Bad memory-lane-type places. I try to concentrate on the sounds of the part of the forest that's shutting down for the night, crows cawing off to wherever they roost, the cardinal singing himself a lullaby. There's a lull at full dark, and the brain tries to move out again. I try mental word games, number games, even though I hate that shit. It's a relief when the woods' night shift comes on duty. Something to listen to.

Sleep's a little slower coming this night. It's shallower and more dream-tossed, too. I wake up earlier, feeling slightly disoriented. It's an effort to stick to the program: piss, eat the energy bars, drop the No-Doz, enjoy the first stirrings of the deer, the birds, do the exercises, get loose and clear.

I hear the Jeep, see its snout, wait out the pause, video the move in, the halt, and the walk of the men, the same men, to the trailer. Check my watch. It's 8:45 A.M. The generator goes on. They cook in there all fucking day, leave just after four.

I write down the time of arrival, time of departure, the Jeep's plate number on the second page of my little pocket notebook. I read the first page. All the digits are the same, in the same combination and order. As it gets dark, my brain gets up and goes. I rein it in with word games, number games. I fucking lose.

At full dark I strap on the night-vision goggles and stare out the slit, hoping for the distraction of a nature video. No good. It might as well be a still photograph. Only movement's two fucking does with wobbly fawns behind, later a single big raccoon. Passersby only. They're in and out of sight in minutes. Then it's just a stumpy clearing and motionless forest.

I keep staring anyway. Pretty soon the stumps are shifting, moving, advancing cautiously on my position. The reticle of the goggles becomes a scope reticle, the scope mounted on an M-4 assault rifle. I zero on one hostile, slam a three-round burst into him, zero on another, zap him too. And another and another and another. But nothing happens. I know I greased the fucks, couldn't miss at this range, but none of them go down. I drop the mag, slam home another thirty-rounder, hose every hostile in sight. None go down. Nightmare.

I rock back hard, slamming my back into the rear wall of the trench. Yank the goggles off my face. Realize I am losing it, bad. When my brain takes off now, I don't even try to stop it.

Dog's first. I feel real sorry about Dog. The moves we made together, banging gangsta dealers. Vassily's up next. I feel sorry about Vassily, sorry for shooting his balls off, for bleeding him like a pig. God, the times we'd had in Sarajevo, the bad guys we'd juked together, the rakia we'd drunk, the women we'd fucked. But the bastard wouldn't stop hitting my homies in Baltimore when I asked him to, begged him to, so I had to take him down. He deserved to die.

Then I'm feeling sorry about the eighty or ninety Serbs I greased from a thousand meters out with a .50-caliber Barrett sniper rifle. I see each one blown to hamburger when a round from the .50 hits. But the bastards kept on hiding up there in the hills, shooting old men and young women and beautiful little kids who deserved a life, and they wouldn't stop, wouldn't face us, just kept sniping and going into defenseless villages, killing and raping and burning, so they had to die, they deserved to die.

Next thing, I'm even feeling sorry about all those fucking Iraqi ragheads. They probably had wives and kids at home, but they were killers and rapists, too, who wouldn't face us like soldiers, so I had to blow their shit away with twin MP5s because they deserved to die hard. Did it even though it killed my army career.

But I do not feel sorry for myself. When it's my turn to die, I'll deserve it, too.

Don't know if I slept at all that night.

■ ■ ■

Dawn slaps me in the face. Hard. I don't know where the fuck I am. Maybe a grave? I start to shove against whatever's sealing me in this hole, freeze just in time when I realize I'm about to blow my mission to hell. I'm shivering and sweating at the same time. I strain to focus on details. In my head I say my own name, I describe exactly what my job is. I pick up and carefully place the night-vision goggles back in the plastic case, put the case in the niche with the Steiners. I check the battery level on the camcorder, calculate if there's enough juice left for one day. There's much more than enough, I conclude. I eat two energy bars, wash them and a No-Doz down with water. I piss into the bladder but I'm a little shaky so some splashes on my camo pants. I peer through the spy slit, recognize the familiar features of the clearing. I sit in a semilotus, do some Zen mind drills. Gradually I begin to feel back in control of myself. Gradually the residue of whatever haunted me at night gets washed out of my brain. I know I'm coming around when I smell my own smell and mutter, "Shit, you fucking stink, man."

I make it all the way back when I hear the Jeep, start camcording it and the same two dudes, hear the generator cough once and then begin its soft purr. To pass the time, I start at the beginning, when I first came up north months ago looking for speed makers and merchants. I even replay the night I got shot, and my date with Russo at the roadhouse. I spend a long time trying to figure Russo out. What's her game here? Is she just a sharp narc, anxious to move her career onward and upward? Is that all that's on her mind? Climbing the DEA ladder, or, rather, trying to reclimb the rung or two it seems she slipped down when they transferred her to Baltimore? Why'd that happen, anyway? Would she be a good fuck?

I laugh to myself at the last thought. Where the hell did that come from—would she be a good fuck? Maybe, if you like it rough and tough. No way I'm ever going to make an effort to find out. I wouldn't fuck her with IB's dick. Or even Dugal's.

I'm getting through the day okay, but dreading the night, even though it's the last. This tour, anyway. Because it looks like there's going to have to be another tour. Busting two cookers would be counterproductive. It'd hurt our chances to trace, track, and roll up whatever network there is. And there's got to be a network, I tell myself. Can't accept that I might have put myself through all this just for two lousy little cookers.

I break a rule, check my watch. Nearly four. Aw, fuck me. They'll be leaving soon. I feel really, really depressed. It was a lot to hope for, I admit, getting what we need in just seventy-two hours. And it's not as if I'll be leaving empty-handed. I've got the cookers on video, I know this place is operational, we'll hit it sometime. I'm just dreading a second or a third or even a fourth seventy-two hours, buried.

Big rush, then. I hear an engine laboring up the track. Get the camcorder rolling. A Blazer appears, faded turquoise where it isn't scabbed with rust, ridiculously oversized tires. A roadhouse-type guy gets out. Looks a lot like Smitty, the ape Russo dropped with her elbow. He ambles over to the trailer like he hasn't got a worry in the world, ducks under the ghillie netting. Comes back out from under in a couple of minutes, toting an OD army surplus tool bag about the size of a carry-on. He puts it in the back of that piece-of-shit Blazer, making it disappear beneath some other bags and opened cardboard boxes with electrical fixtures and stuff sticking out the tops. Soon as he starts the Blazer I punch one button on my cell phone. Panic second when it rings three times, four times. But then IB picks up. I give him the plate number and description of the Blazer, the driver. Tell IB he's carrying product, describe the tool bag, where it is. Also tell him to pick me up at our original drop-off spot at six tonight. And, oh yeah, bring two guys from the squad capable of spending the night in the woods.

IB says he'll get on it.

The cookers leave at the usual time. I wait an hour, pack my gear while I'm waiting, then carefully slide back my roof so there's a space big enough for me to get out.

Bigger rush when I'm standing straight, unconfined, breathing free air. Get a little dizzy for a moment, wobble quite a bit when I shoulder the ALICE pack and hump toward that back road. I stop a few meters in from the road, sit down on my pack, lean against the trunk of a huge oak. I light a cigarette, savor that instant hit of nicotine.

IB's right on time. He's brought Tommy Weinberg and Fowble, who replaced Taggert You Fuck, as Dugal always called that hapless fool, after the dude stupidly got himself capped in a bust gone bad last fall. IB's had the good sense to arm them with shotguns, flashlights attached to the barrels, and pressure switches on the trigger guards. IB read my mind. We wouldn't want anyone to come in and wreck the trailer factory, destroy any evidence, if we manage to bust the Blazer guy and he gets his phone call. I lead them to the hummock, give Tommy the night-visions, tell them to stay on the far side, not the hole side. And either arrest or shoot anybody who comes around. They do not look real happy when I leave.

But I'm so fucking happy, talking my fool head off, that even IB, who loves the sound of his own voice and clearly has a lot of important questions to ask, can't get in one single word all the way back to Towson.

■ ■ ■

Dugal broadcast the all-points as soon as I called IB. A state trooper—thank God it was a trooper and not one of the local county uniforms—pulls over the Blazer just outside of Maryland Line, holds it there until Dugal himself, with Gus the Greek and Petey K. along, shows up. They take the perp and the Blazer back to Towson. Dugal is thinking much better than I usually give him credit for. He comes in very, very slowly, taking a long and round-about route, buying time. He contrives a legal way of getting the perp into an interrogation room, giving him no shot at that one phone call, which might have gone not to a lawyer but to the Winnebergers or whomever the Wynn woods lab belongs to.

I want in on the interrogation, but it's a definite no-go once I look through the two-way mirror. It *is* Smitty. He'll remember my face for sure. So IB does the honors for a while and then, perfect timing, in goes Radik carrying a stack of eight-by-ten color prints. He spreads them out, one by one, on the table, invites Smitty to take a good, long look at some of the grossest crime scene photos I've ever seen.

Smitty's face takes on the pallor and almost the expression he had on the roadhouse floor, just after being expertly chopped in the thorax by Russo.

Radik clues Smitty that he isn't here, with one hand cuffed to an eye-bolt in the concrete floor, just for what Dugal's told me is about $50,000 worth of crystal meth in an OD tool bag. He's prime suspect in a double-quad homicide.

Dugal and I are watching through the two-way, listening over the speakers, when Radik growls, "Tag Lustbader was a guy you knew, wasn't he, Smitty? That photo, second from the left? That's him, or what's left of his face after a dome shot by a .44 wadcut-ter. Cute, huh? The gray Jell-O? That's his fuckin' brains, man. Why'd you cap him, Smitty?"

"Oh, man, he was my friend. Good friend. I wouldn't shoot a good friend," Smitty says.

"I get it. You only kill regular friends, like Randy Schmidt. That's him, next to Lustbader," Radik says. "Or guys you know but don't like. Or guys you don't know at all."

"I wouldn't kill anybody, man. I'm not a shooter," Smitty says. "I don't even hunt in deer season."

IB and Radik look at each other, start laughing like maniacs. Smitty's a husky fella, but IB and Radik must seem like a pair of Frankenstein monsters to him. Insane Frankenstein monsters. IB slaps the table, laughing, and it sounds like a gunshot. Smitty flinches, starts squirming in his chair, eyes flicking like crazy.

I can tell IB and Radik are going to take it real slow, circling round and round Smitty, upping the pressure each time. I'm too antsy to sit through it. Plus I stink. I go down to the locker room, strip off my camo outfit, take a slow shower, very hot. Then I take my street clothes from my locker, dress, leave the station. I'm digging the soft evening air as I walk up the hill and over a few blocks to Flannery's. I wolf down a shrimp cocktail, a porterhouse seared nice and bloody, and two bottles of Grolsch. The reviving effect is great. I feel almost high on something when I walk back to the station, take a seat next to Dugal. IB and Radik have put Smitty in a very bad place by now. He's really sweating, big dark circles under each armpit and a large wet patch on his shirt front. His lips are quivering.

"Well, Smitty," IB says, "you're going to jail for ten years, absolute minimum, on the meth. That's for sure. I mean, you were carrying the shit in your beautiful Blazer. Got you cold on that. No excuses any jury in the county would buy. Am I right?"

"But hey, Smitty, look on the bright side," Radik says. "You won't have to stay in lockdown for all ten, 'cause you're gonna die by lethal injection on that murder conviction. Cool, huh?"

Smitty starts spilling all at once, so fast he's slurring, and IB and Radik have to rein him in, make him repeat a lot, slow and clear. Lots of names, lots of places, lots of details about the timing of pick-ups, his delivery schedule, and drop points.

Dugal looks like he's about to cream in his pants.

"Luther, I deeply regret scoffing at your original idea on this case," he says. He's lowered his normal voice half an octave, the way he does when he's interviewed for TV news. "It turned out to be brilliant. Absolutely brilliant. I can't think of a single way this could have gone better."

I can. The Winneberger twins could have come instead of Smitty, who hasn't mentioned their names at all. But they don't get their hands dirty, they've got lots of Smittys for that. They keep everything at arm's length. We've got a ways to go to nail the twins. But I don't say a thing, just grin at Dugal.

The adrenaline's fading fast. I'm whipped. I tell Dugal I gotta go get some rest.

"Right, absolutely. You've certainly earned it, Luther," he says.

I drive home, almost on autopilot. Key my door open, lock it behind me. Don't even take off my SIG. Just collapse on the futon fully dressed, and sleep for twelve hours.

13.

Dugal, as usual, wants a showy op. Black-hooded tacticals with CAR15s, swooping down on five meth sites. A simultaneous, "synchronize your watches, men" roll up, not only at the cookers' but at the homes of every dude Smitty named.

"Worst idea in the fuckin' world," I say, when IB briefs me on this as soon as I slide into HQ just past noon the next day. Dugal's planning meeting has already adjourned for lunch.

"Fuckin' A, bubba," IB says. "I spent the whole morning trying to sedate Dugal and that asshole who's chief of the tactical squad. They wanna go, go, go! And yet they figure they need three or four days to set it all up. Geniuses."

IB understands what I understand: we do this stunt this way and all we're going to bust is five empty trailers in the woods. For once I don't hesitate to hop across the street with IB, snatch some Big Macs, bring them back to eat at our desks. We need to huddle. We need to figure a way to defuse Dugal's bomb when the meeting reconvenes.

Smitty's given us a way, though that scumbag doesn't know it. After IB and Radik broke him last night, he decided he didn't want to make any phone call. He almost begged to be locked up tight in a holding cell. And kept there. The BCPD was pleased to oblige him. Maybe Smitty's not as dumb as he acts.

"Afternoon, Luther. Get a good rest? I suppose IB's sketched out our strategy and tactics?" Dugal says. It's just Dugal, IB, me, and the big dick from tactical around his conference table. "Have you formed an opinion?"

"Flawless in theory, sir," I say. He smiles, pleased. "But I'm kind of worried. About timing. About the potential of failing to make as big a bag as we all hope for."

"Care to be specific about what troubles you, Luther?" Dugal says. He's tightening up, even though I made as soft an approach as I could.

"Several things. First, if we wait a few days, I'm afraid all we're going to hit is air. The cooker trailers will be abandoned."

"Why should they be? Smitty's locked up. He can't warn anyone," Dugal says.

"It's his obvious absence that will warn, Captain," I say. "Right now the Winneberger twins—Smitty didn't dare name them, by the way, but you know from our reports that IB and I believe they boss the entire north county meth biz—are probably thinking Smitty just burned them, just took off with their meth instead of delivering wherever he was supposed to deliver. They're looking for him, they're really pissed off."

"And?" Dugal asks.

"But they're not rattled. They've got no idea the cops are on their case. Give 'em three or four days, no sign or word about Smitty, and they may start entertaining that notion. They won't hesitate then. They'll take quick evasive action. Empty trailers. Go to ground. No cookers, no pick-up guys operating."

"I follow. But that is only a possibility, not a certainty."

"Yeah, but what is certain is that we have zero on the Winnebergers themselves. We have probable cause to raid their cookers and roll their runners—if I'm wrong and they're still around to be rolled up. But nothing to nail the Winnebergers. They'll just get new trailers, new men, and start again once things cool down."

"You're verging toward the obtuse here. Surely at least one man we catch on these raids will give these Winnebergers up?"

"I don't know, Captain. I mean, even assuming we catch anybody at all," I say, "you rarely see a perp break as completely as Smitty broke last night. He's a pussy. Yet he still never once mentioned the Winnebergers. He wants to stay in jail. Who ever heard of a thing like that? Unless the guy knows he's dead meat on the streets. Feels real sure the Winnebergers will have him capped."

"Let's catch our breath here, Luther. You're getting a bit carried away, I think. Racing right past a great opportunity, a fine plan, to what might, and I emphasize might, go wrong with it," Dugal says.

"But he's right," IB says. "Cookers and runners don't amount to much if we can't clip the guys who're running them. All we'll have on the Winnebergers, best case, is testimony from lowlifes. No hard evidence."

The tactical dick starts looking like a kid who's just been told Santa Claus definitely does not exist. Dugal's tapping his silver pen on the legal pad before him on the table. Which is what he always does when he's getting frustrated. "You have options to offer?" he says. "A counterproposal?"

"A simple one, Captain," I say. "If we move right now, we just have time to do a plainclothes hit on the Wynn woods site where Smitty picked up. Snatch the cookers, stick 'em in with Smitty, wreck the trailer."

"What the fuck good is that?" the tactical dick says, all truculent.

"First thought the Winnebergers will have is that they've been hit by competitors they didn't know they had. Not by cops," I say.

"They get ready for war, but they keep the other cookers running. Let a few days pass, hit another site, plainclothes again. We don't go near the runners Smitty gave up. The Winnebergers feel sure it's competition, not cops. They start making some war moves, instead of going to ground."

"Which will give Luther a chance to get next to the Winnebergers, get some dirt on them personally," IB says. "Shit, he's already had a beer with them, posing as a retailer looking for a manufacturer."

"He has?" Dugal's surprised.

"Yeah, it was in one of our reports last week," IB says. "Maybe— I mean I know you're totally busy handling both narc and vice these days, Captain—you didn't get the chance to read them all thoroughly."

"I'm skeptical, gentlemen. How could you do this today?" Dugal says.

"Easy," IB says. "There are just two chemistry wimps out there. Not even armed, are they, Luther?"

"Nah," I say. "They don't carry, from what I saw."

"So Luther and me drive fast out there now, grab 'em just as they're closing down for the day. We trash the trailer, bring the chemists back here before dark. Then tonight, Luther goes and has another beer with the Winnebergers. Slings around his usual bullshit, sees if he can get them into a deal. Buy-and-bust, if he does. Solid."

"Just a fuckin' minute . . . ," the tactical dick starts in, unknowingly pushing exactly the wrong button, for his interests anyway. Dugal likes to appear bold and decisive. It's something he learned in those management classes he takes.

"Shut up, George," Dugal says to the tactical, standing up like he's General Patton or something. "Luther, IB. Go!"

We're laughing as we hustle downstairs, draw Remington M11-

87s—12-gauge pumps with eighteen-inch cylinder-choked barrels and extended eight-round magazines—and some boxes of shells from McKibbin.

"Grouse season already, lads?" McKibbin grins. "Thought it was months off yet. The Glorious First. Of August."

Then IB and I hit our lockers, put on Level III Kevlar vests under our shirts, do a quick equipment pat-down, put the shotguns and shells in big gym bags, go out to the garage, and climb into the Ford. Only then do we notice McKibbin tucked in the tiny back seat, grinning at us like a leprechaun, a parkerized pistol-gripped Mossberg pump with ghost-ring sights lying across his lap. He's got a leather pouch stuffed with shells belted at his waist.

"Whoa," IB says.

"Very kind of you boyos to invite an old man along. I do like a walk in the woods, having a pot or two at the birdies," McKibbin says. "Especially off-season. Reckon I've a poacher's heart, bless me."

IB looks at me. "Drive," I say. He does. Very fast.

■ ■ ■

IB pulls onto the shoulder, using the Ford to block access to the main track into Early Wynn's forest. We walk fast up that track, ease into the woods just before the clearing, creep up. The Jeep's there. We crouch behind it for a moment, chamber rounds as quietly as we can. We made our dispositions on the way up from Towson. I'm to circle round the clearing just inside the tree line to the ghillie netting, dropping McKibbin off at the footpath that goes to Early's field. When I'm in position, IB'll come straight up the middle. I'm stack-loaded; first two rounds are door-busters, charged with very dense, compressed powdered metal that'll blow hinges off with no dangerous ricochets. The next six are double-ought buck. IB's got eight rounds of armor-piercing slugs. If we're fired on, he'll put them all into the trailer and they'll exit on the far side, guaranteeing anybody inside who hasn't had the bad luck to be hit will be flat on the floor, pissing himself. Then I'll blow the door, cover the fucks until IB comes in and cuffs them. McKibbin will watch our backs, keep an eye out for anyone who might bolt through an alternate exit, a little tunnel, maybe.

I don't believe we'll be fired on. I lift the ghillie netting, see IB moving up the middle, and get ready to just blow that door and freeze the two chemists. Who're gonna be shocked shitless, I laugh to myself.

Boom, boom. Oh, shit. Boom boom boom. Pistol shots, heavy, maybe .44 mag or .45 ACP. I see IB crouch behind a stump. I hit the dirt. He pumps and triggers, pumps and triggers very fast, his Remington roaring and the slugs whanging all the way through the trailer, spraying aluminum shrapnel as they exit. On the eighth whang, I rise, blow the top door hinge, then the bottom. The door goes down. My ears are ringing as I chamber a buck shell and step in. It's smoky as hell, shattered glass everywhere, big holes in the sides where IB's slugs tore through. And, in blood pools on the floor, two dead chemists.

"Fuck me. Fuck me," I hear IB say. He's just stuck his head in and seen the bodies. "I did not want this to happen, goddammit."

I'm scanning. I don't see any pistol. I don't see any weapons at all. Where the fuck did those shots come from?

I hear a piercing whistle. IB and I run outside. McKibbin's squatting near the footpath, pumping an arm up and down, then pointing at the path. We race over, shoving shells into our magazines as we move.

"One, at least. Cut across the path, heading out," McKibbin says. His eyes are bright. "Pursuit, gentlemen? Mind you don't trip, now."

McKibbin takes point, I'm next, IB's rear man as we move in a crouch fast but quiet down that path. It's a bitch, I remember from walking it with Early. Goes up over a hill, down into a hollow, up over another hill. I'm scanning right, IB left. We top the first hill, slither down into the hollow, start climbing the second.

Lots of bullets suddenly snap fast past us when we're almost to the crest, from front and right. Assault rifle ban, my ass. You can buy semiauto Romanian or Bulgarian AKs that'll take pre-ban forty-round mags by mail for three or four hundred dollars from any of a dozen dealers who advertise in *Shotgun News*. That's why a fucking hail of AK bullets are cracking around us now, busting leaves, chopping saplings, throwing up dirt showers.

McKibbin doesn't hesitate. He's a pro, I always knew it. Tactical rule number one: When ambushed, never hit the ground and return fire in place. You and your team will be annihilated. Attack through the ambush with maximum violence. Which is exactly what McKibbin is doing, pumping shell after shell through his Mossberg as he charges the crest, me and Ice Box on his tail blasting buckshot blindly into the woods on the right. We're about over the top; the AK fire is slowing when I hear a distinctive, flat popping on our right flank. Controlled bursts from Uzis. But not at us. The AKs shut up.

We crouch, cram in more shells. The Uzis pop some more on our flank, then stop too.

"The cavalry?" McKibbin grins.

Maybe more Indians. Who the fuck knows? I never expected any of this shit. Then I hear a familiar voice: "DEA, you fucks. DEA. Coming in."

"Not bloody likely," McKibbin calls back, sighting toward the voice through the Mossberg's ghost-ring.

I hear "DEA, coming in. Hold fire, please." Know that voice. I see, a few meters in, blue jackets among the trees. They've got big DEA stencils in reflective paint. McKibbin's still sighted on them when they step out of the woods and onto the path, almost on top of us.

"Fucking Russo," I say. She's cradling an Uzi. So's her partner, the black dude blotched white here and there, the one with the Escalade who drove Francesca away from my place the night she came by. "What the fuck are you doing here?"

"'Tis the cavalry, is it then, Luther?" McKibbin says. He doesn't lower the Mossberg, though. Not yet. Too wise.

"Wrong question, Luther," Russo says, ignoring McKibbin. "What the fuck are you doing here?"

"Our jobs," McKibbin says. "Spot of work."

"Jesus fucking Christ," Russo says. "We've had sensors planted all over this place for a while. Uncle Sam's newest and finest. We're cruising nearby, get a call that the sensors have gone insane, screaming all sorts of shit. So we come to check it out. Didn't expect to walk into a fucking war zone."

"Sensors, Russo? You and your man just happen to be cruising nearby?" I laugh.

"What, you think we weren't conscious to that cookery in the clearing?" her partner says. Don't dig his tone at all.

"Who's 'we,' pal?" I say.

"Luther, this is Ray Phillips, my deputy chief of bureau," Russo says.

"And you're Ewing. Heard a lot about you," Phillips says, extending his hand.

I'm not feeling sociable, so I ignore the hand. IB is up now, backing down the trail a few meters and entering the woods.

"Why so pissed, Luther?" Russo says. "Because Ray's maybe right? Because you're surprised we had this place taped? There's a lot you don't know. Like you didn't know about Bobbie and Butch."

"Oh, dear," McKibbin says. Russo, Phillips, and I go over to where he's standing. A few meters ahead, just on the edge of the path, there's a biker type, down. He won't be biking any more. His face looks like a pincushion, maybe a dozen big needles with little black balls on the ends sunk deep into flesh, one right in the middle of an eyeball.

"Christ, McKibbin," I blurt. "What the hell did that?"

"My flechettes, sad to say," McKibbin replies. "Handy round against blokes lurking in bush or up in trees and so forth. Nasty little darts, about twenty to each shell. Better than buck, in bush. Does look a bit distressing, though, in the effect."

"A bit distressing? In the effect?" Phillips says, then starts laughing. I take a step toward him. Russo grabs my arm.

"Luther, I think you and I need to talk. Fairly urgently," Russo says. "Ray, maybe you and Mr., uh, McKibbin could start looking around like the big guy is down there, check out who we've just been to war with, see if we need to get some medical people?"

I pull out my cell, punch a button. Dugal picks up. "Need a scene team out here pronto, Captain," Russo hears me say into the phone. "EMS, too. Quietly, no cruisers, no lights and sirens. No, we're okay. Turned out to be a few aggressive folks around who aren't. Yeah, I'll walk you through the whole thing when you get here."

Russo cocks her head at me as McKibbin and Phillips move off.

"Appreciate your timely assistance and all," I say to her. "But it's my op, my scene, my people will take care of it. And your deputy's a real asshole. He opens his mouth near me again, I'll clean his clock."

"You are a piece of work, Ewing. Did I offer to cooperate with you or did I not? Now you've got us tripping all over each other.

But Ray, well, he does have a bad mouth. Feel free to close it anytime."

She's smiling. I have to laugh. "Regular goatfuck, right?"

"You ex-military guys have such wonderfully colorful euphemisms." Russo starts to chuckle. "Yeah, I guess goatfuck pretty much says it all. Luther, you punk!"

"Well, are you open to discussing how you and I might unfuck it?"

"I'm willing to listen."

I give her a quickie: the stakeout, the Smitty bust, how Smitty spilled—no specific names or places, though—and how I had to stall my commander from swooping in on all the meth factories we now have pinpointed until we can get something hard on the Winnebergers themselves. How perhaps she and I ought to go see Bobbie and Butch as soon as we can. Like tonight at the latest.

"Maybe," she says. "Let me just mull this a bit, get over being pissed off at you, before I commit one way or the other."

Then there's a commotion behind us, not far into the woods. We move to it. IB has grabbed a biker-type—who's got some buckshot in his legs—by the ankles, hoisted the fuck up so he's hanging upside down, his head about a foot off the ground. The biker's whimpering and moaning.

"You fuckin' pussy," IB says. "Who sent you out here, huh?"

IB jerks him higher. The biker screams. IB repeats, "Who the fuck sent you out here to cap us, asshole? You ain't going to no hospital. You're going to the station with me. I'm gonna hang you up like this in the men's room until somebody takes a huge shit. Then I'm gonna use your head for a toilet brush, like this," IB jerks him up and down. The biker's blubbering. Those buckshot holes must hurt like hell. "Before the fucking toilet's flushed. Unless I hear a name. Name of the fuck who sent you out here."

Lots of moaning and blubbering.

Ice Box drops the guy, turns away. I go over to him. "Hey, IB," I start. There's a pop. I whirl around. Russo's standing next to the biker, little wisp of smoke curling out of the barrel of her Uzi. There's a red hole in the biker's forehead.

"You fuckin' killed him, you crazy bitch," I shout.

"He was going for his piece," Russo says, so cool she doesn't bother to look at me. She just gingerly flips back the lower right part of his vest with her boot-toe. I see a Beretta nine tucked in his belt. But I can't believe he was capable of reaching for it, after the IB treatment.

Decide I'd better have a look around. It isn't reassuring. Besides McKibbin's pincushion and Russo's domer, there are four bodies. One has some buck in his right arm. All the rest have nothing from us. They've been stitched from hip to heart by Uzi bursts. In the back.

"Well, Luther," Russo says when I'm back on the trail. "I decided to accept your offer. Pick you up at nine? Have a beer at the roadhouse, okay? See you later, then."

"You're leaving?" I say.

"Hey, your op, your scene. As you said. We'll just be in the way when your boss and the troops get here."

Goatfuck, getting worse all the time. Dugal'll have our asses if he sees McKibbin. I suggest he might want to make himself scarce, low down in the backseat of the Ford. Pull a blanket over himself and stay still until Dugal's come and we've gone.

"Bright lad," he says. "Believe I'll do just that."

Then I notice IB leaning against a tree, trembling.

"Hey, man. You're okay, right? Not hit anywhere?" I ask.

"Not hit," he says, just staring at nothing. He's in a place I've never seen him enter before. "Sickened. And fucking horrified. Man, Luther, I am not cut out for this shit. Most cops never even have to draw their pistols. Me, I wind up in fucking battles. I can't take this shit. I cannot be taking these kinds of risks. My little girls . . ."

"Easy, IB, easy. Just sit down right where you are. Breathe deep and slow. Help's gonna be along in a few minutes."

Ice Box obeys. But he's still in that bad place, still trembling, still staring at nothing. Or at visions of old Mr. D.

So it's just me who has to do all the talking when Dugal shows up—quiet, like I asked—with the scene team, the meat wagons. One of the EMS guys scopes IB immediately, helps him into a wagon, starts doing trauma stuff.

A whole lot of fast talking. Mostly improvised, and about 75 percent is even true.

14.
I don't get home until well after dark. I call Russo right
away, ask her to make it nine-thirty, ask her to arrange a few other
things too. Need a shower, bad. Even with the extra time, it's
close. That black 'vette with the flame paint is idling impatiently
when I step outside my building carrying an OD bag about the
size of a carry-on. Russo pops the trunk without stirring from the
driver's seat. I toss the bag in. It joins an aluminum Halliburton.
Then I slide into the passenger seat and she tools off, giving the
clutch-popping and controlled skid a miss this time. I start on her
hard.

"You nearly fucked us up the ass, bolting this afternoon," I say.
"Phantom DEA agents, charging in with imaginary Uzis to break
up an ambush that was never supposed to happpen. Jesus Christ!
Do you have any idea, any conception of the trouble you caused?
Any notion how much bullshit my partner and I had to sling to
try to explain that mess to a BCPD captain who's the stiffest fucking suit in three states?"

She just laughs.

"Yeah, laugh. It's that fucking funny," I snarl. "I had to swear I'd sacrifice my unborn children if that invisible DEA, that Fed phantom, turned out to be only a hallucination. Can't fucking bear to mention what I had to promise to get Dugal to release the crystal meth into my hands for a fucking practice sting on the Winnebergers with Fed money he doubts exists because he doubts there's any Fed involved."

"You saw the Halliburton. Money's there, fifty large. You generally get so upset so easily? You're really losing it, slick," she says.

"With fucking reason, I'd say. Here's a promise, Russo. This thing goes wrong any little way, you're doing the explaining to my boss. I am going to haul you straight to HQ. Cuffed, if I have to."

"You mean if you can," she laughs.

I go deep into a fake sulk the rest of the way. She doesn't try to ease me out of it, just puts a Patti Smith CD on the 'vette's player and hums along. Until we park at the roadhouse. Must be a big night, the lot's crowded.

"Put your happy face on, Ewing," she says. "Can't go in looking dark and dirty as you do right now. The bouncers'll think you're a stick-up man or something."

No problem at the door. I'm dressed as usual, she's got the boots and acid-washed jeans. Different top, though. Tight cropped sleeveless T that shows her navel and molds itself tight against her tits. We go to the bar, ask for Rolling Rocks. Quick check. The twins' table at the far end of the bar is empty. Fuck.

Not a lot to talk about. We know what we're going to do. I'm thinking hard about that, about Russo and her moves, while I sip my beer. And I eventually come around to a conclusion I don't much like to admit: she was right, we are a good team, playing off each other smoothly, totally ad lib. Last time, anyway.

By her third beer, me still nursing my first, I'm wondering if there's going to be a this time. Then Russo spins. Somebody must've tapped her on the shoulder. I turn slowly. I figure if she feels like taking down some slob, she can do it herself. But there's Bobbie in white and Butch in blue. No, it's the other way around. Or is it? Shit. And their biker hulk, stone-faced like before. The twins' regular heavy, I guess.

"Hey," Bobbie says. "It's, wait a minute, I'll get it. Yeah, it's Diana and Charlie. Stadtler, retail franchises. What's new?"

"Hey, Bobbie! Hey, Butch!" Russo says. "What's new? Same old same old. Our redneck friends in Grundy County, they're still lost in some kind of time warp or something."

"Too bad," Butch says. Yeah, like he gives a damn. But maybe Bobbie does, or sees an opportunity. Because he says, "C'mon over to our table, have another beer, shoot the shit."

That's what we do. For a while. We might as well be discussing the weather, that's about the level the conversation's on. Then Russo leans a little closer to Bobbie, says, "Okay to talk here?"

"Oh, sure," Bobbie says.

"Absolutely," Butch says.

"You certain? See, it's kind of a strange story. Involves a dude named Smitty."

The twins tighten up, but so subtly almost no one would notice.

"You mean that asshole you knocked the shit out of, last time you visited?" Bobbie says.

"Yeah, and still an asshole," I say. "But an unexpectedly interesting asshole."

"Like to hear all about it," Bobbie says, leaning back in his chair, giving his already shiny dome a couple of buffs with his right hand.

"Oh yeah," says Butch. "But it'd be quieter back in our office, right, Bobbie?"

"Just my thought," Bobbie says, standing up. "Diana, Charlie? Wanna just follow me?"

There's a sudden ruckus over by the pool tables. A longhair and a skinhead are squaring off. Sucker punch draws blood from the skinhead's eyebrow.

"Uh, excuse me a sec, folks," Bobbie says, moving fast toward the tables.

"Goddamned bouncers. Asleep on their feet again," Butch mutters.

Now Bobbie's maybe five feet and some fraction of an inch tall. But that's also about the width of his shoulders. The longhair and the skinhead have closed, each trying to wrestle the other down. Real smooth, Bobbie gets one arm around the skinhead's neck, and half a second later he's got the other wrapped on the longhair. He pulls them apart, a head snugged under each armpit.

"You fucks know the rules," Bobbie says. "You wanna fight, take it outside. If you can."

Then the muscles bunch in Bobbie's shoulders and the two heads slam together with a dull, heavy thud. Bobbie lets go, and the longhair and the skinhead drop flat on the sawdust. Bobbie smoothes the sleeves of his sports coat, kicks each man once but very hard in the ribs, gives the bouncers who've finally shown up a glare, and comes back to us.

"Sorry about the interruption," he says. "Some things I've just got to handle by myself. I find it sort of sets a tone, you know? So. Shall we go?"

We don't go far. A few steps off there's a door in the wall, hard to see because it's made of the same old barn planks the walls are sheathed with. But there's a little cardboard sign thumbtacked to it, red letters on black: PRIVATE. Bobbie unlocks it, reaches around to flick the light switches, ushers us in. Then he and Butch and Stone-Face follow. Stone-Face closes the door, leans on it.

"Take a pew," Bobbie says. There are two corduroy sofas some shade like chewed tobacco facing each other, a table made of a varnished telephone cable spool between. At the far end of the room there's a rolltop desk. A seed company calendar's pinned to the wall, featuring a big color photo of some huge-breasted young girl in a bikini who looks dumb as a cow, just lolling on burlap bags stuffed with seed, above a small page with days and dates. It's five years old.

"Here's the deal," I say. "We run into this guy named Billy Hyde some days ago, have a little talk, give him our cell number. Just fishin', you understand?" Hyde's one of the runners Smitty fingered.

"Don't know a fella by that name," Bobbie says.

"Name's new to me," Butch says.

"Well, we didn't get much past the name stage. And haven't seen or heard from him since," Russo says. "But last night the cell phone rings. Guy says his name is Smitty, won't say how he got our number. Does insist he's got something for sale we're in the market for. I figure it can't be that Smitty asshole from here. I'm very suspicious. He wants to meet. At that truck-stop diner off I-83. I say sure."

"Sounds very kinked, possibly nasty, so we show up an hour early," I say. "Scan that place upside down and backwards for cops. It's clean. And it's crowded, full-house in the cafe and eighteen-wheelers all over the place. Around the time this Smitty guy is supposed to show, a turquoise Blazer with rust all over it pulls in, parks. Dude gets out. It is that Smitty asshole from here. Jesus. So I go up easy, stick my tool in his ribs, suggest we walk around back of the diner, have a talk."

"What a pussy," Russo says. "I can see right off he's nervous as hell. And not just because he recognizes me. He claims he's got fifty thousand dollars worth of crystal that—please don't take offense, this is Smitty saying this—Bobbie and Butch told him it was okay to sell us.

"I'm not trusting his shit at all," she goes on. "It's just so whacked! Why'd he bring your names up? And what's he think, we ride around with fifty large, just in case we see something we wanna buy? Like that's pocket money or something?"

"This story is so weird it's making my head spin. Like round and round and round," Bobbie says.

"Smitty's just some dumb ass who gets drunk here, starts fights once in a while, usually gets his butt kicked," Butch says.

"Yeah, the whole thing felt totally wrong," I say. "So we figure we better make it right."

"And how did you do that?" Bobbie asks. He's cool, but coiling tighter and tighter.

"I told Smitty to show us the goods. He does. We rip him on the spot," I laugh. "Tell him I'll blow his head off, I ever see him again. Put him in that Blazer, and off he drives. Think he wet his pants."

"We go home," Russo says, "check the product. It's good meth, worth just about fifty thou. Already packaged for sale. Brand name in purple ink on each glassine envelope. A really cute name. Dog Bite."

Butch blinks. Bobbie doesn't.

"I am amazed," Russo rattles on. "I am also worried. I think, suppose at least one part of Smitty's shit was true? What if it is— please, no offense meant—Winneberger merchandise? Maybe Smitty ripped it from them, got our number from that Hyde dude."

"So we figure the right thing to do is come tell you all this," I say. "And give the product back. If it does belong to you. Or buy it, if it's yours and you feel like selling."

Bobbie and Butch look at each other for a long time. It's fun to watch, even though they're very cool about it, since I know they're juked by Smitty's bolt with all that meth he picked up in Wynn's woods. And they're feeling real leery, Russo and me being unknowns, just showing up out of nowhere. On the other hand, whoever heard of heat who bring you drugs, then offer to buy them back off you? So the whole lunatic thing, I judge from their expressions, makes a kinked sort of sense.

"Ah, supposing this product does belong to us? You didn't happen to bring it along with you, did you?" Bobbie says.

"Sure. It's in reach," Russo says.

"And I don't suppose you also brought along fifty thousand dollars? Your pocket money?" Butch asks, grinning.

"Sure. It's in reach," I say.

"You guys sure are a crazy couple," Bobbie laughs. "That's a hell of a risk to be taking. When we're just barely acquainted."

"Not really," I say, easing back my jacket. Bobbie and Butch spot the SIG instantly. "Di, too. And, plus, we got a very close friend outside. Ex-Marine sniper. He's got this really jazzed-up AR-15, night-vision scope and all. No disrespect intended, sir. Only, like you said, we're just barely acquainted."

Butch and Bobbie shake their heads. In unison. "You crazy guys," Bobbie says.

"Put yourselves in our place," Russo grins at them. "Wouldn't it be a whole lot crazier for us to've just kept the stuff we ripped from Smitty? If it did actually belong to you boys?"

Bobbie and Butch look at each other and laugh. They're digging this now.

"Well, you might be correct there, Diana. Very correct," Bobbie says. "And sure enough stand-up. So I say we do some bidness. That how your Tennessee friends put it?"

"Hey, great! I'm excited, I'm thrilled!" Russo says. "I see you got a back door there. Open it, please. I'll walk out the way we came in, Charlie'll stay here with you guys. When you see me in back, all three of you just step on outside. Your muscle guy stays put, okay? I'll be carrying a green tool bag in my right hand, and an aluminum briefcase in my left. I'll hand you the briefcase. If you're satisfied with what you see in the case, well, we're already satisfied with what's in that old tool bag. So how about you keep the case, I keep the bag? Charlie and I leave?"

"Sounds like a plan." Bobbie smiles.

"Oh, a fine plan." Butch grins.

I figure they're practically coming, they're so pleased. I figure they'd been pretty much resigned to losing that meth, that they reckoned Smitty was likely halfway to Florida with it by now and no way to catch the fuck. And then here comes good old Di and Charlie with all that nice money.

It goes just like Russo laid it out. Bobbie and Butch take turns pumping our hands after they count. They're chuckling and grinning. "Now don't you be strangers," Bobbie says as Russo and I back away.

"Come around, see us anytime," Butch says. "We might have the start of a very nice little 'bidness' arrangement here."

"Nothing'd please us more," I say. "Been a real pleasure, gentlemen."

"Bye-bye, boys!" Russo cranks up the wattage of her smile all the way, gives them a moment to admire her tits, then blows them a kiss.

Nobody trails us as we move back to the 'vette. I don't feel a single pair of eyes watching us. Nobody leaves the roadhouse. Russo eases out the clutch, and the 'vette just purrs off down the road.

"Damn, we're good!" Russo says when we're well away. I've been watching for tails. There aren't any. "Goddamn good! And that was brilliant, Luther, your improv about the ex-Marine sniper!"

We agree Hyde is no problem. He'll deny it all, he'll be telling the truth, but Bobbie and Butch? They'll never believe him, after what just went down. They'll figure he was in on Smitty's scam attempt, and they'll disappear him. Tough luck for that fuck. We have a laugh over it all. And then Diana and Charlie talk and trash like new best friends, all the way home.

. . .

"One thing, Luther. You know, you're really doing a number on my self-esteem," Russo says. It's after midnight, we've just pulled up in front of my building, I'm holding an army surplus tool bag with fifty thousand dollars worth of first-rate crystal meth in my lap.

"Because I don't come on to you?" I say. It's calculated.

"No, dickhead! Christ, the male ego. Enormous. But dumb. Probably why I get more reinforcement in that particular area than I actually like." She laughs. "I'm talking about professional self-esteem."

"How could I be doing anything at all to that? When you've got so much of it?"

"If I knew the how, I wouldn't be having the problem, would I?" she says. "Usually I'm good at reading people, what they're all about, what they really want. Very, very good. But you keep surprising me, confusing me."

"I doubt that, Francesca. With me, what you see is exactly what you get."

"Oh no, it is not. What's worse, you have this way of looking different all the time. The Luther of one day scarcely resembles the Luther of the next. You do that deliberately, or do you suffer from multiple-personality syndrome or something?"

"I don't do any such thing. Consciously, anyway. Maybe it's the other thing. But I'm not quite following where you're going with this."

"Maybe nowhere. Maybe I just like to have clear images of

people, based on what I know and what I've seen. But I can't get you into focus. It's complicated."

"Why don't you park this shark, come up for a beer? Maybe we can uncomplicate it," I say.

She grins, does it. It's only a matter of minutes before we're sitting on the futon in my living room. She seems to have a clear enough sense of what I consider the boundaries of my personal space. She keeps just the right distance, physically. We sip Grolsch from the bottle.

"You know I know your history," she says. "Know you're bitter about losing your army career, know you worked as a Company merc in Sarajevo. Know you got capped in the head there, wound up with some brain damage and a permanent commitment to anti-seizure drugs."

"So you've claimed. Before."

"I know you dig violence. Get a rush, popping caps. No problem. You're not the only one."

"You making a small but intensely personal confession here?"

"You'll figure that out. Like you've figured out that both Braunstein and the NYPD don't know shit, even though I'd bet a year's salary without hesitation that you personally took out Vassily."

"You'd lose."

"Would not. But never mind that. What confuses me, given the stuff we know I know, is your other side. The good-guy side. Going to see Dog every Sunday. Family dinners at your large partner's home. That solid friendship with your colleague, Annie's her name, right? Has a place in Federal Hill? The solid affair with the college kid, Helen. That sweet real-life action."

All my sensors are going nuts. She's deliberately tripped them. I know how she got my history, she admitted her sources. But this stuff? Has she had me under surveillance? Or maybe it's the CIA, feeding her data. Either way, she's juked me now. And she's timed it perfectly.

"Ever notice how people in our line of work dig the hell out of spreading disinformation?" I say. "How they're so into conspiring and stuff that they'll grab any little piece of bullshit, make it totally real in their minds? Like what I've heard about you."

"And what have you heard?"

I take a shot. "That you're bent. That you've gone rogue."

She laughs. "Hey, that might really be true. Never know, do you? Anyway, what confuses me is that the pieces of your life do not fit together. Some pieces are touching, okay? But they're not the right pieces. And there's lots of the jigsaw just missing."

"Hey, Francesca," I say. "I think we've danced around enough. What do you really want to know?"

"Whether you're so into this Winneberger case because you're a dedicated cop, or because you just dig any sort of action, or because you see some possibilities, some opportunities?"

"Got a rule, Francesca. I never go all the way on the first date."

She laughs, stands up to leave. "I do, sometimes. But not this time, I think. Ask me what I see in this case next date, maybe. I'll give you a straight answer then. If I'm talking then to the same Luther I've talked to tonight."

15.

Next date? The only next I care about, the only one worth going on, is a buy-and-bust—face-to-face and hand-to-hand with Bobbie and Butch. Di and Charlie will need to make some slick moves to set that up.

But there is definitely a next question, aside from how Di and Charlie will manage a sting. Who the fuck is she, this Diana Stadtler, this DEA Francesca Russo? Very talented professional, very acute, doing far more damage to my professional self-esteem than she claims I'm inflicting on hers. And she damn well knows this. She knows I can't make her, what she really wants, what she's really all about, what she's really up to.

Except that she's a woman who can put a nine from her Uzi into a man's forehead as coldly as anyone I've ever seen, and not so much as blink.

I'm deeper into Russo's mysteries than the problems I've got to look forward to as I hit the station next morning, early for a change. I'd phoned IB just after Russo left my place, filled him in on the roadhouse deal. He'd seemed his usual self, seemed past his post-ambush shakes. He'd suggested we get together to talk about the deal and the Wynn woods action before Dugal can grill us. Which he is defintely going to do, big time.

IB's in his cubicle as agreed, but buried in the first edition of the morning *Sun*.

"Ever wonder why cocaine use did such a fast fade? Here's the best fuckin' reason ever," he says, rattling the newspaper at me. "Dig this. Guy in New York City, likes to sometimes shoot a coke solution into the hole in his dick, 'cause it makes him stay harder longer. This time, the hard-on decides to stay that way. Fuck's walking around with a boner for three days, hurtin' bad. So he goes to to the hospital. Docs've never seen anything like it, think it's kind of funny. Until the guy gets blood clots in his cock, arms, and legs. Then the docs take it serious, but by the twelfth day, guy's got fucking gangrene, man! They have to amputate his legs, nine fingers, and—oh, I hate the thought of this—his cock!"

Still jittery, IB is. Residual shock, I think. Can't blame him. The man's tough enough, no question. But he is not real accustomed to taking a lot of fire, doing a lot of shooting. Yesterday at Early's was way outside his boundaries. What happened there would juke most people. Only sociopaths dig firefights. And IB's just a solid, centered family man.

But I chill the newspaper thing, take us straight back into the firefight, and the roadhouse meet. We're in accord on the best way to present what went down, ready as we can get, when IB's phone rings. He picks up, listens, says, "Right."

"Postmortem time," he says to me, gesturing toward Dugal's office very unenthusiastically. "Sounds like it's probably ours."

Dugal's radiating tension so intense I can almost smell it the moment we open his door. So I start the talking and keep on talking. Jump in hard with the good stuff, before Dugal can hit us with whatever's got him wrapped so tight.

"This is making no sense, goddammit," Dugal raps out before I get very far. Heavy sarcasm next. "Enlighten me, Detective Ewing, if I've lost the thread. You talked me into releasing the seized meth to you. You then met the alleged masterminds, these Winneberger twins, at a biker roadhouse last night. You offered to give them the meth. After a quick chat, you gave them fifty thousand dollars cash, so you could keep the meth. Which we already had. Am I going mad? I feel like I must have lost my mind, permitting this."

"But it was only DEA money," I say. "Who gives a fuck about Fed cash? They've got tons of it."

"Levity is inappropriate at the moment, Ewing," Dugal snaps.

"Sorry, Captain. Two points. First," I say, "I did this with a DEA agent, with the express purpose of gaining the Winnebergers' trust. As I explained last night when I asked for the meth. So that we could go back later and do another deal. With maybe five or ten times that much money, wired and backed-up, and bust the twins when they hand us meth for the cash."

"I never sanctioned any joint operation with the DEA, Ewing," Dugal barks. That pen of his starts drumming a fast, angry tattoo.

"That's second. That's the neat part. It's no joint op. The local DEA chief of bureau—you met her, that woman Russo who came here with the NYC DEA guy months ago—agreed you have complete tactical control. The DEA's only role is to provide the money, and the only other DEA involvement is that Russo will accompany me to meet Bobbie and Butch. As she did last night. Seems fair, since she is the one who got us contact with the Winnebergers in the first place."

"Agreed? She *agreed*? Who the fuck . . . ," Dugal starts.

"Otherwise, it is totally your operation," I race on. "You plan and execute the Winneberger bust. You plan and execute the roll-up of the cookers and runners Smitty gave us. Your show totally, with your people. You, I mean the BCPD, gets all the collars, all the drugs. The works. Plus all the credit."

"Oh, excellent, Ewing. Very, very good," Dugal sneers. "Too fucking good to be even halfway true, in fact."

"Had the same thought, sir," I say. "Worked Russo for all I was worth. Searching, probing. Why would she do this? What's in it for her? She was already onto these guys."

"So why is she doing it?" Dugal says. "I suppose you've got some brilliant answer."

"No choice, I think. We beat her to the punch when we busted Smitty," I say. "She's smart enough to know that gave us the initiative on the case. Smart enough to realize that if she helps us carry it off, then the door to future cooperation with you is wide open, Captain."

He ponders implications for a while. His temper's still out there, his mind is still deeply suspicous, but his ego? His ego is pushing the other way. My guess is he's seeing some big triumphs down the road, maybe things we couldn't do without DEA support, for which he'll manage to snag the laurels. Or enough of them to keep pushing his butt up the ladder.

"Future cooperation? I'll be the judge of that, thank you," he says. "It is yesterday that concerns me at the moment. You told me you were very simply going to arrest two unarmed chemists. Instead I find a battlefield. How did this happen? I've thought over everything you told me at the scene. It does not add up, goddammit. I want it to add up."

"I'm still thinking what I told you out there," I say. "The Winnebergers got nervous about Smitty never turning up, put some of their boys around the site for protection, just in case."

"Which sounded reasonable. Until I got the preliminary scene report this morning," Dugal says. "The chemists were not, repeat *not*, killed by IB's shotgun slugs."

"Oh, man," IB sighs. "I been feeling so shitty, thinking I capped them."

"You did not. They were executed by pistol. Most likely the first two shots you say you heard," Dugal says. "The next three may, repeat *may* have been fired in your general direction. But no pistol bullets were found lodged in stumps or anywhere else. No pistol brass was found around the trailer."

Oh, fuck, I think. This is getting weird.

"Can you tell me why the Winnebergers would kill their own chemists, Ewing? No, you cannot. Your theory is complete garbage," Dugal says. "It is also extraordinary that these people were able to set up a military-style ambush so quickly. Unless they were expecting visitors. Police visitors. Which becomes even harder to credit. Aside from those Russians, I have never known criminals to deliberately set out to kill police officers in this county."

Think fast, Ewing. Very fast.

"Well, Captain. Looked at that way, it is very strange," I say slowly. "Since they capped the chemists, they weren't Winneberger shooters after all. And they lured us into that ambush. Remember? Saw the one man, maybe the guy who shot the chemists and got out while I was eating dirt and IB was swiss-cheesing the trailer, run across that footpath. Deliberately showed himself, in other words. Since he could have got away clean through the woods."

"Where are you taking this nonsense?" Dugal demands.

"Here: We were not made for cops. We were made for Winneberger boys. And the Winnebergers actually have real competitors, like we wanted them to think. Those competitors were the shooters. They come to take out the factory, we stumble on them. They cap the chemists, like they'd planned. Then they try to kill us."

"In a preplanned ambush on the trail?" Dugal's laugh is mean. "You can't seriously expect me to accept that."

"Not exactly preplanned, if one or more them was ex-military. They would have had fallback positions worked out, just in case," I say. "I definitely would have, if taking out the factory was my mission."

"No doubt, considering your previously demonstrated inclinations," Dugal says. "We'll know better once the men are ID'd."

Oh, shit. I'm almost ready to go down on my knees and pray none of the dead guys turns out to be on the list of names Smitty gave us.

"And then, a miracle, of course," he adds. "This DEA Russo and a partner, luckily carrying their Uzis that day and being nearby, rush in at the crucial moment and save your asses. An extraordinary happenstance, wouldn't you agree?"

"Yeah, very odd. I said just that to you at the scene."

Dugal stares at me. "However, the scene team did find a number of movement sensors, as you said Russo claimed the DEA had planted," he grudgingly admits. "And some hidden cameras. All infrared triggered, I believe. Though I am not up to speed on the technology."

That's about the only hopeful thing, I think, in what is shaping up as possibly the goatfuck of my life. IB, I can see, isn't giving much thought to any of this. He's too busy feeling relieved that he didn't kill anybody.

"I do not like extraordinary happenstances, Ewing. I do not like incredible coincidences. Everything stays on hold until I get a full report from forensics and the scene team," Dugal says. "Interesting, though, that the preliminary indicates all the dead, aside from the chemists, were apparently killed by Uzis. Except the one with those dart things in his face."

"That was me, Captain. Flechette rounds. Better in bush than buckshot," I say.

"Certainly seems so, in this instance," Dugal says.

. . .

Ice Box slides into a very strange state after we're finished being hosed by Dugal. He's so radically unburdened, so extremely pleased he'd taken no lives at the trailer that an almost lunatic grin seems grafted to his face. It won't shift, it won't moderate, it won't go away. Seems like the hosing didn't register.

But the man's aura—the first I think I've ever actually seen, not just vaguely sensed—is in total contradiction. It's pure biohazard acid green, the color of the worst sort of toxic industrial waste.

A lot more is juking IB than some postfirefight shock. I'm sure of this. Because I'm in the same spooky shadowland, and maybe a couple of steps ahead of him.

"My brain seem to be functioning normally?" IB asks. We've walked over to Teddy's Gyro, he's slurping what passes for coffee there and I'm sipping a Coke. "I'm awake, alert, no delusions or anything? I'm wondering about this a lot right now. Since I'm feeling so weird about a lot right now. Like I'm having some kind of bad, bad dream."

"Night and fog, man," I say. "Just walking and breathing feel kind of dreamlike after bang-bangs like yesterday. You'd be weird if you weren't feeling that way."

"It isn't yesterday that's doing this to me, Luther. It's today. What Dugal brought up. What you told him, Luther. About real competitors hitting the Winneberger trailer. That's the freak part."

"Hey, I tossed the boss a theory, that's all. Got us out of being completely barbequed for the goatfuck, didn't I?"

"What freaks me is that the theory is completely crazy. But I can't come up with any sounder explanation, can't put the thing in any more rational context."

"And that's bad?" I say, not really wanting IB to get deeper into this just yet, not wanting questions I don't have answers for.

"Fucking horrible. First, how likely is it that those Winneberg-ers actually do have real competitors? Second, how about the timing? Them, us, that DEA bitch, and her buddy all at once? Third, how come she murdered the only live body who might have been able to tell us what the fuck the whole thing was about?"

"Hey, scumbags like the Winnebergers always got enemies," I say. "The DEA had that place taped tight. All those sensors and shit. Maybe the guy Russo domed really was going for his tool. I don't make her for a thrill-killer, do you? Only funny thing I see is the timing bit. And all I can say about that is coincidences do happen, and we're lucky this one did."

"Too damn many coincidences," IB says. "And you know it, man. There's the reality: what went down, which we know. And why it went down, which we don't, yet. And then there's a second level! There are players near us who are fucking invisible, Luther. Who the hell are they, and what the hell is their game? 'Cause I'm feeling it ain't exactly the same game with the same rules we're playing."

"Stress reaction maybe, IB?" I say. "A little paranoia developing?"

"You wanna blow it off, then blow it off," he says. "But I'm telling you, there is a second level. And we're gonna get blind-sided by ghosts if we don't find it."

"No problem," I laugh. "If you aren't just going paranoid on me, we'll know soon enough. We'll find the phantoms, or they'll find us."

"Now that's real comforting. They find us first, we'll likely wind up like those guys out at Early's yesterday."

"You're forgetting one thing, IB."

"What?"

"Those guys did find us first," I say.

■ ■ ■

We go back to our cubicles, and IB starts struggling to peck out a full report of yesterday's encounter on his iMac, cursing every few seconds when his big fingers hit two keys when he only wants to tap one. Which is why he hates that machine as much as I hate mine.

I'm staring at a green pressboard folder, with a yellow Post-it attached. It's Eddie Blizzard's jacket. The note, from Tommy Weinberg, says he drew a zero on the alias "Angel Dust." But I'm thinking of IB's "second level." And I suddenly feel, just as surely as I feel when I squeeze off a round with my SIG whether the bullet will be kill-zone or a flyer, that Francesca Russo is conscious of that level. A synapse or two later, I'm conscious of the possibility that Francesca Russo may fucking *be part of* the second level.

Save and store, I tell myself. Brain's like the iMac in some ways; open too many windows on the screen at once, the bastard crashes on you. I do some breathing, some mind-clearing. Then I dive into the Blizzard jacket.

Career scumbag. First pop: at fifteen, Blizzard sells five ounces of grass to an undercover, walks on probation. Second: stomps a forty-five-year-old man nearly to a pulp in a mall parking lot for no apparent reason, gets six months in the BC juvie facility because he's only sixteen. Over the next four years: arrested seven times for first-degree assault—which means he beat the shit out of seven people. No convictions; the victims refused to press charges. At twenty-two, Blizzard gets his first taste of hard time. Three years in the Jessup lockup for armed robbery of a video

rental store, plus possession of five rocks of crack. Out of jail for
six months, arrested for possession of cocaine. Acquitted. A year
later, arrested for possession with intent to distribute cocaine. Acquitted. Six months later, arrested for armed car-jacking with two
other men. They go to Jessup, Blizzard walks on a technicality.
Two years later, arrested for manslaughter—got into a scuffle at
the fucking Winneberger roadhouse, left one guy dead in the
sawdust from multiple blows to the skull with a pool cue, and another dude alive but looking like a carnival freak show attraction;
Blizzard cut up his face with a broken beer bottle so bad it took
123 stitches to close the wounds and left him minus a nose. Hung
jury. Ten witnesses swore the two attacked Blizzard.

I stare at the mug shot from that arrest. It's only two years old.
Long, narrow face. Long nose, thin lips. A little white scar bisects
his right eyebrow. He's an even six feet tall but only weighs one-
hundred forty pounds, the data reads. The story's all in the eyes,
though. Black, cold, reptilian.

A better story: employed by Winneberger AgriCorp, in Westminster; occupation, salesman.

Bet he sells tons of seed.

I open the case file on my iMac, add the most important Blizzard data. Then I take the jacket over to the scanner, do his mug
shot, and enter that into my computer file, too. A routine. Don't
really need to do it; the brain scan's enough. I'll know this fuck for
sure, if I ever see him.

And I do want to see him. I'd very much like to see him. I'm
feeling cold and clear about that, about taking him down hard.
All the way down, if I get lucky and have a nice shot. A clean bust
is no good. Too many fucking snakes like Blizzard slither right
through the system. And the few that don't almost never do the
time they deserve. I don't want this fuck in prison, watching all
the videos and making all the phone calls he wants, getting high

on contraband dope whenever he feels like it, turning some younger, weaker inmate into his temporary wife. I want Blizzard, and all the fucks like him, pincushioned like the dude McKibbin took out with that flechette round. I want them gone for good.

Bad zone. I feel at some fundamental level I'm not much different from all the Blizzards, the ones who don't give a fuck for anybody's rules, who believe they've got the right to make their own. I stand up so fast my chair slams into the cubicle's partition—though the beige padded fabric damps the sound—some small part of my mind violently mutinous. Then a worse flash: Where the fuck was Early Wynn when the caps were popping? Why no mention from the scene team of an old coot with an Ithaca pump storming into his woods, demanding to know what the hell had happened?

I bolt down to the garage, check out a Crown Vic, slam a red flasher on the dash, and terrify a couple dozen solid citizens by weaving wildly in and out of the traffic flow at homicidal speeds. I don't kill the flasher and slow down until I'm only a mile from the farm. I force myself to chill, to ease into Early's drive and park like a sane man.

The SIG's out of its holster, round chambered, before I'm out of the car. Combat scan, quartering the area, peripheral tuned to catch any movement to the sides. I can see about half the front porch and the entire north side of the neat white house. Nothing seems off, out of place. I can hear the slight ruffle and shiver of leaves on the old oaks that dwarf the white house. Half-turn, and I see the tractor's still and silent near the barn. I check out the greening fields. Nothing. I ease into the barn. All the tools are neatly racked, the place is nearly as tidy as Early's kitchen.

Seems clear. I leave the barn, start to ease around the rear of the house, calling, "Mr. Wynn? Early? It's Detective Ewing. You here?"

Nothing.

I make a wide cut around the far corner, come up the side to check the half of the porch I couldn't see before. I stop before cutting the corner. Leaves still rustling in the breeze. Then, beneath that, I catch a regular creaking, wood on wood. I move, SIG at low ready.

There's Early's white-painted pine rocking chair, slowly moving back and forth, back and forth. And there's Early Wynn sitting in it. But it's only the breeze moving the chair. Early is still, staring out at nothing, the front of his khaki work shirt stained dark maroon. His tongue is lolling down through the slit in his throat that gapes just beneath his chin.

I cell Radik.

"Jesus!" he says. "Colombian necktie. Thought that was only Cali cartel legend shit."

"Yeah," I say. "Legend shit. Except what I'm staring at is fucking real. Too fucking real."

"I'm on my way," Radik says.

16.

Helen's lime green Bug is in my parking space that evening. I find another, pull the TT into it, kill the lights and the engine. Then I just sit. I could be sitting anywhere in the world, not necessarily in the soft black leather seat of my own car, outside my own apartment building. For my mind is still at Early Wynn's.

They'd hurt Early before they'd killed him. There'd been circlets of blood around his wrists and ankles, which were bound tight to the rocking chair with braided steel mirror-hanging wire. They hadn't worked on his face, but each of Early's fingers had been bent back until it snapped. Probably one at a time, between questions. His thumbs were stumps, cut off with pruning shears. Radik found the shears in the flower bed around the porch.

No sense to it at all. No reason. There was nothing Early could give up, besides a vague description of two guys who'd come by claiming they were BCPD detectives. And two names, Ewing and Cutrone, if he'd even remembered them. Completely useless information.

Unless somebody else had come calling some other time. Un-

less somebody wanted to be very sure Early hadn't told those detectives anything incriminating, and never would.

Can't get clear on this. Can't get cold. Too much rage. All I want
to do—I want it so bad my hands start to shake—is walk into that
roadhouse with my MP5 on the most crowded Saturday night the
place has ever had, and go full-auto. Not because I'm sure whoever did Early would be among them. Just because they're bikers
and shit-kickers. Just because I feel a certain truth in Poppa's old
Nam jive: Kill 'em all, let God sort 'em out.

Then I'm doing it. Ripping off mag after mag. Not with Geneva
Convention–sanctioned "humane" FMJ rounds. Fuck humane.
My mags are stuffed with notorious Winchester Black Talons, the
kind that mushroom on impact and punch horrendous ragged
holes through people, turn human flesh to shredded meat.

Let God fucking sort that out. If He can.

I'm only into this fantasy for about as long as a real-time mas-
sacre would take: two minutes, tops, plus another minute to
dome anyone who's still twitching, still drawing breath. Then I'm
out, but still in a shitty precinct. Sweat's beaded on my forehead,
my pulse is up to about a hundred-twenty a minute, my hands are
still shaking. I push a Cat Powers tape into the Audi's deck, volume way up, let the acoustic melancholy and the girl singer's
haunting voice envelope me. I start my breathing exercises, the
Zen mind drills. Do a slow fade from Early's porch, a faster one
from something Radik mentioned there: that the marks on the
brass lab-fired from that .45 found at the house with seven bodies in the basement match those on the shell they found when
I got shot, right here in this parking lot. Not a positive, court-
admissable ballistic match, which can only come from bullets.
But close enough.

So many fucking dots to connect. No picture I can even guess
at from the ones we've drawn lines between so far.

Breathe. Fade from all of it. When I feel I can go in clean, no chance of soiling Helen with the scum and slime of the world I move through, I get out of the Audi. Check my watch on my way to the front door. I've been sitting in the car for thirty-three minutes.

. . .

"Quintana Roo?" I say.

"Didn't you listen? It's pronounced Kin-tana Row. Coast of the Yucatan Peninsula," Helen says. "We have to fly to Cancun, but we drive a hundred miles or so south because Cancun and Cozumel are where all the college jerks go. It's like Florida or the Redneck Riviera up there. Down where we'll go it's still quiet, small. Great reefs, great snorkling. If you want it even quieter and smaller, we could go to Roatán. But that'd mean a couple of flights in four-seater planes after the nonstop to Cancun."

We've been out to dinner, seen a film called *Chocolat* at some cineplex. Now we're naked in bed, lights out, and Helen's talking about going away for a week. Her prefinals break is coming up. "My last one, babe," she'd launched in as soon as we'd come home, the wistful pitch off just a bit, so I knew it was serious, but not crucial. Though maybe a hint about our shortening time horizon.

"Why don't you just go down to St. John?" I say. Her parents have a place there.

"I want it to be we. And St. John would be the last place you'd like. Full of old farts tooling around in golf carts, everybody always talking about the stock market and whatever will the Federal Reserve do about interest rates."

"Problem is," I say, "I'm right in the middle of something fairly major. We don't get breaks in the middle."

"How about five days? Any five of my ten days. As long as they're consecutive," she smiles. "Surely you can take five days?"

I probably could. Dugal's put everything on hold. Nothing will go down until Russo and I take a shot at setting up a buy-and-bust of the Winnebergers. And we can't do that for a while. We approach them now, so soon after scoring that fifty large of crystal, and we'll set off every alarm bell in their heads. Nobody moves that much meth that fast and comes looking for a whole lot more, unless they're doing bulk deals, maybe have cartel connections or arrangements with gangstas. Di and Charlie are supposed to be small to medium retailers, successful and ambitious. But still retailers, not players.

I probably could go. If it wasn't for an old man wired to a rocking chair, I definitely would. It'd be the perfect antidote to that, and the ambush. Might even clear some of the clouds of confusion about just who's doing what with who that are filling my head, making it so hard for me to get the sort of clear view I usually have this far into a case. Usually by now I know exactly who I'm hunting, how I'm going to get them. This time's different. That fucking "second level" of IB's. I'm believing in it now, just not truly seeing it. Only the inexplicable things it does, like wiring a harmless old man to a rocker on his own front porch.

"Yeah, five days might be doable," I say. "Most likely nothing will break. But it could. If it does, I've got to be here. Can't be thousands of miles away, stretched out on a beach with you."

"Want me to show you how fast you could get back?" Helen says, running her hands down my front, kissing me, and then, when I'm kissing and stroking her back, straddling me. She goes slow and sweet right up to the edge, pauses a while, then takes us both very slow and very sweet right up to the edge again and over it. After, she laughs.

"It's a three-hour flight, Luther. You'd only have maybe two hours and fifteen minutes left before your plane would land."

"You're forgetting one thing," I say, grinning.

"Am I?"

"Drive time. What about drive time?"

"I know a way," Helen whispers gayly, "to make you wish that would last forever. If you'll do the driving."

I hold the girl as close to me as I can, clutching the realest thing in my warped life. I say, "I'd love to go anywhere with you. Just let me check a few things out, the next few days. Let you know on Sunday for sure, okay?"

"Perfect," she says. "Because I've got two tickets on the Continental flight that leaves early Monday morning."

■ ■ ■

Captain Dugal's as shaken and edgy as I've ever seen him next morning, IB and me across the table and Radik's two-page preliminary on Early Wynn snapping like a snare drum under the rapid beating of his pen.

"Will one of you, if either of you are capable, give me a complete appreciation of this case?" he says. "In simpler terms, what the fuck is going on? I send two experienced detectives into a low-to-moderate-intensity drug zone. I expect, reasonably I think, a systematic gathering of information that will lead to warrants, followed by arrests. What do I get?"

IB mumbles something inaudible. I'd brought him up to speed on Early and everything else I know earlier. He was very unhappy. He was dismayed. "Fucking spookier and spookier," he'd said. "Getting a real bad feeling here, Luther."

Dead bodies!" Dugal suddenly screams. IB flinches. "Seven—or was it eight?—at that house. Six—or was it seven?—at the trailer site. And now an old farmer. Goddammit! I did not ask for dead bodies, did I? The chief dressed me down like I was some errant schoolboy already today. And that will be mild compared with what will come down once the media get their canines into this damn mess."

"We didn't do the killing, remember?" I say, pushing back. "We've got bikers and shit-kickers capping each other, with DEA triggers taking out anyone left standing. That's our fault? Bullshit. We're clean on this. Sir."

"Clean? *Clean?* Good God, Ewing. This is happening in our backyard! From any angle it is going to look as if the BCPD has its collective thumb stuck up its institutional ass. We will never be 'clean' unless you get out there and start putting these people in jail."

"I think, right now, that Homicide has to get out there and put some people in jail," I say, feeling bad for deflecting some of this shit Radik's way. "Our mission is to nail the speed kings. The Winnebergers. Which, as you know, is nearly halfway done."

"With the DEA, which seems at the moment to be part of our problem, not our solution." Dugal is still shouting. "We cannot depend on some dubious sting plan. Something's got to be done right fucking now, Ewing."

"Yeah. By Homicide, not by Narcotics," I snap. "I understand your emotional reaction, Captain. But intellectually you're as clear as I am why we have to wait before we do the Winnebergers."

"Are you patronizing me, Ewing?" Dugal snarls. He whacks his silver pen so hard on Radik's report the cap flies off.

"No sir, I am not patronizing anybody," I say, trying to ratchet things down a notch. "We're all stressed out about this. We're generating more heat than light, sir. I think we need to look at this as coolly as we can, get our team back to being a team. That's all, sir."

This shuts Dugal up for a minute. He can't bear the idea that he might be losing command presence here, even if it's just in front of me and IB. He makes a visible attempt to chill, adjusting the knot of his tie, tugging his suit-coat lapels straight, even semipolitely asking IB if he sees that pen top anywhere. IB retrieves it from the carpet, hands it to Dugal, who slips it onto the pen, then slips the pen into his shirt pocket.

"All right, gentlemen," Dugal says in a near normal tone. It's plainly taking lots of effort for him to manage this. "That's all for today. Proceed according to plan."

"Now poor Radik's gonna take real heat," IB murmurs after we've left Dugal's and are heading back to the narc room. We have to pass through the Vice Squad warren. We get bad looks, some mean muttering.

"The fucks still haven't forgiven us," IB smiles, first time he has today. After the Russian Rattle, when Dugal got command of both Narcotics and Vice, there was a sour reaction, a lot of resentment. It didn't help when some joker used an indelible marker to print, in big block letters on the wall of the men's room, "Vice Squad detectives will please stop eating the urinal cakes. Effective immediately!" Over a reasonable facsimile of Dugal's signature.

It took a week of nightly scrubbing for the janitor to reduce the heavy black words to a faint outline. IB's sure Tommy Weinberg wrote the message. Tommy's kind of pleased people think it was him. It was me.

"Eating the fucking urinal cakes!" IB's laughing hard when we hit our cubicles. It's good to see him loosen up. You look at a guy like IB, you figure he's the fucking Rock of Gibralter, unshakeable and unbreakable. Easy to assume his feelings are the same—if you even bother to consider he might have feelings. Yet he's got more tenderness, more true care, in one massive hand than most men have in the depths of their souls. I've seen it so often, in the way he is with MJ, in the way he radiates love when he's holding his twins, one cradled securely in each arm. In his eyes, when he thought the slugs he'd pumped through that meth trailer had killed two men. IB's got to be pushed real hard before he'll use his great strength, even against the worse scumbags out there. Then he'll go all the way. But he'll feel real shitty after.

Not like me. Never like me.

I decide I'll wait a day or two before I ask Dugal for five days' leave.

I go into my iMac, call up the case file, which I've labeled Crystal. Crystal doesn't have much to tell me today. She seems scattered, evasive, all over the place. Energy's there, I sense it. But it's random. Even when I do the most basic chronology, all Crystal gives up is a list of discrete events that seem to make little sense in time or place. I need humint to make links.

Maybe Annie. We go over to Flannery's for a bar-food lunch: Cobb salad for her, steak sandwich for me. She reads a one-page printout of Crystal, shakes her head.

"What a bitch," she says.

"You see any pattern? You intuit any reasons for what went down when it went down?" I ask.

"Not on this," she says, giving me back the paper and devoting herself to her salad for a moment. "Only a weird contradiction. Seems like every time there's heavy static, especially the super-static of the last few days, this DEA babe is around. But no clear cause-and-effect. Not always physically present, but somehow hovering near. I'm just speculating here, you understand? But I'm getting the sense she's the pivot. Maybe what that book—damn, I forget the title—calls 'the tipping point.' Make any sense to you?"

"Some," I say, explaining IB's conviction that we're playing on the obvious, hard-evidence level but that simultaneously there are people we're not conscious of moving and manipulating. And how much this freaks him, because it's something outside any of his experience.

"Getting a similar feeling myself," she says. "Don't discount it, Luther. Just because it's new doesn't mean it can't be real."

"Know that. I should be hyperalert. But somehow it isn't happening. Christ, I still don't know why I was shot, but I'm not even thinking about solving that mystery." I laugh. "Must be getting old and slow. I'm beginning to believe that Russian thing completely dulled my edge."

"What about the ambush? What about the old man yesterday? You revved about that? You okay about that?" Annie's scoping my eyes now, my gestures and movements.

"Not the way I used to be. Still the usual sequence. Rage rush, ready to kill some people, wanting to. Then the despair. Hating this world, feeling it's too fucked up to go on. But now I just feel so fucking weary of it all."

"But you're clear the world isn't that way," she says. "You know we all feel the rage and the despair sometimes because our jobs put us in the shit up to our eyeballs. Tends to twist us, doesn't it? Regular people living regular lives don't get the way we get."

"Yeah. Maybe I've just got some battle fatigue."

Annie pushes a few bits of salad around the bowl with her fork. Then she gives me that lopsided grin I love.

"Listen, Luther," she says. "Last thing I want to do is put you back in that combat mode you used to almost constantly be in. If I tell you something that's pretty strange, pretty provocative, think you can guarantee a reasonable, reasoned reaction?"

"Hard to promise anything, with a lead-in as vague as that. But I think you'd have to jolt me with a stun-gun to get me very excited about anything."

"Never mind. I've got to tell you anyway, because it might be important," Annie says. "I'm here last night, just having a tequila shot and a beer all by myself before I head home, when that Russo babe slides into a chair at my table. All smiles and patter, like we're girlfriends or something. So I give her that right back. Pretty soon, though, it gets different. She's very smooth, very subtle, but my new girlfriend is working me for information."

"About what?" I ask.

"About you," Annie says. "Not the meth case or anything. Just you."

■ ■ ■

"What it is, home? You think you be gettin' fed, you got the wrong time and the wrong day," Dog says when I show up at his momma's house Thursday morning.

"Fuck that," I say. "Let's go shoot some hoops."

Dog cocks his head, gives me a bad stare, then grins. "Gonna wax your ass, man. You down with bein' humiliated?"

"Show me what you got, nigger," I say.

Dog's in sweats. He makes it up from his chair, out the door, and down the outside back steps on those aluminum crutches, me carrying his folding wheelchair and the basketball. He makes it about halfway up the half-block to the playground when I unfold the chair behind him, lever him into it, steal his crutches. Don't want to diss the man by waiting 'til he has to ask.

"Kiss my butt, shorty," he says as I'm wheeling him onto the court. The backboards are metal, rusted here and there, no nets on the hoops. Four teenagers in baggies are playing at one end. Dog and I get into a one-on-one—he can't maneuver real well but he's got a wicked one-handed set shot. Takes me twenty-one to twelve the first game. About halfway through, I notice the kids have drifted down to our end, dissing me hard. They know Dog, they dig him.

"First time I play since I got capped, and I crush you, home," Dog says at the end, spinning his chair with one hand on the wheel and dribbling the ball with the other. One of the kids asks Dog if they can play, a three-on-three, half-court. I got one on my team who can slam-dunk. Not enough. Dog's team beats us four straight games.

Afterward we sit over by some monkey bars, watching the kids go.

"Told you, nigger. Told you I'd wax your butt," Dog says. He's tired, I can see it, but he's feeling good. "Now you tell me what the fuck you doin' here? Shootin' hoops ain't your game."

I give him a quickie on my problem.

"Shit," Dog says. "My homie Pick, he left my squad just before you and me got together. Joined the D fuckin' E fuckin' A. We're still tight. Whatever he knows about this Russo bitch, you'll be knowin', nigger. Stay loose a while, man. Dog's on the case."

I go see Dugal. Tell him I'm burned out, urgently need a break. That night I tell Helen I've got the days. Monday morning we're on the plane to Cancun.

17.
"Wrong flight, pretty? I think we're in Miami," I say. "Except there'd be more Latinos and more Spanish spoken in Miami."

Helen's looking dismayed. The arrivals concourse, which appears brand-new, is teeming with Germans, Italians, and French. I hear a fair amount of Texan and Midwestern American, loud and nasal above the European. I see a few soldiers lounging here and there in pale green uniforms, side-folding stock assault carbines slung on their backs. No clear make, probably old FAL para models, or Daiwoo 5.56 mms. Very loose security. A relaxed and happy crowd for an airport these days.

"It wasn't like this before," Helen says. "I swear it was just a sleepy nowhere place."

"When was 'before'?"

"Ah, I think around eight or nine years ago."

"Which means you were still a girl, just a hint of tits," I laugh. "Things change."

"Listen, it'll get better when we head down south. Promise," Helen says.

It does, but not for at least fifty kilometers or so. Helen's rented a Jeep from Avis, and as we head down Route 373 with her at the wheel, she starts a running complaint. "Jesus, this was the only highway in the entire eastern Yucatan. A narrow two-laner. Nothing but bush on either side. Maybe three gas stations between here and the Belize border. Which is at least four hundred miles south. Maybe a dozen small side roads, all dead-ending either at the sea or inland at some little place like Coba. I can't believe this."

What she can't believe seems normal enough to me. On the right there's a road running parallel to the highway that's purely commercial: some mini-malls with shops and convenience stores, a cement factory, even a Chevy dealership. All backed by a dry, scrubby jungle. On the left, every quarter-mile or so, tarted-up entrances to big, self-contained resorts. The sea's a mile away, but the resorts have private roads, and a lot of buses from the airport full of Germans or Italians are turning into them. Huge billboards everywhere, all in English: "Welcome to the Maya Riviera," "Swim with the Dolphins at Sian Kaan," "The Grand Hotel Royal Mayan."

"Terrible, terrible," Helen says. "I am so bummed. I'm so sorry, Luther."

"Don't be. I wasn't expecting a South Seas paradise. Just Mexico."

"But this isn't Mexico, not really. Which is why it was so special. The Mayans here fought a war against the Mexicans starting around the 1840s, surrendered finally in 1930," Helen says.

"These Mayans must've had a serious dislike for Mexicans," I laugh.

"Oh yeah. And when the Mexicans finally did win, they stopped bothering the place. Figured there was nothing here worth having. So they mainly stayed away, just let the Mayans get on with their slash-and-burn corn growing—same thing Mayans have been doing since maybe 500 or 600 A.D."

Helen lightens up when the four-laner suddenly funnels into a worn, narrow two-laner and the billboards and resort entrances finally disappear. Low bush on both sides of the road now, but the place is so flat you can't get a look at the ocean. I see some dirt tracks heading inland into the jungle, a few clusters of houses built of tree branches with thatched roofs, women gathered around a single well, all wearing the same style white, sliplike garment. I see men in tattered straw hats hacking around small burnt-out patches of bush with machetes.

"Kind of little, these people. Kind of short," I say.

"Because there never was any Spanish blood, like there was in the rest of Mexico," she says. "A lot of people down here still speak Mayan, not Mex-Spanish."

But the Mayans working at Akumal do speak English. I would've missed the entrance to the place, but Helen spots it, hangs a left, takes the Jeep maybe half a klick down a rutted, potholed road. She starts complaining again about how the place has changed, but it looks okay to me. Akumal's bay is calm, green and turquoise, protected by a coral reef from the deep blue Caribbean that breaks against it. There are only two small hotels and, along the northern horn of the bay, a row of white stucco casitas. She's booked us one near the end. Lovely spot, built on a spur of limestone a few meters higher than the beach. The casitas all have lush gardens out front. Then there's a narrow sand path, a low seawall with steps down into the bay here and there. I spot an iguana poised on the rocks like a miniature predator dinosaur. Except he's chewing a bright red hibiscus flower.

"This at least hasn't changed," Helen says, once we're installed and have gone out on our patio to drink a Montejo, the Yucatan beer. Then she leads me into the water. I know the snorkling drill, but I'm not prepared for the reef. It's an astonishing thing, this wide live wall. Some of the hard corals look like enormous boulders coated with some mossy sort of stuff, but the colors run crazily from green to rusty orange. Among and attached to these are huge, delicate fan corals doing a slow sway, and red corals that resemble small trees after autumn's leaf fall, except the branches are as thick as the trunks, and they're tubular, soft, and a shade of red I don't think I've ever seen. Fish of every color and shape are everywhere, some solo and some in close-packed schools that move abruptly in perfect unison, better than any flocks of birds on the wing. I don't much like the way a pair of barracuda—as long as I am tall—eyes me, but I dig them anyway. They're silvery, sleek as missles, and almost, it seems, as fast. When they want to go. It's their choice; they seem to regard an approach by me with complete disdain.

We dine that night on a *frijoles negros* soup laced with spices I've never tasted before, and grilled grouper. The Mayans we meet are warmly friendly, polite but not subservient. Nothing like the Mexicans I've come across in other places. I get no sense of machismo, no feeling that you could score anything you wanted simply by offering enough pesos. No narcotraffick here, I figure. No hitters for hire, no whores of either sex.

"Long way from Tijuana," I say to Helen.

"Another world," she says.

And by the second night I'm in another world. Hours cruising easily among the fish and coral during the day, soft evening hours eating and then just sitting on our patio or the seawall, listening to the lazy lap of the water. Making love, then sleeping deeply, without dreams. If our time together is running out, Helen and I don't notice it, don't speak of it. And it isn't until the last morning, when we're tossing our gear into the Jeep for the drive to Cancun airport and the flight home, that I'm startled to realize I haven't had a single thought about meth, the Winnebergers, Russo, poor Early, or the whole fucked-up case since I got to Akumal.

I want to thank Helen for that. There's no way I can explain what she's given me, with these five days. The best I can do, knowing as I do it that it's lame, totally inadequate, is to stop at a boutique on my way back from returning our masks, snorkels, and fins to the dive shop. We'd passed the place a couple of nights walking home from dinner, and she'd admired a particular silver bracelet, crafted locally and incised with old Mayan symbols. I buy the bracelet, slip it onto her left wrist just before we get into the Jeep. "Souvenir," I say. I get a tight hug and a deep, sweet kiss in return.

But by the time our plane lands at Baltimore-Washington International, it's almost as if I'd dreamed Akumal. I'm deep, deep into meth-dealing bikers and shit-kickers, and getting, finally, a feel for the pattern, a sense of who's manipulating those puppets. No hard facts, but strong instinct. It is not totally the Winnebergers, I decide. There's a bigger, faster barracuda in the waters.

■ ■ ■

First thing I do when I hit the office Monday morning is drop in on Radik.

"Man, I think I need to get on Prozac or something," he says. "Never been so fucking depressed. Scene team and forensics got absolutely zip on those dead dudes at the trucker's house. Except they got capped with a .44 Special. Like that really helps. They got nothing on that old farmer, except he was strangled to death before the necktie. Like that really helps. We've muscled every snitch we ever had. Zip. We've interviewed every vic's family members. Twenty-nine interviews. Zip, except for a few names of the victims' buddies. We grilled the buddies, fucking toasted and roasted them, man. Zip."

"Shit," I say. "Now I feel like double-dosing Prozac."

"Tell you, Luther, I've never seen anything remotely like this. Ran by Dugal the IDs of those dudes who went down ambushing you; he says none of them are known, none of them are on the list that guy you busted with the meth gave up. I'm starting to feel I'm just in the middle of a real bad dream and pretty soon I'm gonna wake up to a normal world. 'Cause if I don't, I'm gonna have to start believing in phantoms. How the fuck do you nail a phantom for multiple homicide?"

"Killer ghosts? Forget the Prozac, man. I think you need Thorazine, some kind of antipsychotic."

"That what you been on all these years? Maybe I'll give it a try, then. I mean, anything that's kept a lunatic like you acting half-sane at least half of the time has got to be fine stuff." Radik laughs.

"Wouldn't help you," I grin. "It's in your fucking genes, dude. All your relatives back there in the Carpathians or in Transylvania still believe in vampires and werewolves and shit. Just make yourself some handloads with silver bullets for your piece, start carrying a cross. Oh, and take one of your empty Pikesville Rye pints, sneak into a Catholic church, and fill it up with holy water. Vampires really hate getting splashed with holy water."

It's no joke, though. Radik's good at his job, and it troubles me a lot that he's getting nowhere. I get more troubled when I go down to the narc squad room and huddle with Ice Box.

"You down in Mexico shacked up with your pretty little señorita, and IB's here taking shit from all sides," is how he greets me. "Ain't fucking fair, Ewing. Dugal's got PMS or something. Wants reports every day. I got nothing to report. Plus that DEA weathergirl just walks into my personal office here not once, but twice. You got a thing going on the side with her? Because she asks a hell of a lot of real personal-type questions, gets all huffy and icy when I tell her you're south of the border."

"You told her that, IB? You told her I was off with Helen? I can't fucking believe it, man."

"Well, yeah." IB sort of hangs his head. "But hey, it wasn't on purpose or anything. The woman is one damn sly operator, pushes buttons you didn't even know you had. So it just sort of popped out. Sorry about that."

"Ah, don't mean nothing," I say. I can't be pissed at IB because he got twisted up by Russo. Not when I've gotten twisted up by Russo. One of the things that hit me on the flight home. Somehow she'd managed to lock me into the role of her partner—her junior partner—in what's supposed to be my case. No way out of that place just now, either. Not if we're going to pop the Winnebergers.

IB does have at least one fresh thing on the case to tell me about. One thing only, but it's a large jack for me. Persons unknown hit one of the meth factories up north. Nobody would've known about it—since we'd pulled back surveillance to the lowest level—if the trailer hadn't combusted and started a forest fire. Exactly the sort of message I did not want the Winnebergers to get. They might bunker up, they might now be unapproachable to Di and Charlie. Shit. Means I've got to set a meet with Russo real soon.

I call her office. Some dude—sounds like that Phillips shit who was handy with his Uzi in Early's woods—says she's out. Try her cell; it tells me it's busy or out of service range. I don't ID myself or leave messages either call. I phone Dog.

"Got some shit for you, home," he says. "What's tonight look like for you?"

"Looks like maybe dinner at that Chinese joint you dig, the one where the chicken's really cat," I say.

"Hey, haven't had any of that tasty cat for a long while, nigger. You're on. Pick me up, say seven or so?"

"Party starts then. Later, man."

No way Dog can ride in the TT. But the Chink place is a wheelable distance from his momma's, just a block west to Greenmount Avenue and a few blocks down. The man won't let me push. He's got fingerless leather workout gloves, and he can roll his cart fast. Which he does, until I ask him to slow it down so I can walk, not jog.

Dog orders about six dishes. They all taste like cat to me, just different sauces: black bean, garlic, some Szechuan thing so hot my nose starts running. He works those chopsticks like he was born using them. The plates are about half cleared, second bottles of Tsingtao beer have been uncapped and sipped, when he gives.

"So, what my man hears about your Russo is this," Dog starts. "Hears, you down with that? 'Cause he can't rob files or nothing. Wouldn't if he could. My man's stand-up, dig?"

"Hears is good. Hears is a fuck of a lot better than nothing," I say.

"Age thirty-one. Joins the CIA fresh out of college, transfers to DEA after two years or so. Fast-track from the start. Either real talented, or knows the right guys to fuck. My homie figures real talented. Couple of years out, she's banging, high intensity. Undercover in Miami, major busts, Jamaicans, Colombians. She's a star, so naturally the big dicks use her up, burn her out too quick. Can't get undercover anymore; she's known to all the players. So she's pissed, she's resentful, blames her bosses for misusing her as an asset. But she's a star. They toss her something they know she'll like a lot."

"Such as?"

"A transfer to Phoenix, a key spot on the team trying to nail the Sonora cartel."

"Details?"

"Plenty. One of the biggest, baddest crews in the world. Run until 1985 by Rafael Caro Quintero. Big surprise to everybody, specially that dude, when a fucking Mexican court gave him life and threw away the fucking key. Not for being a narcotrafficker. For murdering a dude name of Salazar. Who happened to be American, not Mex. And DEA."

Dog chops up some more of whatever it is we've been eating, takes a long pull of beer. "But they got a real sweet system, down in Mexico," he goes on. "You pay the right generals, the right top cops, the right politicians, and you stay in biz. Only now the top dude is Rafael's little bro, Miguel Caro Quintero. These fucks got a thing about formality with names. Weird. Anyway, Miguel don't live like the criminal everybody knows he is. Shit no. He be big in Mexico, goes where he wants, does what he wants. Goes on radio talk shows and shit.

"And when he's not out frontin', and fuckin' all the pussy he can find, he's taking delivery direct from Cali of tons of Colombian cocaine at a lot of ranches he owns in Sonora. Then he sends his mules over the border to Arizona, New Mexico, California, Texas, spreads that coke along the interstates."

"So. The Feds got that big Colombian cartel boss, that Pablo Escobar," I say. "Why not this Mikey Quintero?"

"They been trying. For what, fifteen fucking years? But they can't get a Mexican to touch him. Every once in a while Washington gets bad and nasty with the Mex government, but still they don't do shit to this dude. DEA keeps slipping agents into Sonora, but Miguel's crew is army-size. Anyhow, last time the DEA did a kidnap, the U.S. courts turned the fuck loose, I think."

"So my girlfriend's one of the agents they send into Sonora. Something happens, she winds up here," I say.

"Yeah. My homie, he don't know what, though. What he hears, she got closer to Miguel than anybody had before. What he hears, maybe too close. Too involved, maybe? Nothin' illegal, but something the DEA chief in Phoenix didn't dig. He pulled her sweet ass right out, shipped it Fed Ex as far away as he could. Fucking B-town, nigger. Our hood!" Dog's laughing hard.

"Lot of ways to read that shit, man," I say. "She could've been too fuckin' good, or too fuckin' bad."

"Couldn't have been too bad, home. She'd be dead. Or at least unemployed," Dog says. "But saved the best for last, nigger. This Miguel, richer than shit on Colombian money for doing nothin' but sending his niggers to do the dirty work, he's got it made, dig? Private jet, big Mercs, Land Rovers, lots of nice big houses, imported live-in Yankee snatch, top quality from Vegas and L.A. Sensible man be content with all that, you know what I'm saying?"

"I'm digging it," I say.

"Miguel, he's some crazy Mex, though. He be cooking speed on his ranches, making his coke mule niggers double-hump across the border. How fuckin' dumb is that?"

"Dumb as it gets," I say. "Why risk the meth by smuggling it, man?"

"Yeah, fuck that border risk. When you could just put up some cash, finance some Americans to cook it and deal it for you." Dog holds my eyes. "Shit, you could have factories anywhere, real close to the markets. Even trailers in the fuckin' woods up the north county, you know what I'm saying, nigger?"

I do. Not for sure, nothing to move on, but close enough. Now I'm thinking it probably doesn't matter if we nail the Winnebergers or not. Because possibly they're being taken out for us. Now I maybe know why, and maybe even by who. That second level. Cool. We could just sit back and let it happen, then jump all over the new guys, the ones that torched the factory IB told me about. Except there's a little problem with just sitting back, seeing what goes down: Dugal. No patience at all. I got this Winneberger thing in motion and he wants to go, go, go. Shit.

. . .

"Your security sucks, Luther. Took me about ten seconds to pick your lock."

My apartment's completely dark, but I don't need to see to know I'm hearing Francesca Russo. Probably sprawled on the futon in my living room.

"What? You think I got anything here I'd give a fuck about if it got stolen?" I say.

"Your life?" she says. "Generally people in our profession are at least a little security-conscious about their lives."

"That's the least thing I worry about," I say, flicking on the lights. Little surprised to see Russo lean over my table, snort up a line of coke with a tightly rolled hundred-dollar bill, then wave me over with the bill toward the other line that's laid out there. And not by the drugs. Francesca isn't wearing her business suit or her roadhouse tart outfit. She's dressed for sex, at least the kind she thinks I'm into. College-girl style: low-slung baggy pants, cropped jersey top, navel showing. Helen's style.

"Try this," she says, pointing at the line. "Cali's best. Pure. Never been touched, let alone stepped on."

"I'll pass," I say. "And I don't mean to be cruel, but that outfit just doesn't make it. A little too young for you, maybe."

"It'll make it perfectly," she says, snorting the second line, "with the guy I'm going to see after I leave here."

"Don't let me keep you, then." I feel like jerking her chain, maybe asking if the dude's got three names and a good tan. But I squelch it.

"I've got a while. It's not like I'm going to Akumal for five days or anything. Just a date."

"His place? Or one of yours?" Stupid, but I can't resist. Dog'd laid a few other details on me, like the fact that Russo had an apartment downtown, but spent as much time as she could on a little farm across the Bay in Caroline County, along the Choptank River. Word was the place was an inheritance from her grandmother. Russo kept some horses there, loved to ride. Also into some kind of dog breeding. Probably Chesapeake retrievers.

"No way. My favorite spot's this cheap motel down around Arbutus," she says, ignoring my shot. "I like some really garish neon leaking around the drapery at the window, some bedsprings squealing from the next room. Those romantic kinds of touches."

"So, what's holding you up? What is it that just wouldn't keep until office hours tomorrow?"

"Bobbie and Butch. They lost another cooker while you were on vacation with your little girl. You probably heard that from your big partner this morning." Russo does a yoga stretch that lifts her breasts, makes her top ride higher on her belly. "I couldn't reach you when it happened, so I took the decision to speed things up, accelerate our plan. A meet with them in Westminster Wednesday? Noon? They suggested lunch. I see a diner with Naugahyde booths in our future."

"Just let me check my Palm Pilot, see if I'm free."

She laughs.

"You're free," she says. "Trust me. I know these things."

"I've been getting the sense for a while now that you know everything, Francesca," I smile at her as she gets to her feet. *Except that I'm catching up with you.*

She turns at the door. "A pity," she says.

"What is?"

"I sometimes look at you and think we might have some nice times together," she says. "If we weren't business partners."

"That doesn't seem to get in the way for Di and Charlie," I say.

"Transparent, Luther." She laughs. "I'm gone. Phone Helen. Get her over here in her green Beetle."

18.

"Guess I was wrong about Naugahyde," Russo murmurs as we walk into the Carrol Inn precisely at noon on Wednesday. The restaurant's in one of the few old stone colonials that rub shoulders with red-brick Victorians in the neat little center of Westminster. Not a suit in sight, but what passes for serious business attire here. Lots of men who've doffed their sports coats, revealing crisp white short-sleeve shirts and narrow ties. Lots of middle-aged and old women in dresses or buttoned-up blouses and ankle-length skirts, light cardigans draped like shawls around their shoulders. Floral's the dominant motif in skirts and dresses. Everyone sitting around tables on spindly legged maple Colonial-style chairs.

I don't see our guys anywhere. And all the tables are full. "We're supposed to be meeting the Winnebergers," Russo says when the hostess approaches and starts apologizing for being unable to seat us.

"Oh, of course," the hostess says, brightening. She leads us through the main room, takes an unexpected turn, and we're in a side alcove with a single large table. Two identical faces look up simultaneously.

"Bobbie! Butch! Great to see you!" Russo cranks it up. She's not wearing her roadhouse gear, I've skipped the Deere ball cap and my jeans and boots are clean. But we are a little underdressed by Carrol Inn standards. Nobody seems to care.

"You guys, you crazy guys," Bobbie smiles.

"Take a pew, don't be shy," Butch grins.

"Not late or anything, are we? We drove up and down the street three times before we spotted this place," Russo says, easing into one of those chairs with the skinny legs.

"Punctual to the minute," Bobbie says.

"We always come a little early, have a Bloody Mary prelunch," Butch says. "Like one?"

"Love one," Russo says. "Charlie?"

"Not me, hon. You know I'm a one beer a night guy," I say.

"That's Charlie, all right. I noticed that about you, Charlie. Sensible habit," Bobbie says. "Got a regular routine myself. One Bloody Mary before lunch, one shot of Black Jack every evening. No more, no less."

"Except for special occasions, Bobbie," Butch says. "I do think I've seen it more like half a bottle of Black Jack. On special occasions. And you forgot all those Rolling Rocks."

"It's true, what can I say?" Bobbie smiles, shrugs his shoulders. "I always do regret it next morning, though. Every single time."

"Tell me about mornings after the night before!" Russo laughs. "Once I get going, I never have sense enough to stop. Charlie has to stop me. And next day? Oh, I'm nasty. It's a wonder Charlie hasn't divorced me, I'm so mean."

"Uh, Di," I say. "Don't want to upset you, but I did divorce you. Three years ago. Think maybe you were too hungover to notice."

The twins are nearly howling. "You guys! You crazy guys! What did I say about Charlie and Di, Butch? Didn't I say they were our kind of people?"

"You said they were our kind of people, Bobbie. Your exact words."

Russo drains about a third of her Bloody Mary, half opens a menu, closes it quickly. "So what's good here? I've got a real appetite today."

"The fried chicken's the best anywhere," Bobbie says.

"No, the chicken pot pie's the best," Butch says.

"So who do I believe, boys?" Russo grins.

"That's a hard one, Di," Butch says. "I always have the pot pie. Bobbie always has the fried chicken. I've never tried the chicken, and Bobbie's never tried the pie."

"Big help. Guess I'll toss a coin in my mind. Tails, it's the fried," Russo says. "Whoops! Came up heads. Pot pie for me."

"How about you, Charlie?" Bobbie asks.

"Nothing better than fine fried chicken, in my book," I say.

"The right choice, definitely," Bobbie says.

We go back and forth like that, total horseshit, until we're about halfway through our food. Then Russo rachets things up a notch.

"This is terrific, really special," she says, waving a forkful of pie. "And you know what else was really terrific, really special? That Dog Bite. We never sold anything so fast, it was like a Blue-Light Special or something. Never had so many happy customers."

"That makes us very happy, Di. We like our clients to be satisfied," Bobbie says.

"Satisfaction guaranteed," Butch says. "That's our motto. Not a money-back guarantee, of course. I mean, how can you give any customers money back when they've already consumed the product?"

The twins giggle. "Bidness," Bobbie says.

"Which is why I called you boys," Russo says. "We're sold out! Can you believe it? The shelves are empty, we've got customers lined up at the front door waving their dollars at us. And we're sold out."

There's an almost imperceptible eye-flick between Bobbie and Butch, the faintest scent of worry in the air.

"Well, let's all of us just go back to our office when we've finished and talk this over," Bobbie says. "Apple cobbler for dessert, first."

"No, pineapple upside-down cake," Butch says.

Russo laughs. "Guess I've gotta toss that coin again."

■ ■ ■

Winneberger AgriCorp is most definitely a going concern. Russo and I follow Butch and Bobbie's black Lincoln about a half-mile past the heart of Westminster to a light industrial area edging the old Baltimore & Ohio railroad tracks. The tracks are rusty, the siding switches probably frozen, because no trains have run that line in years. Instead, there's an acre or two of asphalt parking lot for eighteen-wheelers and smaller trucks, a big corrugated metal warehouse with loading docks, all of it looking no more than five or six years old. Butch and Bobbie's office is perched up on a very wide second-story balcony-type thing that runs all the way around the warehouse. It's glass-fronted; from it, you can look down on pallets stacked with five-hundred-pound bags of seed and fertilizer, four or five bright yellow forklifts scurrying around them, once in a while lifting a pallet and driving out barn-size doors to a dock.

They settle in behind identical gray steel desks; Russo and I sit on a sofa the same chewed-tobacco color as the one in the roadhouse, facing them. Bobbie buffs his bald dome with the palm of one hand.

"Well, boys, like I told you, Charlie and I are sold out," Russo starts in. "Cash-rich, product-poor. Think you can help us out?"

"That depends, Di," Bobbie says, still polishing his scalp. "Couple of factors involved."

"Couple of factors." Butch nods.

"Now, if you want the same quantity, same price, why, we can get right down to bidness," Bobbie says. "You have something else in mind?"

"Absolutely something else," Russo says. "We did so well last time, Charlie and I are convinced there's a lot of opportunity we're just missing. It's always a shame, missing opportunities."

"So what are you thinking?" Butch asks.

"Exactly—not ballpark, mind—nine times our first deal," I say.

"Done some informal market research, customer-survey types of things," Russo says. "We want four-hundred-fifty-thousand worth. Same quality, but at this level I think a volume discount would be in order."

Another eye-flick between the twins. They're cool about it, but I can feel some surprise, some anxiety. Maybe some hesitation, because after the two hits they took on their cookers, they might not have anywhere near that weight to sell, much as they'd like to. But they can't let us know that.

A smile spreads across Bobbie's face. "Well, my gosh, Di. That is a what I'd call a very major expansion. Are you liquid enough? Because, much as we love you crazy guys, it's always cash up front. No credit."

"So liquid we can pour four-fifty large into your pockets day after tomorrow."

"That's what we like to hear," Butch says. "Of course, you have to understand we don't generally inventory that sort of weight. It would take us a while to gather it up."

"How long's a while?" Di asks sweetly. "You boys wouldn't keep a girl waiting too long, would you? Being the gentlemen you are."

"Can't give you a definite answer to that, Di, until we talk to our foreman," Bobbie says. "I believe I can promise it wouldn't be long enough to disappoint you. I'd hate to disappoint you guys. But let's take one step back here."

"One step back," Butch says. "What sort of volume discount do you have in mind?"

"Oh, teensy, really. Nothing outrageous," Russo says. "Charlie did one of those spreadsheet things on his laptop. I didn't quite follow the math, but his numbers came up 12 percent more product per fifty than what we got for the original fifty. Sound fair?"

"Almost," Bobbie says.

"Actually, 10 percent would be more usual," Butch says. "If we could agree on ten this time, twelve would be a very strong possibility for a reorder down the line."

Russo and I look at each other, trying for a husband-wife kind of consideration when they're negotiating to buy a new house or something, the wife silently sending "It's a steal, let's grab it, honey" messages, the husband sending back "I'm really worried about how high the monthly mortgage payments will be, darling." I catch Butch and Bobbie doing the same, but about the weight, not the price, I figure.

"Well, twelve was our number," I say after what I judge is a decent interval. "But what the hell, ten this time and twelve the next? That sound like a deal? Okay by you, Di?"

"Sounds like a deal to me," she smiles.

"Then hey, you guys! It's a deal," Bobbie says.

"But one thing," Russo says. "How quick can we do it? And I'm not quite up to an exchange behind the roadhouse. I mean, it won't just be one briefcase and one canvas bag. I think we need a little less public venue, don't you, boys?"

"Now that is simply no problem at all, Di. Your concerns are our concerns exactly," Bobbie says. "We'll do it very privately, very securely. Guarantee that."

"But the timing, Bobbie. I don't want to press you boys, but time's a big factor for us," Russo says.

I hear heavy work boots clanging on the steel-grate catwalk outside the office, a sharp rap on the door.

"Hey, here's our foreman," Butch says as a lean guy all in denim slides in.

"Eddie, meet Charlie and Di," Bobbie said. "A crazy couple. We love 'em."

I turn to look. It's fucking Eddie Blizzard, looking back with those cold lizard eyes. Then he gives Russo the stare. A smirk flickers across his face so fast I'm not sure if I've only imagined it. Maybe it's just a flash of what Dog told me about how close she got to that Sonora drugista, but goddammit if I don't suddenly feel like Francesca Russo's met Eddie Blizzard before. Maybe more than once before. And the Winneberger twins haven't got a clue.

■ ■ ■

I know it's all very, very wrong because I'm getting no rush at all. Nothing. Nada. There's nearly half a million dollars, nice banded stacks of bills, in two Samsonite suitcases in the trunk of Russo's 'vette. It's getting near midnight, ten days after lunch in Westminster, and we're waiting for Bobbie and Butch to show with a shitload of methamphetamine. Dugal, IB, and a bunch of tacticals Dugal always gets off on using are within shouting distance but totally out of sight.

The Winnebergers are going down tonight. If they bring Blizzard and Angel Dust and some others in their crew, we might even get to do some shooting.

And I've got no rush at all. I am flat. Never felt like this before an action. Never. It's wrong.

Everybody else is revved and ready. Dugal's behaving like a competent but combat-virgin battalion commander about to launch a major assault. Before we left Towson, he'd gone over his plan with all the key players for maybe the fifth time, even though it's simple as shit, nothing complicated or innovative or risky about it. He, IB, five tacticals, and five plainclothes, carrying shot-guns or CAR15s, will trail Russo and me to the rendezvous and get hidden. They got night vision; when they see us complete the deal with Butch and Bobbie, they're gonna pop up and bust the fucks.

Then Dugal's gonna say "Racer! Racer!" into his mike, and teams of narc squad members and tacticals are going to sweep right in on the four or five trailer factories in diffent parts of the north county, seize and hold them. Nobody's going to be at any of these places, I'm sure of that, but Dugal wants them captured and de-fended, just in case any of the Winneberger crew gets word out of the bust, and some bad guys go in to destroy the sites.

Just before we all drove off, Dugal even inspected the troops, gave 'em a bracing speech about how important each and every swinging dick and dickette was to the success of this mission. He gets into his black Crown Vic, accompanied by the tactical chief, like it's a Loach, and he's an Air Cav commander going airborne to direct the attack.

Seen too many movies, read too many books about Vietnam, I figure. This thing could be handled by me and IB and a troop of local Boy Scouts, it's that simple.

Now we wait. It don't mean nothing, to me.

Even Russo, who's got to have seen much, much heavier action in Miami, in Phoenix and Sonora, has got an edge on. She's pretty cool, but the adrenaline's doing its job anyway. Her conver-sation's about two beats faster than normal, her hands uncon-sciously moving repeatedly from the 'vette's steering wheel to check-pats of her tools, her wire.

"Hey, Francesca, about the other night? The one when you let yourself into my apartment?" I bait her.

"Yeah? What?" she says. Not looking at me, not paying much attention, too busy scanning the abandoned quarry where we're meeting the Winnebergers even though it's total blackout and she can't see a thing, won't see a thing until headlights come up a little hill, crest it, and head down to the quarry pool we're parked near.

"I was just wondering," I say.

"Wondering what, Charlie darling?" Oh, she's good, but I pick up impatience in her voice.

"Uh, just what color neon you dig? Red, blue, green? What makes you look best when you're naked in a cheap motel room?"

"Fuck off!" she snaps, then recovers quick, laughs. "Red, what else? Even you'd get off on me, naked in a motel room with a little red neon glowing on my body."

"You know, I might. I can sort of see it. Yeah, I might dig it."

She laughs again, then does a one-eighty. "Going to be some unhappy people and some very happy people, after tonight," she says. "Going to be a nice vacuum in the regional meth market. Somebody's going to notice it. Somebody's going to step right in."

"Wow. Dugal'll be so surprised," I say.

"Sarcastic bastard, Ewing."

"Nah," I say. "Dugal really will be. You and me are maybe the only ones who won't. Somebody besides the BCPD has already started creating the opening. Tonight we finish it for them. Point is, though, I just don't give a fuck. Already cleared it. Butch and Bobbie go down, I'm off this chickenshit. Reassigned. Shit-kickers bore me. I like to party with the big boys, the smack and coke crews. I like to bang."

"Tell me something I don't know," Russo says. I see, just

vaguely in that dark, her hand brush her wire, checking it's still off. She knows I'm not wired.

"Like what?" I say.

"Like you don't see some opportunity in the vacuum? Like it hasn't crossed your mind that maybe a career in law enforcement has a shitty risk-reward ratio?"

"When I cross the line, it'll be for something a lot more worth my while then a little meth merchandising."

"Thought you were smarter, Luther. You are badly underestimating meth, in terms of risk-reward. I've seen it up close. Best ratio going."

"You learn that down in Sonora, did you? Miguel lay it all out for you?"

"Now you're dropping from half-smart to dumb, Luther." She's chill, more in control then she's been all night. She has to've taken a wicked hit, but she doesn't flinch a millimeter. "You got yourself some industrial waste from the DEA rumor mill, which churns out whole landfills of the shit. I'm supposed to swoon or something?"

"It'd be cute to see, Francesca," I say. "But light entertainment only. Since you're always right, though, I'm curious. How about, when we're done with this job, we maybe get together and discuss some basic mathematics?"

"Had that thought long ago. You blew it off."

"People change, Di darling."

"Later, Charlie," she says. Two beams shine up from behind the hill, blind us for a moment as they crest it and head down. Few seconds later, a repeat. All as planned. Butch and Bobbie'd balked a bit when we'd insisted on dealing with them personally, but Russo'd gone so convincingly hurt and pouty that they'd agreed. Provided they could bring backup, in a vehicle carrying the product. And we promised to limit our backup to our one ex-Corps sniper pal.

"Bobbie! Butch!" Russo's calling, out of the car and hand shielding her eyes from the glare of two pairs of headlights, which flick to high beams twice, then cut out: the arranged signal. I've got my eyes closed tight. Don't want my night vision temporarily weakened.

"You guys, you crazy guys," Bobbie says. I exit the 'vette when I see two figures get out of the Winneberger Lincoln. The other vehicle's an SUV, looks like a Pathfinder. It turns, backs into the space between the Vette and the Lincoln. As agreed.

Handshakes all around. Bobbie and Butch go with Russo to the back of the 'vette, where she pops the trunk and they pop the Samsonites. I stand back as Stone-Face opens the rear of the SUV. There's another biker-type dude I've never seen before about two steps from the passenger door. He's cradling an FAL, probably Imbel license-made in Brazil, not the real Belgian model. Poor choice either way. Classic battle rifle, but much too long and much too slow for any close-quarters situation. Dumb shit-kicker.

"Where's Eddie?" I ask as Stone-Face pulls a big army surplus duffle out of the SUV, keys the brass lock at the top, opens it wide. I'm wearing a Petzl LED light on my left wrist. Turn it on, pull out a pack of Dog Bite at random from the duffle, open it in the narrow but brilliant white beam.

"Busy," Stone-Face says. Flash on that glance at Russo at the twin's office. Nasty flash.

"Lookin' real good up here, Di hon!" I call when I've tasted what's in the single pack, hefted the whole duffle.

"Good here too, am I right, boys?" Russo says.

"You guys," Bobbie says. "Awright!"

"Hey," Butch calls as he and Bobbie come around the 'vette,

each hauling a Samsonite, "you wanna bring that duffle, see if you can cram it in the trunk, Angel?"

The dude with the FAL slings it, lifts the duffle with one damned big arm, hauls it around to Di. After a moment, "Hey, it won't fuckin' fit!" Angel says.

Angel. Eddie Blizzard and his buddy Angel Dust. Fuck me. I'm thinking of an old man wired to a rocking chair. I'm thinking I don't want Angel going down soft on a drug arrest. I want him and Eddie going down hard for Early Wynn.

"No problem," Russo says. "I'll take the spare out. I'm ice-picking it to let the air out. We can toss it in the quarry. What's one five-hundred-dollar mag wheel on a night like this?"

I hear the spare hit gravel.

"You got that sucker in yet, Angel?" Butch says, sliding his Samsonite into the SUV.

"Just fuckin' making it fit," Angel says.

"You guys, you crazy guys," Bobbie says. His Samonsite's in the SUV too. "I know you love your 'vette, Di. But next time, take my advice. Don't use your pretty car on something like this. Get an old Cherokee or something."

"Am I dumb or what, Bobbie?" Russo laughs. "Charlie, am I dumb or what?"

"All set, hon?" I say. "Bobbie? Butch? All set?"

"Perfecto," Bobbie says.

I douse the Petzl, ease my SIG out, let it dangle against my right thigh. Russo moves up even with me but two meters left.

"Couldn't be better," she says, and I close my eyes.

We're lit up bright, bright. Wait a beat, open my eyes, point the SIG at Bobbie's gleaming dome. Five or six of those superintensity handheld spots from four directions make it look like we're on the fifty yard line of a football stadium. Lots of running, shouting, the traditional asshole "Go! Go! Go!" from the tacticals. Bobbie, Butch, and Stone-Face are nailed, still as jacklighted deer. "You're under arrest," I say. Peripheral catches Russo's Glock swinging between Angel and Butch.

Angel bolts, jigging hard around the 'vette, unslinging his FAL knockoff. Dugal's screaming "Freeze! Freeze! Drop that weapon!"

Russo pirouettes like a dancer, double-taps. Angel goes face first into the gravel. She swivels back, and IB and some tacticals are cuffing Bobbie, Butch, and Stone-Face.

"You guys?" Bobbie starts, but Dugal starts booming the Miranda. I see cruisers crest the little hill way too fast, go airborne a couple of feet, wham down hard. Stupid fucks probably just split their oil pans wide open. Overexcited uniforms. Fucking menace to themselves and others.

It's over for me. I holster the SIG, turn, and settle into the soft leather seat of Russo's 'vette. Put my hands behind my head, close my eyes. Let my mind drift where it will. It heads south, toward Quintana Roo. Russo has to elbow my ribs, hard, to get my attention. It's dark, quiet. Must have been zoned out for thirty minutes, minimum. Everybody's gone.

"Buy you a beer, Luther?" she says.

"Sure," I murmur. Don't really click on completely until I'm holding a cold bottle of Rolling Rock, at the bar in Bobbie and Butch Winneberger's roadhouse.

19.

It's her. It's that brilliant, devious bitch. I dream it clear that night, see the pattern perfectly in the morning, through a shower and a couple of cups of coffee. I'd been staring right at it for weeks, months even. Just not seeing the real shape. Like one of those optical illusion drawings you're absolutely sure is a glass or a cup or something. Until you finally see it's the outline of two faces.

Two. That fits. That's perfect, 'cause she's been playing us—playing me—two sides at once. From the get-go.

It *is* her. Problem is, how am I going to get anyone else to stop seeing the cup, start seeing the faces? You can't just explain the thing. They'll have to stare and stare until the reversal snaps into clarity in their own brains. And she's set everyone up so well they won't want to stare, won't want the switch. Because they're so fucking pleased with what they're looking at.

Dugal, for instance. She showed him so many dead bodies, so many otherwise inexplicable homicides. Plus a half-million dollars worth of crystal meth. Shit, today he'll be giving interviews, tonight he'll tape himself with his home VCR appearing on the evening news. It's deeply engraved in his mind that the Winnebergers are big, bad, and dangerous. He won't give that up, he won't allow himself to see that those fucking twins are nothing but very greedy yet pretty small-time operators. He won't give up the glory, won't admit he busted a couple of semi-tough shit-kickers. Who are not the clear and present threat to society that he's going to tell the media today he and his team eliminated.

IB? He might come around. He's the one who sensed that second level. He'll look, and he'll see the faces. Radik might too. Radik, baffled by the body count, might see the sense of it, the why of it.

I don't take it much further. Because the next problem's bigger and tougher. The bitch is clever, she's in the clear. I haven't got one piece of hard evidence, one single scrap of proof. Just a theory that's convinced me but won't wash at all with the powerful people who can take her down. I go to Dugal, I go to some big dicks at the DEA, they'll think I'm crazy, dismiss anything I might say. She's kept herself so squeaky clean I'll never make a case. Fuck the bitch. I will. I'll take one step at a time until I've ferreted out what I need, something so solid it'll be irrefutable. Or until she makes a mistake, a misstep that gives her away. That could happen. She is not perfect. Just very, very good.

She is going down, no matter how long it takes. But not like Vassily. Down by law.

■ ■ ■

Everybody's still jazzed, everybody's still congratulating everybody else when I roll into HQ that morning. I see that dumb-ass tactical chief moving around like a football coach in the locker room after a famous victory, high-fiving his players, slapping butts, growling manly praise. Five cooker sites were seized, held, and the evidence is flowing in. I see the LT who led the uniforms on the field in the final minutes of the game doing about the same. I see IB grinning at me from his cubicle.

He tells me Dugal never went home last night. Stayed up real late talking to the Winnebergers and Stone-Face. Angel isn't dead, he's under guard in the hospital and might survive Russo's double-tap. He says Dugal's made the unprecedented step of summoning the DA from the county courthouse to his office, and the two men are in there now, making arraignment plans.

Big fucking deal. Only surprise is that IB says Russo is in Dugal's office with the DA. She's got a federal prosecutor for backup. That sure was never part of the deal. The deal was BCPD—meaning Dugal—all the way. A little Fed help on the op. Not any Fed prosecution.

"Like to be a fly on the wall," IB laughs. "Wonder how Dugal's taking this Fed shit. Oh man, I bet he's just hating this, just chewing his own gut."

Doesn't look that way an hour later when the door to Dugal's office opens and four people exit. Looks like each one is satisfied, each one is happy. Russo does a quick scan of the squad room, catches my eye. She waves. "Charlie! Love ya," she calls. "All to pieces, honey."

IB, Tommy, and a couple of others look at her, grin at each other, look back at me and start laughing hard.

Dugal does not glance my way. He knows he's dissed me, excluding me from the meeting. He knows he'll have to weasel his way out of that mistake later.

Fuck him. I get busy with the report. Figure I'll give things an hour or so to get calmer.

Put it to IB over lunch, not as an optical illusion, though. I use chess as a metaphor, the bitch playing herself, moving the black pieces and the white pieces. He gets it faster than I ever expected.

"I fucking told you there was an invisible player, Luther," he says. "Did I or did I not? Did you or did you not scoff?"

"Hey, what can I say, IB? You were right."

"Damn straight! Maybe I couldn't see who it was, true. But I knew the player was there. Now we know who, man. Shit, it all fits so perfectly I can't believe I didn't clue to it right away."

"Nobody did, IB."

"Doesn't matter. We've got a target now. We can move now."

Except IB doesn't have any ideas about a move we could make. Still, I'm feeling revved when I head out to Westminster after lunch on a little gambit that came to me. I drive the TT, I've dropped the Deere ball cap and all that shit. Don't need cover anymore. I'm going to drop by Winneberger AgriCorp, see what's shaking there with the bosses still in lockup.

"Eddie Blizzard," I say when I walk into the twins' office, see that mean-faced fuck behind Bobbie's desk. He's all in denim, but he's wearing Tony Lama lizard-skins instead of steel-toed work-boots. He's got the Lamas up on top of the desk, he's leaning way back in the chair. Down below, men are working, the forklifts are scuttling around. Eddie doesn't even blink.

"Charlie," he says. "Of Charlie and Di. 'You guys, you crazy guys.' What Bobbie always said, right? Never said you were cops. Never guessed it, the stupid shit."

"Aren't you troubled, Eddie? Butch and Bobbie in jail, telling us everything they know? Cross your mind I might be here to bust you?"

"No. Because you can't," Eddie says. That smirk flickers, then locks into place. "No jurisdiction in this county, no fucking cause. I'm just the foreman at AgriCorp. I make sure the assholes working downstairs put the right pallets in the right trucks, don't get the forklifts into a demolition derby."

"So capping people's just sort of a hobby for you? You go bass fishing, too?"

"Weedless bush-hog's my favorite lure for bass. Capping people? That some kind of cop jargon? Never heard of that. Never been around cops much."

"Guess not. Just long enough for them to handcuff you and drive you to the station," I say. "You dug prison, didn't you, Eddie? All you trash hillbillies like prison's sexual opportunities, am I right? Tight young butt's a lot better than sheep slop. So shit-kickers tell me."

Blizzard's chill. He's cooler than I expected.

"Charlie. I mean Luther. It's Luther, I know. I'm surprised."

"Why's that?"

"I heard you were smart. I like smart. But you come on real stupid with these insults, this jailhouse fag shit. Like that's gonna rile me, rattle and roll me."

"Hey, I am stupid. So help me out. Being foreman at AgriCorp is looking like a job that's going to disappear. What with Butch and Bobbie headed for hard time. What're you going to do for a living?"

"I got my resumé out," Blizzard says. "But you never know. Some smart investor might buy AgriCorp from Butch and Bobbie. Some smart people might see a real nice balance sheet, might realize goodwill's got value, too. And that customers like to keep dealing with a man they know, not some stranger. I figure I might get a raise and a promotion. General manager, say."

"It could happen," I say. "Yeah, I can see it. Either way, I'm sure of one thing."

"Are you?"

"Yeah. Be seeing you soon. One way or another."

"Hey, Luther. Check my boots. Shaking like crazy, aren't they?"

. . .

I start laughing as I run the TT pretty hard down Route 140 toward Towson. Blizzard was genuinely cool, not just putting on some con bravado. But he's still a dumb fucking con. Asshole said my real name. Only one source for that. Conclusion's clear: he's her man, her wet-worker. Thinks he's important to her, because he did some efficient sacrificing of a lot of her pawns. Doesn't have a clue the bitch'll sacrifice him in an eye-blink too, if it suits her game. Because he's only another pawn.

Hope I'm there when it happens. Hope there's a moment, just before his lights go out, for Blizzard to feel the awful surprise, the piss-yourself terror. Only thing better would be a situation where I get to kill him, kind of leisurely, with my bare hands.

I'm into images of that when I get back to HQ. Wipe 'em before I hit the squad room. I don't want to be like that anymore. Shouldn't indulge myself, thinking shit like that. But it's a hard habit to break.

"Breakfast tomorrow with Radik? IHOP, say eight-thirty?" IB says to me. "Yeah, I know you don't dig it, but Radik likes a big stack of blueberry pancakes. We want him in a good mood, don't we?"

"We do," I say. "I'll be there."

"And how about being at my place at seven tonight? Some downtime, man. Already set it up with MJ. Annie's coming. Helen's coming. No shoptalk. Spaghetti carbonara, salad, glass of Chianti. We just eat, take a little girl-abuse. Okay?"

"Love girl-abuse. I'm a junkie for it. You're the one that cringes when they go after you."

"I'll try to stay strong."

"Believe it when I see it, dude."

It's a good night, a nice break in a clean, real world after so long lately deep in the shit. My secret thing for Annie's been so clearly out of the realm of possibility for so long that it's never gotten between me and Helen except the first time they met, and that was, what, eight, nine months ago? Anyway, I like flirting with MJ.

Which I'm happily doing—the ritual cooing over the sleeping twins done, and dinner at about the midway point—to Helen's evident amusement. MJ's lost everything she gained during her pregnancy plus eight pounds; she's slimmer and prettier now than in all the years I've known her.

I say that. "Why don't you finally follow your heart and run off with me, MJ?" I say. "Think of the times we could have."

"Time, Luther," she grins. "Not enough of it. I'm only two years younger than you. When I'm your age, you'll think I'm an old bag."

"He's already beginning to think I'm an old bag," Helen jabs. "You should see him whenever he comes on campus. He's drooling over seventeen-year-old nymphettes."

"Where'd you get that Lolita complex, Luther?" Annie laughs. "It troubles me to think of you in your forties, trying to seduce junior high school girls. Because I'll have to bust you for it."

"No, it'll be even worse," MJ says. "He'll be crushed because women in their early thirties will run away screaming when he gives them that awful leer he thinks is a seductive smile."

"That's what all the girls at Goucher already do," Helen says. "They think I've got like some sort of father complex, hanging with him. 'Helen, he's sooo old! How can you let him touch you, my God, even the idea is gross!' I get a lot of that."

"You digging this, man?" IB murmurs to me. "You still an addict for it?"

"Of course he likes it, IB," MJ says. "That why he begs for it, starting up with stuff like 'Why don't you follow your heart?' Luther, you'd be hurt and depressed if we didn't pay all this attention to you, right?"

"Devastated. Crushed." I'm grinning. "Because I know women

mock men when they're trying to mask their true feelings: a deep and mysterious sexual attraction."

"He's uneducable," Annie says. "He really believes that nonsense."

"Ohhh, they're takin' you down hard, Luther," IB says.

"Only proves what I said. They're all deeply, madly, truly in love with me, and they don't want each other to know it. MJ especially doesn't want you to know it, IB."

A chorus of laughter then, all kinds of eye messages racing between MJ and Annie and Helen. I do dig it. My smile broadens. Then does a quick fade when Helen pulls out a thick stack of photos from Akumal and starts passing them around the table. She'd worked her Nikon CoolPix digital overtime down there, and I've never seen what she shot before. I don't much want to see when they get to my end of the table. Not after the comments.

"Jesus, they're bad as a bunch of rookie uniforms looking at a really poor centerfold in a skin mag," IB says.

He's nailed the tone exactly.

And I soon know why. That damned digital's too crisp, too sharp. The bright Yucatan sun hasn't done me any favors, either. In the close-ups, I see wrinkles at the corners of my eyes I never knew I had, a little loose skin on my neck. In a couple, taken just as I've left the water, my hair looks lank, thinner than it used to be. All those white scars in the long shots, hell, they're just badges that show I've lived an active life. But my body and legs look scrawny, my ribs are even visible in some. And in every one where I'm clambering onto the rocks, flippered and masked, I look as awkward and strained as a stringy old man.

"Man, you're about fifteen pounds too light," IB says. "You gotta eat more, get in some gym time."

He's right. I'm at least fifteen under the weight I'd carried from boot camp all the way through the Russian Rattle. And that was only about a hundred fifty-five. A hard, toned hundred fifty-five, the waist size of my pants only twenty-eight inches. Maybe I've gone too Zen with my body, like I did with my apartment.

"You skipping lunch most days? Drinking coffee all day long? Dinner only sashimi and rice a lot of nights?" MJ asks.

"I don't know about that, but when we go out to dinner he leaves about half the food on his plate," Helen says.

"Look at his plate now. More than half full still," MJ says.

"Bad, Luther. Very bad. You've gotta get your weight back up to normal," Annie says. "Go down to the gym one day, see what you can lift. I bet it's a lot less than you used to handle. What're you going to do if you get in a tussle?"

"What you think the guns is for? as a friend of mine once said," I say.

"Oh, really bright. Excellent attitude," Annie says.

"Maybe we need to form a Feed Luther Committee," Helen snickers. "I'll be responsible for breakfast. Maybe you could see to his lunch, Annie?"

"I could freeze a lot of lasagna and baked ziti and things for dinner, but somebody'd have to make sure he bothered to take it out, microwave it, and actually eat it," MJ says.

They all laugh.

"Glad I don't have a weight problem," IB says. "Uh oh," he says, realizing the magnitude of his error, when three pairs of pretty eyes turn on him.

■ ■ ■

I try to match Radik and IB pancake for pancake next morning, but fail miserably. I must have shrunk my stomach these past months. Things taste good, but it gets too full too fast. I suppose

I'll have to endure a kind of self-imposed force-feeding for a while, ditch the coffee, too. Worse, hit the department gym for at least a half-hour each day. Making myself an object of ridicule to all the pumped-up muscle-heads in their twenties.

Shitty prospect. But the breakfast's a success. I lay out my idea—not completely, not mentioning the bitch—then IB chips in his bit, and Radik sees a possible way out of the complete dead end he's in on all those unsolved homicides.

"Will Dugal buy it, though?" he asks.

"He promised me I could do something different for a while if and when we popped the Winnebergers," I say. "So he owes me. And he's got his agenda, remember?"

"Fucking agendas!" IB says.

"Dugal's is written large and clear," I say. "Soon as he made captain and got Vice, what'd he do?"

"Chernobyl'd the squad. Squeezed the Vice LT into resigning, transferred about half the men, and replaced them with his own guys," IB says. "Shit, that first meeting the first day, Dugal scream-ing 'Vice detectives? You dicks are supposed to be sweeping up numbers runners, bookies, con men of every sort, street hookers, and classy call girls. Easy duty. But look at your conviction rate. You pussies couldn't handle a wet dream.'"

"And he's never appointed a new LT for Vice or Narcotics," I say. "The man's a control freak. He wants to run it all himself, hands-on. So he'll see my request for temporary assignment to your squad as a double plus, Radik. He'll see it as a way to rattle your cage and start exerting some influence on yet another squad. Another rung on the ladder to Assistant Chief. He just has to stay unconscious to the fact that you and I colluded on this."

"That slime-bucket," Radik laughs. "But you're in the X-ring, man. The fuck does want Homicide under him, along with Narcotics and Vice. Next it'll be Sex Crimes and Robbery. Every fucking detective unit we got. Let me welcome you to the Homicide squad, Luther. Do your thing, man."

I go in to see Dugal soon as we get back from the pancake house. It takes less than five minutes. Dugal's in an elevated mood, he got a full minute on the evening news last night. He's also real happy I've given him a way to make up for my exclusion from the meeting with Russo and the prosecutors. And very eager, though he tries to hide this, to bang Radik. Win-win for him. First, *I* asked for the transfer, which keeps him politically clean. And if I close some cases, everybody'll know it was Ewing, his best narc, who showed Homicide how to do its job. If I don't, he'll still have the pleasure of jerking Radik around.

Done deal. Dugal okays my temporary assignment to Homicide.

Afterward, I give Radik what he needs to get started: Eddie Blizzard's jacket, and my belief that Blizzard and Angel Dust were the hired hitters who took out those guys in the basement, that Blizzard capped the two chemists and organized the stumblefucks who ambushed me and IB at the meth site while he slipped away. And very probably personally gave poor Early the Colombian necktie, with Angel's help.

"I'd work Angel first," I say. "He's so fucked up from the double-tap he took at the Winneberger bust they've got a fentanyl drip in his arm at the hospital. He'll babble all sorts of shit. Oh, his real name is Kit Butcher. Didn't have time to pull his jacket.

"And I'd put big money that you'll find connections between a lot of those stiffs and Blizzard. Maybe even arrests together, prison time together," I say. "Plus, I've met Blizzard. He's the kind of asshole who might not like to get rid of his favorite gun just because it's sure conviction-type evidence in a murder rap. He might still have that .44 Special somewhere."

"He does, he's goin' away," Radik says happily. "Shit, thanks, Luther. I can make things happen with this."

"But we're agreed you won't move on Blizzard himself until I've had my shot at the drugista I think hired him. All copacetic there, right?"

"Damned straight. We'll just find all the little ducks and put them in a row, then let 'em sit until you say go."

"May be a couple of weeks. That okay?"

"No probs, man," Radik says. "I'll need a couple of weeks anyway."

"Then no probs anywhere," I lie.

20.

It's early Saturday, one of those May mornings when the air's soft and even a full sun's light is buttery, not harsh and hard-edged like it is in midsummer, or midwinter. The light gilds the waters of the Chesapeake instead of ricocheting angrily off it as I take the TT over that long high curve of the old Bay Bridge, almost alone. After Memorial Day, it'll be bumper-to-bumper all day most days, an irritation that will blot out just how beautiful this crossing is.

Not a cloud anywhere I can see. And I can see for miles, the Bay rippling south to the horizon, the Eastern Shore spreading flat over three compass points until it too meets the sky.

The Audi feels good, smooth and responsive. So do I.

First time in the past week, for me. I'm a cripple for three days at the start, my head throbbing through bad caffeine withdrawal even codeine tabs won't ease, my belly bloated and heavy from forcing down three full meals a day. Next three days, every major muscle group in my body burns and aches from a couple hours of replicating my Special Forces boot camp PT. I sprawl facedown on my futon each night, let Helen massage my abused body. I can't return the favor. She says she doesn't mind. Maybe it's true. But I mind.

Left all that behind this morning. I know I'm no stronger or faster—need at least six weeks of my new regime for any physical result at all—but it was enough for my brain. Enough to clean it, snug up all the circuitry, get it purring in neutral but ready to race the instant I step on the pedal. Like the TT's engine.

I feel good. I'm going to see the bitch.

I accelerate when I leave the bridge, cross Kent Island. Push the needle some digits higher on Route 50, moving south toward Cambridge and the Ocean. But I'm not going that far. Ease off passing through Easton, take a left on Route 328, northeast toward Denton. Somewhere midway between those two towns, some-where among the mix of manicured gentlemen's farms and work-ing family corn-and-hog spreads that edge the Choptank River, I'll find Russo's place, down at the end of some dirt drive off a nar-row strip of country asphalt.

Don't know exactly where, so I'll have to ask around. I'd tried Dog at the beginning of the week: could his DEA homie get me a precise location on Russo's farm? The callback: she keeps it quiet, except maybe from Ray Phillips, the Uzi man. And he ain't talk-ing. But Dog's had another homie hack her credit report, got her mother's maiden name. The farm came from her maternal grand-mother. The locals'll know it by that name. Oh, the old Kelland place? Why, sure, mister.

Lucky morning. That's exactly what I get from an ancient black man in overalls—hair little tufts of white fuzz like just-picked cot-ton and one gold front tooth—behind the dusty glass counter of a grayed clapboard country store with one busted gas pump out-side. I take a Coke from the big red cooler. He still stocks those old glass six-ounce bottles you hardly ever see anymore. I drain it while he tells me the rights and lefts, a couple of landmarks to watch for. Then I go take another bottle, pop it on the cooler's built-in opener, lay a five on the counter, and drive off.

Jesus. It could be Early's, except the land's perfectly flat, and the white house, almost hidden by old-growth yellow poplars and horse chestnuts, is a single story raised slightly on a fieldstone foundation, with a couple of wings angling off it, instead of a square two-story Victorian. The front porch is only two steps up, and it's screened in. As I get out of the car I know why: I can smell slow-moving water, and through a gap in the thin ranks of trees a few hundred meters behind the house I see the river. Mosquito country.

Nobody seems to be around. Nobody's reacting to a shitload of furious dog barking coming from someplace I can't pinpoint. I do a little recon. All the acres in front of the house—and there are a lot of them, running far down the road in both directions—are packed with new corn plants, just rising. She must lease that acreage to some local farmer. The barn's in good shape, and at least ten acres toward the river are pasture. I see three, no, four horses cropping grass, tails flicking now and then. The 'vette must be back in the DEA garage, because the only vehicle's a Volvo station wagon, navy blue. As I round the barn, I see an olive-drab hood poking out of a shed. I go up close. The dogs get louder, more hysterical. It's a Steyr-Puch Pinzgaur, the Austrian army's version of the Humvee, but narrow and not any larger than a 4-Runner or a Cherokee. Pretty rare to see one in the States, though it's a perfect thing to have around a farm.

Or perfect for bopping and busting through that rough Sonoran terrain.

I go back to the TT, sit on the hood, sip the last drops of my Coke. I see her before she sees me. She's coming up out of the gap in the forest from the river, a long fishing rod in one hand, a big bucket that's holding something fairly heavy in the other, judging from her list to that side. Landed a big one this morning, I figure. Bringing it in live, water in that bucket.

She's still two hundred meters off when she looks up from the path, spots me on the TT. The sun's behind her, she's just a silhouette with a shadow face. If she's reacting, surprised maybe, I can't tell. She doesn't alter her pace, shift her grip on her load. We're just looking at each other for the couple of minutes it takes her to close the distance.

She walks right past as if I do not exist, toward the back door of the house. "Kitchen's this way," she calls. "Me and my fish are going there. You come, too."

. . .

I'm sitting at a scarred old pine table the color of honey, enjoying a little jolt from the first cup of coffee I've had in a week. She'd poured it and put it before me without saying a word. Now she's spread newspaper on the counter by the sink and is intently gutting a fairly large rockfish, her back to me. She's wearing a man-size flannel shirt, sleeves rolled up, over loose and dirty khakis. Her L.L. Bean gum boots are by the door, just where she'd slipped them off.

"I was wondering when you'd come by," Russo says. "For that math lesson."

"Maybe no math today. There are a few basic things I feel I need to learn first," I say.

"Naturally. I'm ready when you are. Start asking."

"How come the DEA didn't dump your ass, after whatever happened in Sonora?"

"My sweet ass!" She laughs. "And big fear. A couple of heavy suits happen to have found that TV-anchorwoman look I affect just too fucking sexy to resist. Happily married, very buttoned-up, and superambitious suits. You know how kinky that type can be. Now, if Francesca, who may have been naughty but has such a fine record as an agent, gets cross, starts talking and crying her pretty eyes out, maybe even retains an attorney, there go a couple of careers, there go a couple of marriages."

"Yeah? Simple as that? Unbelievable."

"Don't be coy, it doesn't suit you, Luther," she says, using her long fingers to scrape clean the gutted fish's belly, then washing it inside and out under the tap. "You know as well as I the guys who rise in Fed service—including the armed forces—are expert ass-kissers but ball-less wonders. They'll violate any rule, concoct any cover-up, perjure themselves before Congress, betray their best friends, if they figure that's what it'll take to save their careers when trouble comes calling.

"So I'm insured, double indemnity. Hell, I am probably overin-sured. But I paid all the premiums a long time ago. In full. So that Russo bitch is the terror of high Washington bureaucracy."

"Sounds to me like that Russo bitch might be a walking target, then."

"Oh, I can handle that, I think. DEA, you can pretty much for-get. Even the Company is very short of competent wet-workers. And afraid to use them. Has been since the Carter administration, when we were only kids. Assassinations? America is above such morally dispicable acts, remember?

"They were never all that good at it anyway, even before the rhetoric and the watchdogs," she goes on. "Did they get Castro? Hell no. Did they send in teams of guys like you on black ops to take out the key Colombians and the rest of the drug lords? Hell no. The war on drugs could've been won in a year. But it'll never end, because the bureaucrats are too timid to break the rules. They waste years negotiating with completely corrupt governments over arrests and extraditions. Once in a while they get tossed a bone, like Pablo Escobar. Washington declares a famous victory. But does the dope stop flowing, even for a day?"

"Hell no," I say.

"So one day the Mexicans will probably toss Washington Miguel Quintero. Another famous victory. Sonora cartel chopped." She laughs. "Miguel'll go down because he's got a big mouth and a bigger ego and decides one day he's paying the generals and police commanders way too much. Somebody else will make them a nicer offer. *Adios,* Miguel. *Buenos días,* whoever."

"Ever cross your mind I might decide it's *adios* time for you?"

"Sure. But if you were going to do that, you would have tried after I capped that wounded ambush guy. Or after you found that old farmer with his throat slit. Which, by the way, I had absolutely nothing to do with. It's a toss-up whether you'd have been as succesful as you were with Vassily. But you would have tried."

She wraps the rockfish in brown kraft paper, puts in it the fridge. "Hey, gotta show you my puppies," she says, moving toward the door. There's a cattle prod hanging from an old iron hook. She takes the prod with her left hand. I follow her outside.

■ ■ ■

The day's warming up considerably. The mad dog chorus crescendos as we pass the shed where the Steyr-Puch sits. Behind it there's a big prefab metal kennel, with a run about ten meters square fenced in with heavy chain-link at least eight feet high. Dogs are charging it, dogs are jumping, dogs are swirling and snapping so fast it takes me a moment to realize there are only five of them.

Five dogs from hell. All black, with the look of pit bulls but noticeably taller, leaner, longer jawed.

"What the fuck are they?" I ask.

Russo laughs. "An experiment. Something I started when I was living in Phoenix, just for the fun of it. Wanted to see how mean a dog could be."

"You could have saved yourself the trouble. Bought a couple of fight-trained pits."

"I did. Truly ferocious. But too damned dumb to use as tools. Dobermans, now they're *smart* and ferocious. They can be trained to take orders just as well as German shepherds. So I've been crossing pits with Dobermans. The two big ones are the second generation. The other three are the third, just over a year old now."

"Kind of a weird hobby, Francesca."

"Yeah, some might think that. But it's not exactly a hobby. Watch this." She pulls a silver whistle from her pocket, the kind pitched so high humans can't hear it, and seems to blow just once. The smaller three freeze instantly. The two big ones stop attacking the fence, but roam restless around the yard. She unlocks the gate, walks into the run, the cattle prod before her. The two big ones snarl and snap at it, but are careful to keep their distance. She backs them into the kennel, closes the door. She opens a big wooden box fitted against the kennel, hauls out a man-size dummy, walks it toward the three young dogs. They stay frozen. Only their yellowish eyes fix on the dummy, follow its every movement.

Then she hangs it on the fence, takes a few steps back, blows the whistle twice. In an explosion of black, the dogs are on that dummy, mauling it to pieces in an eye-blink. Russo starts trying to beat them off, using the prod as a club instead of shocking them with it. The dogs ignore the blows, take the pain, keep ripping that dummy with their teeth. She blows the whistle once. The dogs instantly come out of their frenzy, back off a couple of meters from the dummy, and freeze.

She takes her time unhooking the dummy, half-shredded now, and putting it back in the box. She strolls slowly past the dogs, sliding a hand over each of their heads as she passes. They don't move a muscle, don't even twitch. She leaves the run, locks the gate behind her.

The dogs don't move.

"Think I've got just about the perfect mix now: ferocity, tenacity, absolute obedience."

"Not sure I'd feel confident about that last quality," I say. "A little bit more of that pit instinct pops out one day, they'd eat you alive."

"Not a dog person, Luther?" She's grinning. "Terrific tools, these guys. They won't move until I tell 'em to. We could stand here for three hours. They still wouldn't move."

She turns, and we start walking. I look back just when we're about to lose sight of the run. The dogs are frozen. When we reach the kitchen door, Russo blows the whistle once. Immediately there's a whanging of dogs hitting the fence, growling and barking.

"Let's do lunch," Russo says. "That fish'll take about forty-five minutes to broil. Would you settle for sandwiches and potato salad? Because I'm really hungry right now."

"Sandwiches sound good," I say.

Russo slices a baked ham, still studded with cloves, that she's taken from the fridge. She puts the ham on multigrain bread that looks homemade, though I doubt she made it. She places a colorful Mex-looking ceramic bowl of potato salad on the table, then brings over the sandwich plates, paper napkins, and forks.

"Beer, or iced tea?"

"Iced tea, please," I say.

Ham's great, and the potato salad's got something special to it. I ask her about it.

"Standard grandma recipe. I just add some cumin. Gives it some whip, cuts the mayonnaise-y flavor."

We eat quietly for a while. Then I say, "Tell me about the opportunity here."

"Speed, lots of speed. As I told you before. You head a Mex organization. You're making a fortune transhipping cocaine for the Colombians. But hey, suddenly there's a burgeoning American market for high-grade marijuana, which the Colombians don't do. A real renaissance in grass. What would you see as your best growth opportunity?"

"I'd keep the Colombian biz as my core enterprise, move into grass independently, in a big way," I say. "Leave a dumb drug like meth to gringo shit-kickers."

"Exactly. That's what Miguel figured. So the Sonora cartel's getting out of meth. That leaves the domestic producers, the Grundy bunch and others like them. And what could be easier than eliminating shit-kickers, eating their lunch? How hard was it to get rid of the Winnebergers? Remember what I said about risk-reward ratios? This one's off the charts."

"So, Di," I smile, "you've got the plan, you've got the start-up facilities, you've got a home market. Ready-made business, ready for you to grow it nationwide. Why are you talking to me?"

"Coy again. Coy really irritates me, you know that?" she says.

"Okay, okay. I just dig foreplay," I say. "The deal's simple. You get me—or someone like me—to build and run the biz in the Mid-Atlantic and Northeast regions. You get others to handle the South, the Midwest, the West Coast. All of them cops if possible, fed or local. Because who's better placed, better able to direct and protect a narcotics business than narcs?"

"Very good. Much improved," she says. "I was getting doubtful about you for a moment there."

"And you can forget the math lesson," I continue. "I did the math before I came down here. A beautiful thing, those numbers."

"Aren't they?" she grins. "My banker in the Caymans is already sending a limo to meet me at the airport when I fly down there. But there's something even better."

"I know. The action. The sheer fun of it. I've been missing that kind of rush."

"That was pretty obvious. You were just radiating it, that day we met in your boss's office about the Russian thing. Got me interested in you."

"And you still are. Or we wouldn't be talking."

"Correct."

"Well," I say. "Could be a go."

"Don't be hurt, but I started without you."

"Your DEA pal, Ray?" I shake my head, look skeptical.

"Yeah, not the best, but good enough. And now I think he can put in for that transfer to Atlanta. Which is what we planned, as soon as I got everything settled here. If it is settled?"

"Not quite yet. I'd need a lot more details, operational and financial."

"Of course. Any time you like," she says. "Right now even, and you can stay for dinner. I'm broiling that rock."

"Like to, but I've got to get back," I say, glancing at my watch. "Should head out about now."

"Come another time, then. Stay the weekend. We'll fish a little, ride a little, get comfortable with each other. Lay the entire plan out in detail, fine-tune any part that needs it."

"We should do that."

"Only don't wait too long. Or your window of opportunity won't be there anymore. I'm moving ahead with this pretty quick."

She walks me out to the TT, I get in, look up at her. The slant of the sun gives me a clear, sharp sight of her eyes. Just what I want.

"One thing," I say. "Why'd you shoot me?"

Her eyes stay perfectly clear and steady.

"Oh, that? Finally figured who done it, have you?" She laughs. "I came to kill you, actually. It was early days, and it troubled me that a guy who'd do what you did to Vassily was moving on the meth biz. You looked like trouble. You looked like a serious problem I'd rather not have."

"But you didn't eliminate it."

"Last-second inspiration. Wild boy like you might be a valuable asset, not a problem. But I needed to see which way you'd go, seriously provoked, understand? So I gave you a little push. Just a love tap. And waited."

"Worth it?"

Russo smiles. "Got your attention, didn't I?"

21.
"Here's the story of the week, and it's only Monday," IB says, cheerfully rattling his *Sun* to get my attention as I enter my cubicle. "Get this: 'A Massachusetts insurance executive who slit his wife open with a butcher knife and impaled her heart and lungs on a stake in a neighbor's garden after she chided him for burning a pot of ziti repeatedly asked a court pyschologist: Is this a big case?'

"Big? Big?" IB laughs. "Oh, hey, don't worry, man. Think of it like you maybe ran a red light, had a fender bender. You gotta have full liability coverage, right? I mean, insurance is your business and all."

"Sicker every day, IB," I say. "You got this very ghoulish side, you aware of that?"

"Hey, I told you why I collect this stuff. I'm gonna compile it all in a book, true crime stranger than fiction. Probably make enough on it to pay for the twins' college."

"But you laugh at it, man!"

"That's something else," he says. "You know I wouldn't be laughing if I was on the scene. Too fucking gross. But when it's a newspaper story, just straight reporting with that ho-hum tone they always give these things? I mean, how can you not laugh? Shit like this is just too crazy to take seriously. Like that airline pilot in Connecticut or someplace a few years back who stuffed his wife through a rented wood chipper, then returned the thing without even bothering to wash out the blood and bone slivers. Who could take that seriously? It's just too unreal to register as real. Right up there with those UFO snatches and shit in the *National Enquirer*, right?"

"You ever think it's time you talked with Annie, or the department shrink, about this obsession you've got, big man?" I say.

"You ever think about doing that yourself? You, the only guy I ever saw smile after he just shot and killed a man?"

"Fuck off, pal."

"Hey, I'm sorry, Luther. I didn't mean anything by that. I know the smile was just some kind of involuntary reflex, some kind of stress reaction. Forget I said it. Please?"

"On one condition," I say.

"Anything."

"You want to clip these sick stories, build a file, write a book, just do it," I say. "But stop reading every one of the fucking things out loud to me, okay?"

"Okay, sure, whatever."

I don't enjoy coming down on IB like that. Hell, some of those stories are so whacked it's hard not to laugh. But he'll feel a little hurt, kind of abashed now. And I'll have some quiet time to consider my day with Russo, think about what's happening with her, and how I might deal with it. Didn't even try on Sunday. Wanted to give my mind time to absorb it all, work on it way down deep, below consciousness. That's where lots of answers come from, if you let the process happen.

So I'd spent a great day with Helen. A day that, in between the good stuff like making love with her, gave my frontal lobes something completely different to brood on: losing her.

She graduates from Goucher in a couple of weeks. She's got some great options. She's been accepted in the English Lit master's programs at Princeton and Penn, either one perfect if she wants to go on through to a Ph.D. and an academic career. And she's also been admitted to the MFA programs at Columbia and Stanford, which mostly lead only to teaching creative writing at some lesser place, but once in a while produce people who actually write fiction that gets published.

"That MFA crap is such a racket I wonder why it isn't illegal," she'd said last fall, when she started applying. "It's like the lemming thing. The universities charge huge sums—as much as top medical schools—to turn out MFAs who then work for peanuts turning out more MFAs who then do the same, nobody ever writing the great American novel. Until there's such an overpopulation of MFAs they start starving, and run in masses off cliffs into the sea."

But she's said nothing about any of that since. I've never brought it up. We've had tacit but strong agreement to keep our time horizons short. From the very first time we made love, we were clear it was just a fun affair we'd walk away from smiling when she graduated—if it even lasted that long.

Things change. They always fucking change. I used to dig that, want my life that way. Always looked forward to whatever might come next. But after that Russian episode . . . hell, I don't know. Something crept up on me, a feeling I never had with any woman before. Crept up so stealthily I only just recently realized it.

I think I need Helen.

But Helen, even if she thinks she does, most definitely does not need me.

She seemed to be leaning that way a bit, Sunday. She'd seemed kind of sentimental, a little saddened, when we talked about what she was going to do when she was done with Goucher.

"Maybe not being able to make up my mind's a sign," she'd said, after she'd laid out her prospects at Princeton, at Stanford. "Maybe I ought to take a year off, get some easy kind of job, just hang out and have some fun. Grad school'll wait. They aren't going anywhere. They'll still be open a year or so from now."

"Sure. But if you're going to do that, you can't waste the year managing a Gap store in a mall," I'd said. "Sign up for just one gut course, and your parents'll happily finance a year in Paris or Florence."

"They would. Already ran it by them," she'd grinned. "But I'm afraid I'd be missing you."

"For about a week, maybe. Until you met some good-looking young Frenchman or Italian."

She'd laughed. Then, "I know what'd be real fun. I could become a cop-ette here. Like Annie. I mean, it's not like enlisting in the army or something, is it? I could just quit in a year if I wanted, couldn't I?"

"Absolutely." I'd said. "And think how cool you'd look in one of those great khaki BCPD uniforms while you spent eight hours every day in a cruiser with some young muscle-head yammering on and on about the Orioles and the Ravens. Bored right out of your pretty mind."

"Guess I couldn't just do the training course, then hang out with you and IB, huh?"

"Generally doesn't work that way," I'd said. "Generally you don't get a detective's shield until you've been a good beat cop for some years."

I'd stayed awake wishing, long after Helen had fallen asleep, that there was something worth her while that would keep her within reach. Couldn't think of a single thing. The girl's going. The girl's already half gone. Never dreamed that would hurt the way it's starting to.

. . .

Now, hollowed out and facing the big nothing in my personal life, I zero on Russo. She's got my total attention. I'm gonna juke her. Don't know how yet. Don't know when. I can't just start working with her in the meth biz. No brief from Dugal to go undercover that way, no way he'd even consider giving me a brief to target a federal official, even if I had solid, convincing evidence. I'm not even sure we can do that, legally, anyway. So I'd be totally unprotected. I get anything on her while actively particpating, it's on me, too. Get enough to take her down, I go down with her.

And, with what I've got, it's beyond absurd to think of walking into DEA headquarters in Washington and telling them their Baltimore bureau chief is not only bent but moving to build her very own drug cartel. Shit, they'd hustle me off to St. Elizabeth's and punch in an antipsychotic drip.

"IB," I say, after almost an hour of circling, backtracking, racking my brains, and getting nowhere. "Ready for a true crime stranger-than-fiction story I know?"

"Sure, man," IB says. He grins at me.

I tell him everything I know, eveything I suspect, explaining how certain seemingly unrelated bits connect perfectly. IB and I talk for a long time about my day at the Shore, Russo's plan.

"Un-be-fuckin'-lievable!" IB says, shaking his head. "If there was a Richter scale, something like that, for totally outrageous schemes, this'd be a seven or an eight. Heavy duty, dude. She really think she can get away with this?"

"She can, IB. Just listen to yourself. Who the fuck's gonna believe this? But Russo can actually do it. Create and head an all-American meth cartel. Unless she makes a truly stupid move, who's gonna even think of going after her, let alone take her down? She's so well insulated, so fucking clean."

"So we got to get her dirty," he says. "Only way."

No way I can see it, then. But a little later IB's idea gives me one. Can't decide whether it's brilliant or a dumb fraternity-boy stunt. I can jerk her chain a few times, see which way she moves. Maybe get her off balance, maybe rattle her into making some bad mistake.

After lunch I go down to the lot, fenced and topped with coils of wicked razor wire, where we keep impounded vehicles and recovered stolen cars. I talk to Slow-Mo, the shuffly old uniform who's serving out his last year until retirement supervising the lot. I give him a bullshit story of a sting I'm setting up, tell him I desperately need some hot license plates, plates from a jacked car that he hasn't yet registered, plates that'll pop up on the computer in any cruiser as Stolen Vehicle.

Slow-Mo buys the bullshit. He's got a BMW M-series rocket that was just brought in a couple of hours ago. No, he hasn't yet had time to wipe its plate numbers off the computer system. (He isn't called Slo-Mo for nothing.) But together we're pretty quick about taking them off the Bimmer. I swear him to secrecy, and cover my ass further by telling him he's got to get the young uniform who brought the stolen BMW in to swear he found it without plates, ID'd it through the vehicle ID number. Shouldn't be a problem; the young uniform's his son.

I put the hot tags in a paper bag, go back upstairs.

Then IB and I hit the evidence cage. He distracts the old uniform sergeant. Starts telling him one of those news stories. "Here's a flight you'll be glad you weren't on," he starts. "A coffin in a jet cargo hold leaked fumes from a decaying body into the passenger compartment, forcing an unscheduled landing of a United Airlines flight from Las Vegas to Chicago at Denver, to get seven nauseous passengers to hospitals."

"Very funny. You pay people to make up shit like this for you?" the old sarge says.

"Hey, it's true!" IB goes all huffy. "That was a direct quote from a story in the *Sun*."

"Horseshit. You can't air-freight stiffs."

"Probably half the passenger flights every day are carrying corpses," IB says.

"Potential corpses. If the plane goes down."

"No, you knucklehead. Your grandmother dies in Florida or somewhere, you want to bring her home."

"My grandparents are all dead."

"What the fuck difference does that make?" IB says. "My point is, people wanna bring dead relatives back, bury them at home. Maybe they already got family plots in a cemetery. So how do they get the bodies back here. Federal Express? Trailways bus?"

"I don't know."

"By commercial airliners, how the hell else? Look, I got the clipping from the *Sun*. I can show it to you."

"Ah, nobody'd ever fly if they knew there may be corpses down in the luggage compartment. Gotta be horseshit."

While they're going round and round, I nick some meth from the Winneberger seizure. Not much. Nothing anybody would notice. Just enough weight to make a charge of possession with intent to distribute, not simple possession.

Now I've got what I need to jerk Russo. When it's time.

Next we go see Radik.

"Hey guys, how's it hangin'?" he says.

"About halfway to my knees," IB says.

"In your dreams," Radik says. "Luther, man, you were pretty fuckin' on about the vics having connections with that Eddie Blizzard. One or two arrested with him, a couple of others did prison time that overlaps with Blizzard's. All of them seem to've hung with a lot of the same people. And Blizzard seems to have known everybody the dear departed knew. The whole crew, like, they don't all know each other, but they all know Blizzard. He's right at the center, with Angel Dust in real close orbit around him."

"Somehow I'm not surprised," I say.

"Nothing I can arrest Blizzard for, unfortunately. But there's some good shit," Radik says. "We got enough live bodies saying the same things about Blizzard that I figure I can convince one of our harder-nosed judges to give me a search warrant. Anytime I want one."

"Can you get one, and just not execute immediately?" I ask.

"No probs, man," Radik says. "I'll go see Judge Goldstein tomorrow morning, first thing. He loves issuing warrants on homicide suspects. Hell, I think he wants to go with me when I toss some scumbag's place, he's that into it."

"Jammin'," I say. "You'll be ready to move soon as I let you know I've got what I need from my side?"

"Shit yeah," Radik says. "We can be in a car and on our way in like two minutes."

■ ■ ■

Next morning Russo and I have a date we didn't arrange ourselves. At the county courthouse. Bobbie and Butch and Stone-Face have been arraigned and indicted, bail set so high they're going to be guests in our lockup until trial time. The prosecutor's psyched herself into a sure conviction—hell, only a moron could blow a case as solid as the one against the Winnebergers—but she's obsessive even on the easy ones. I've worked with her before.

She wants to interview Russo and me yet again, this time together first, then Russo privately and me privately. Wants to be absolutely sure there isn't a single detail, no matter how small, that contradicts.

Russo and I are synched as good as Di and Charlie in the joint talk. It lasts about an hour, we tell the exact same story from beginning to end four complete times. Russo gives me a big smile when I leave and she stays with the prosecutor.

It's about an hour before lunch when I step out into the sun. The courthouse square's almost empty; everybody's hustling to get their morning tasks complete before streaming out to go eat. I find Russo's 'vette in the parking section reserved for official vehicles. Takes me less than a minute to remove her license plates, substitute the hot ones. Takes not much longer to pop the front door lock, slip a double ziplock of speed into the carry sleeve on the back of the driver's seat. I leave a corner of the ziplock peeking out. A gamble here, but I don't think Russo'll notice either new tags or the planted drugs. She'll be too anxious to get away, after another half-hour of extreme boredom reanswering the prosecutor's questions.

I'm waiting outside the prosecutor's office when Russo emerges. She shakes her head, grins.

"You know anybody more anal than that girl," she says, "do me a favor. Keep me away from the bitch. Catch you later, Luther."

"Sure," I say. Except, with any luck, you're the one who's about to get caught, Francesca, I'm thinking as I go in for my session of obsessive-compulsive torture.

I'm half dazed when I finally escape that prosecutor—and her invitation to lunch. I cell Radik, ask him if he can toss Blizzard's place later this afternoon, early evening.

"One toss, coming right up," he says. "Got Goldstein's search warrant here in front of me. Consider it done."

22. I've pulled two chains at once. Nothing to do now but wait.

Helen comes by that evening bearing gifts. She's got tortellini stuffed with porcini mushrooms, a big bag of fresh mesclun lettuce, a crisp-crusted loaf of ciabatta bread, nice bottle of Vernaccio. I eat like a wolf; I'm still off coffee, still putting in an hour working out each day. My body craves calories.

"Great!" I say, leaning back in my chair.

"How'd you know?" Helen grins. She's still savoring the tortellini, nibbling at the salad. "You're a human trash compactor all of a sudden, Luther. I think that could have been gruel and you'd still say 'great.' No way you could have tasted it, when you didn't even chew it."

"Ah, the delicate, slightly nutty flavor of the porcini contrasted beautifully with the tart notes of balsamic on the mesclun," I say. "And the wine? A smooth but saucy little number, with just a hint of presumption."

The girl laughs. "You sound like the caption of a *New Yorker* cartoon. Next time I'll just throw everything into the blender and you can drink your dinner. Like the gym freaks drink that super-protein stuff."

A little later we're watching a video she'd brought along, a Swedish thriller called *Insomnia*. Not even vaguely related to American films. It's about a top Stockholm detective, slightly arrogant, who's sent to a little town above the Arctic Circle to investigate the murder of a young girl. It's midsummer, the sun never drops below the horizon, he can't sleep. Each day his judgment gets fuzzier, even as he and the local cops are closing in on the killer. Then, fired on through light fog along the seashore while in close pursuit of the chief suspect, he accidentally shoots and kills his partner. Split-second decision time: he chooses to do a cover-up, so it looks like the killer did it. They catch the fuck, everybody buys the cover-up. Except one smart young woman, one of the local cops. She lets the detective know she knows with one simple gesture, then does nothing more. He goes back to Stockholm. Case closed.

It's all so subtle, so very, very possible. Everything that happens could happen. A nightmare so close to the real there's no way to know which it is. Helen thinks it's a small masterpiece, quiet and deft in the writing, acting, and directing. I feel shaken, unsettled.

I twitch when the phone rings around ten. It's Radik.

"Blizzard's in lockup. You are not gonna believe what this asshole did," he says.

"Try me," I manage.

"We bang on the door for a long time. No response," Radik says. "Finally the fuck cracks the door, chain in place. He's in his fucking underpants, with a hard-on! Bolts soon as I flash my badge."

"Come on, get to the good stuff," I say.

"We bust through, chase him down the hall. Into his bedroom. There's this naked girl lying there, a real sweat hog. All that banging *we* did must have interrupted *his* banging. Anyway, Blizzard yanks open the night-table drawer, pulls out a piece, starts to turn toward us. One of my guys dives over the sweat hog in the bed, takes him down hard. I step on Blizzard's wrist, grind it a little, til he lets go. We cuff him, start to haul him out to the car. And the sweat hog calls out 'Aw, Eddie, don't go now. I ain't come yet.'"

Radik cracks up then. He can't stop laughing.

"The gun? What about the gun?" I say.

"Oh yeah. Well, what else? A .44 Special," Radik says. "Ballistics check going on right now. Gut feeling? It's the gun that domed those basement stiffs. Blizzard's gun. Blizzard's the shooter. It's all fitting, Luther. Like you said."

"All we need's a ballistic match."

"I bet my left nut we get the match of the decade," Radik says. "Now if you'll pardon me, I'm gonna go sweat Blizzard. He's got this smirky kind of face, you know? I'm gonna have fun wiping that off him."

"When you get him real loosened up, ask him if he works for a bitch named Di," I say.

"What?"

"Something from my end. Just see if you can get him to spill anything about Di. Nice-looking woman, late twenties early thirties, smart. Tell him Di gave him up. See how he reacts."

"No probs. But I'm working on that fuckin' smirk first. It really gets on my balls."

"You're the man," I say.

"Soon as I get anything, I'll let you know, Luther. And hey, thanks for tipping me to this piece of shit."

"Cop stuff!" Helen snorts when I put the phone down. "Now compare that with *Insomnia*. Policemen who use language properly, speak the way normal people speak. You guys, on the other hand, make an effort to sound like De Niro or Pacino when they've got bad lines to begin with and then go over the top with them. And I only heard your end."

"It's no effort," I smile. "We are over the fuckin' top."

"Hopeless, Luther. Beyond redemption," she says.

■ ■ ■

First thing next morning I check in with Radik. Ballistics hasn't finished yet. But I can sense things happening. I can feel momentum. I can feel events I started in motion gathering speed. I'm on a roller coaster that's been slowly clanking away up that first hill, the lead cars have just crested the top, we're looking down at the steepest, longest fall, and the operator's just released the brakes.

IB is the first to squeal.

"Holy shit! She's gotta be going nucular," he says, soon as I appear in his line of sight in the squad room. I sit down in the extra chair in his cubicle. He's heard from a state trooper friend of his.

"She leaves the courthouse yesterday, gets on I-83. A young trooper radars the 'vette at ten, maybe fifteen, over the limit. Slow day, flashy car, babe at the wheel. The trooper's bored. So he punches in the tag number, follows her a while, then pulls her over up around Hereford." IB's talking low but fast. Grinning, too.

"She tries to badge him off, all superior-like. Guess it generally works for her. But it pisses this kid off. He takes her license and registration back to his cruiser, sees the computer's already flashing a stolen vehicle alert. He doesn't check the license or registration. He goes back to the 'vette, pistol unholstered but pointed at the ground, orders her out of the car.

"She's pissed. But the more shit she gives him, the harder-nosed he gets. He sees, as she's getting out, the baggy in the pocket behind her seat. Knows he's got probable cause to search, so he pulls it out, has a look at exactly what's in that baggy.

"Next thing the bitch knows," IB goes on, "she's cuffed, stuffed in the back of the cruiser, and headed toward the nearest state trooper barracks, where she's promptly thrown in a holding cell. Charged with possession of a stolen vehicle, possession with intent to distribute a controlled substance, speeding. And, get this, resisting arrest!"

"So what's happened?"

"My guy don't know, it's not his barracks. He's pretty sure she spent part of the night in a cell. Maybe all of it. Complicated situation, the way you set her up. Takes a lot of phone calls to establish she is who the badge and ID says she is, that the plates on the 'vette are from some other stolen car, all that shit. And a lot of talking about why she's carrying meth. Hell, she may still be in that cell."

IB's laughing again.

"I don't think so," I say.

And I'm right.

Russo's lounging against the railing on the steps when I walk out of HQ's front door at lunchtime. She looks me straight in the eyes, holds the look, then says "Let's walk," and strides off. I catch up. We go to the courthouse square, stroll around in the manicured grass there under majestic old oaks and tulip trees. I sense a tail. Confirm it as we turn a corner. Shaved head, goatee, black suit. And sunglasses. Great disguise, Ray, I'm thinking.

"Suppose you know what happened to me yesterday," she says.

"Yeah, just heard about it this morning. Bad luck. Any idea who'd set you up like that?"

"Idea? Don't play with me."

"You can't think it was me?"

"Fuck you, Luther," she says. "Thought we were in accord. Thought we had a contract."

"In theory only," I say. "I reflected a lot on our discussion. Had a last-second inspiration. Give Francesca a little love tap, see which way she goes."

"What works is smart. What doesn't is stupid," she says. "This was truly stupid. Yeah, it's amusing, the DEA area chief busted on a drug charge. She skates, naturally. Everybody has a big laugh. Except the DEA bureaucrats. Now they have to look into the matter, maybe place the area chief on administrative leave. Very awkward. Very definitely attention we did not need. You've just moved back from asset to problem again, Luther."

"Oh, sorry. I fucked up," I say. "Twice maybe. I'm scared to tell you now, but guess I'd better, before you hear it from somebody else."

"What else?" she demands.

"Well," I say, "I sort of gave Homicide Eddie Blizzard. They got all aggressive about it. Went out to toss Blizzard's place real fast. He didn't dig it. Reacted badly. So that asshole's in jail right now. Facing a bunch of murder ones."

Francesca Russo makes the first critical mistake I've witnessed. She stays quiet for just one too many beats. And then says, "You mean that scumbag who worked as Butch and Bobbie's foreman? So what? Blizzard was as dirty as Angel Dust and the twins. Too bad we didn't nail him when we busted them. But he's got nothing to do with our current difficulty."

"Which is?"

"How you're going to turn yourself back into an asset, you dumb punk," Russo says, turning suddenly and walking back toward Phillips.

■ ■ ■

The coaster's committed now, to speeds that press you back hard into your seat, to screaming curves that make your stomach lurch, to loops you're sure no one will survive. No way to get off, no way to stop it. It'll race on and on until it ends.

I hit the first stomach-churning curve two nights later, with a phone call from Helen. Pretty Helen, smart Helen, smart-aleck and fearless Helen, now nearly hysterical. She's in the GBMC emergency room.

I react. I don't think. With a red flasher on the dash of the TT, I'm hitting seventy and eighty on roads where the limit's forty, weaving in and out of traffic like a madman, before it hits me that she's conscious, she was able to call me, that she can't be badly hurt at all, just scared. I take the TT down a few hundred rpms, I stop the controlled skids and the crazed weaving. But the tires still squeal in protest when I jerk to a stop in front of the emergency room entrance, and I leave the TT's lights on and the door open when I sprint inside.

I must look crazed, for Helen stares at me like I am when I burst into her room. She isn't even in bed. She's sitting in a chair, a small bandage on her forehead. She's calm, she even grins at me as she touches the bandage. "Five stitches," she says. "And I did it myself. Cracked my head on the Bug's door, trying to get out too fast. Because I was so pissed, Luther. I was so pissed I wanted to kill the bastard."

"What bastard? What the hell happened?"

"The fucker who ran me off the road. He did it deliberately, Luther! He even looked at my face while he was doing it. And he smiled. That black motherfucker," she says. "Oh, Jesus, that sounds awful, doesn't it? Forget I said that. He was just a plain mother-fucker."

I crouch next to her, take her hands in mine. "They check you out thoroughly here? You're okay? Just the cut?"

"Yeah," Helen says. "I'm fine. But my Bug's half-totaled. The right side's dented and scratched to shit. Sort of slid against the guardrail for a long way. Goddamn it. That motherfucker."

"But you're all right, pretty. That's what matters. That's all that matters," I say. "Think you can tell me exactly what happened?"

"Just what I told the policemen who brought me here. I was driving down Charles Street in the far right lane. Just before it makes that big long curve around the Shepherd Pratt place, this huge, huge SUV comes up in the left lane. He doesn't pass me. He looks at me. And he starts edging his monster toward me. I speed up, I slow down, he still stays even with me. Still keeps edging that SUV toward the Bug. I'm half on the fucking shoulder already. I start yelling and honking at him. He just smiles, keeps moving into my lane. Next thing I know I'm hitting the guardrail pretty hard, bouncing and scraping. I slam on the brakes, lose control a little, I guess, because pretty soon the Bug kind of slams to a stop against that rail. Then the motherfucker really speeds up, races off. And no, I didn't get the license plate number. I whacked my stupid head getting out."

"You saw his face, though? Saw it clearly? You can describe it?"

"I did," she says. "But I'm sorry, Luther. He was just this black guy. Not a kid or anything. Just a black man in a black suit in a huge fucking black SUV. I saw him, but—shit, I know this is terrible—if you showed me ten pictures of black guys in suits, all maybe early thirties, I don't think I could pick anyone out. Except for one thing. This guy was freaky, really strange."

"How?"

"He had like a couple of patches on his face that looked as if his skin had been peeled off or something. Because they were really white."

Helen wants to go back to her dorm. But I insist she's staying with me. I drive her back to my apartment, draw her a hot bath, bring her a glass of white wine while she's soaking in it. I call HQ, get the dispatcher to patch me through to the uniform who was first responder. He's still out cruising. He's sorry, but he can't tell me much. All he knows is what Helen told him. He thinks it was just some real carelessness by the guy in the SUV. Judging by the length of the Bug's skid marks, Helen couldn't have been doing more than thirty-five when her car hit the rail and she hit the brakes, he thinks. No marks on the left side of the Bug. He figures the SUV never made contact with Helen's car.

Didn't need to, I'm thinking. The SUV man could have got her killed anyway, panicked her into turning hard away from him, hitting the guardrail at a sharper angle.

Just a black guy in a suit. Right.

Last time I saw that fuck up close, he was carrying an Uzi.

23. And I know where Ray Phillips goes when he goes home at night.

I know he parks his car in an underground garage beneath his apartment building. A little extra detail in the intel package Dog's DEA homeboy put together on Russo.

I'm there two nights after Helen's crash when Ray Phillips pulls into his personal space just past eleven, kills the lights on his personal vehicle, that gross Escalade he keeps so buffed and polished.

Nobody else is around.

He's wearing the black suit. He doesn't see me coming until I'm maybe three paces from him. "Fucking Ewing," he says. "What?"

"Nothing," I say, taking one more step, my hands in the pockets of my windbreaker because I don't want him to see the lead-loaded black leather slap gloves I've got on.

"What the fuck kind of answer is that?" he says.

I shrug, take one more step. He's tensing.

I'm loose, not tensed. Speed's everything. You're faster when you don't try to be fast. Just let it all go, let your nervous system make the body move, no conscious intervention.

I let go.

Black blurs smash into his face, just below his eyes. The lead loads crack his cheekbones. Blurred black backhands hit lower, left and right. His jaw fractures on both sides.

Now he screams. Now he tries to reach for the pistol in his shoulder holster. Too fucking late. A black blur hacks down on the bridge of his nose, flattens it with a sickening crunch. Blood spurts. Backhand blurs slap his mouth, right and left. His lips split wide, spray blood.

He staggers. He's not reaching for his piece anymore. His hands are cupped below his chin, as if he's trying to catch the teeth that are falling from his ruined mouth. Or begging for this to stop. Pure reflex.

Phillips collapses to his knees. He's helpless with pain and shock, doesn't react when I remove his piece, one of those special .45s Springfield made for the FBI hostage rescue team. Doesn't resist when I seize the collar of his suit jacket, drag him between the Escalade and the car it's parked next to and prop him against the wall. His eyes are barely slits, the swelling's that bad already. But I'm sure he can see.

I take some things out of the fanny pack I'm wearing, open the driver's side door of the Escalade. With a mini-Maglite held in my teeth, I find the main electrical harness high up under the dash and clip every wire with a small pair of wire cutters. Wire cutters go back in my pack, box cutter comes out. I razor the beautiful black leather that covers the seats, front and back, until it looks like it's been through a paper shredder. I use a heavy screwdriver to destroy the CD and tape players, and punch it through every speaker I can find. I pry open the air bag containers, pop holes in the bags. With the butt of the screwdriver, I smash the glass covering every instrument dial on the dash. I take a big crescent wrench out, tighten it on the gear shift, and bend the thing almost in half

Then I get out of the Escalade and get serious. Under the hood,

I cut every hose, tube, and belt. Poke holes through the radiator, wrench the alternator off its base, crush the fuel injection system with a pry bar. Pop the valve covers and ding, bend, or break everything that's visible. Wham the air conditioning unit until it cracks.

Pry bar goes back in the pack. I take out a small, spring-loaded tool EMS guys use at car crashes. It shatters the windshield perfectly. So I move around and shatter every other window, plus all the lights. Ice-pick all four tires. Finally, I take a baggy full of sand out of the pack, pour the sand into the gas tank.

I figure Ray's looking at a minimum twenty-grand repair bill right off, and ten thousand later if nobody figures on the sand and he ever drives his patched-up piece of shit.

Ray isn't looking too good. I check his pulse and breathing. Both okay, considering. He needs a hospital, but not urgently.

I feel disgusted as I take off the gloves, stuff them in the pockets of my windbreaker. No pleasure in what I've done. Too fucking crude. I could have killed him with two fast, sharp strikes. The first with my bare thumb, the second with two fingertips. No, not a clean kill I could walk away from feeling clean.

But this wasn't combat. It was a message. RSVP was scrawled all over the one I'd been sent via Helen. Here's my reply, Francesca.

Almost feel sorry for her messenger boy, lying here. I know exactly what Phillips's future holds: Pain. Multiple reconstructive surgeries on his face.

I pat him down, lift his wallet, so it'll look like he got jumped, mugged, and robbed. I'll ditch the pistol where it'll never be found, burn the wallet. I turn, walk fast out of there. Three blocks away, I unlock my TT, slip in, and start driving home.

I cell Russo on the way.

"You're gonna have to get yourself a new boy to work Atlanta, if you were planning on starting there anytime soon," I say. "It looks like Ray's not going to be able to unfold the stock of an Uzi for maybe a month at least. Let alone fire it."

I break the connection before Russo can say a word.

■ ■ ■

Helen's curled on the futon wearing nothing but one of my shirts, watching some DVD movie that looks like it's set in early-nineteenth-century England. Lots of bonnets and big dresses, horses pulling a gleaming black carriage up a gravel drive to one of those huge stone piles with fifty rooms and servants fluttering all over the place.

"Pride and Prejudice," she says. "Not bad. Not bad at all."

"Need a shower, pretty," I say. "Then I'll join you."

Go into the bedroom, strip, put windbreaker, jeans, boots, and the gloves in an old Gap bag. I'll destroy them tomorrow. Pretty certain Phillips will never talk. But it's best to make certain there's no forensic link anyway. Then I walk naked into the bathroom, shampoo and scrub under water hot as I can bear. Do a little brainwash exercise, too; each stroke of the loofah rough against my skin wipes out an afterimage of a move or a blow I made on Phillips.

So I go to Helen unsoiled, body and mind. Or at least under the strong delusion I'm clean.

That's important to me. I want tonight to be more than an ordinary night. I want to specially please her. Because I don't know if there'll be more than just one or two more nights before there are no more nights with her at all.

She's graduating day after tomorrow, a Saturday. Her parents—the father and mother I've never met, the father and mother she's never told about my role in her life, or even of my existence—are coming down from Westport for the ceremony. They'll be expecting Helen to come home with them, I figure.

The girl's conflicted. She's made that plain by showing she's lost some of her usual clarity of thought. She'd pleaded with me, a few days before she crashed her car, to come to graduation, meet her parents.

"Too late now, Helen," I'd said. "What do you think the reaction will be if you spring a surprise like that on your folks? It'll resonate, even if you don't push me in their faces in public while we're standing on the college lawn and you're in your cap and gown. Suppose we have a quiet dinner together the night before? What's your dad going to think, seeing me, learning what I am and what we've been up to for almost two years?"

"Uh, pretty pissed, probably," she'd conceded. "He's not a jerk, but you don't get where he's gotten on Wall Street without being smart and tough. He'll hate feeling deceived. Well, not deceived. Out of the loop. I never lied about anything. Just never told him anything."

"Getting pissed off would be a justified reaction," I'd said. "I'd probably feel the same in his place."

"Ah, it's my own damn fault, Luther," she'd said. "He's really a decent guy. Not a class snob at all. If I'd introduced you a year ago, if you'd spent some time with him, shot some sporting clays, done a little sailing together, I'm sure he'd have liked you. Man to man. And he doesn't have any grand ambitions for me or anything. So you're a cop. He'd have gotten used to that. He might have started digging the idea, me with a cop, an ex-soldier. He was a platoon commander in Vietnam, did I ever tell you that? Right out of college. Went back and got his MBA at Wharton after the army. He could relate."

"That's a large maybe, I think. And you're forgetting the age bit.

Fathers get disturbed when men not all that much younger than them are fooling around with their daughters. What is he, just past fifty?"

"Turned fifty-two in March," she'd said. "He still thinks he's about thirty, though. Behaves like he is, anyway."

"Worse and worse. Because that's closer to what I am. You see that, right?"

"Yeah, I do. I guess it's a bad idea. Dad might deal with it, he's cool under pressure. It's my mother who'd get crazed, really," she'd said. "So, bad idea. For now."

Bad idea forever, I'd thought.

"It's not like graduating from college is such a major deal or anything," she'd said after a while. "But damn, I'd like you to be there and celebrate with us. Oh, I'm an idiot. What I'm really wanting is for us to be us, together, in front of my parents. Guess I pussied out, babe."

I'm deep into all this when the movie ends. Helen turns off the system with the remote. "Remember that great line in *Casablanca*? When Ingrid Bergman says to Bogart: 'Oh, kiss me. Kiss me as if it's for the last time'?"

I remember. I do it now. And it grows and deepens until we slide into a slow, bittersweet lovemaking that grows and deepens and goes on and on for as long as we can make it last.

We stay entwined, stroking each other's bodies for a long time afterward.

"When are you driving home with your parents? Sunday?" I finally ask.

She sighs. "I sort of have to now, yeah. But I don't have to stay in Westport forever. I've got to come back here and get my Bug when it's fixed, remember? Luther, can you take some time off? Could we go away someplace when I come down for my car?"

"Depends," I say, part of me glad she's going to be safely out of here while I take care of my not nearly finished business, and another part thinking it's over, so make the break now, don't drag it out with trips and visits. "Got that big trial starting Monday. It could take a while. You never know how long a trial will drag on. And I've gotta be here through all of it."

"Doesn't matter," Helen says. "I could just stay here with you, tell my folks I'm going to the beach with friends or something."

"Sure," I say. "Or something."

■ ■ ■

Saturday, about the time Helen must be getting handed her degree, I drive the TT down the Jones Falls Expressway and then though the city to Federal Hill, where Annie lives, in the constant dirt and disorder of her endless renovation of a large, hundred-year-old house. I have to pay for the visit, which she knows without a word from me is more than just a friendly drop-by. I'm hardly inside before she's handed me goggles, gloves, a small propane torch, and a scraper.

"Your mission," Annie grins, "is to help me strip the paint from the dining room door frames."

"Aw, Annie, it's too pretty a day to stay inside," I say. "Let's go down to the harbor, have a nice lunch."

"Un-uh, Luther. You're on the clock. Get started," she says. "I can listen while we strip."

I light the torch, tune the flame just right, start moving it over a small section of frame until the paint starts bubbling. There must be eight or ten coats, all kinds of odd colors. Everybody who ever owned Annie's house covered up somebody else's taste with their own. I slide the scraper under the bubbled layers, reveal a patch of wood. Annie claims the frames are solid mahogany, they'll be beautiful when they're bare, well-waxed, and polished. The wood I've bared looks lighter than any mahogany I've ever seen.

I flick that scraper a couple of times to shake off the mess of paint. The goo doesn't want to go. I scrape the blade against the edge of the waste bucket on the drop cloth. Then I start torching again. Shit, this could take days.

"Well?" Annie asks. She's working the other side of the frame.

"You sure this is mahogany?"

"Yeah. And I'm sure I'm working next to a man who thinks his heart is breaking, wants very badly to talk about it, but, all of sudden, feels too shy to speak."

"Close. Too stupid's probably more on target than too shy, though."

"You can't mean that what I've been telling you for years has finally gotten through your thick, metal-reinforced skull?"

"I can. I do. I've always set things up with women so there'd be no future. . . ."

"And finally you wish you hadn't, with this one. You want it to go on with Helen."

"Yeah. I'm not ready to give her up. I don't feel we've reached a natural conclusion. That's the really stupid part."

"It is. You know you only got her in the first place because she was age-vulnerable. And even if she's turned out to be what you imagine at the moment is the love of your life, she won't stay age-vulnerable. If you manage to stretch it out—and you probably could—she'd leave you eventually. No way you're the love of her life."

"Okay, point made, doctor," I say. "Can we talk shop?"

"Sure. That trial coming up?"

"That is the very least of it. That doesn't even signify. I've been had."

Annie laughs. "This I've got to hear."

She isn't laughing, she isn't even scraping paint anymore after I've given her a detailed briefing on the Russo situation.

"Christ, somebody tattoo 'Born to Lose' on your butt when you popped out? How can you keep getting into such deep, deep shit, Luther?" she says. Then she gives me that eye-scan she's so good at.

"Oh no, Luther. You swore never again after the Russian thing. IB and I risked a lot for you on that one. You swore you'd never cross the line again. And you're thinking of doing it again, god-dammit."

"If there was another way . . ."

"There is. Maybe there wasn't with Vassily, but there is this time. Definitely."

"Like what?"

"Walk away from it. Just walk away. Let this woman become someone else's problem. Just dump everything you've got on Du-gal. If he wants to walk it up the federal ladder, let him do it. If he doesn't, so what?"

"Might be too late already."

"Look, if she's as smart as you say, it isn't. All you have to do is walk away, stay completely clear of her. She'll see that, and she'll see at once she's better off staying clear of you. She'll realize going to war with you would be dangerous and distracting. That it'll be much better for her business to leave you alone. As long as you leave her alone. As long as you don't mess with her."

"Yeah, that sounds logical. But I keep remembering that old man wired to a rocking chair on his porch, with his tongue pulled through a slit in his throat. There was no reason for that, Annie."

"Yeah, there was. She had to rachet up the action, make it real bad and bloody, to demonize the Winnebergers. I know you've had that in mind, you talked to me about it. Well, they've been demonized, they've been busted, and they're going to be convicted. She's all set. Her field's clear. If you stay out of it."

"And if I don't?"

"Then you're asking for it, like I just said. She'll have to react. But if you stay quietly out of the way, moving on you would only cause her problems she doesn't need. So please, please let it go, Luther. It may take a while, but the DEA will clue to her eventually. Let the DEA take her down."

"Those fucks?"

"Luther, you know Russo's a rogue. There have to be some smart, straight people at the DEA who will see that sooner or later. Leave her to them."

"You're right," I say. "I mean intellectually, I know you're right. But I feel like I have to do something, take some kind of action. It's gotten personal."

"Stay cold and clear. Isn't that what Gunny always told you?" Annie says. "The last time you didn't, the last time you let it get personal, it cost you your army career. What'll it cost you this time?"

I don't answer.

"More than she and the shit she's trying to pull are worth," Annie says. "Much more. Maybe everything."

24. "Luther! Hi!"

Russo's in anchorwoman mode when I walk into the court-house Monday morning, her hair and makeup just right. But she's giving me straight Di. Di and Charlie, those crazy guys. Partners in a booming retail biz. Great couple. Tight, those guys. Really tight.

She's good. She's cool, she's so chill it's scary. I do my best, but I know it isn't up to her level.

"Hey, what's going down?" I say.

"Bobbie and Butch, pretty soon," she laughs. "Way down, after we leave the witness stand. That prosecutor, Trotter, I saw her a few minutes ago. She looked like she was anticipating the first orgasm of her poor deprived life."

"God, no," I say. "She wins, she'll be wanting to start dating us."

"That's when I ask for a transfer to Fargo. ASAP, please."

"Atlanta might be a better bet."

"Christ, Luther!" she lowers her voice to just above a whisper. "I know we've got a lot to talk about. I know there's been some serious misunderstanding. Things that need straightening out in a hurry. But this is not the time or place. We do our court act, okay? Then we talk everything through."

"Okay on the act. I don't know about the other."

"I can live with that. Just do the act. Whatever happens after, happens."

. . .

What happens in court is short and sweet. There's Bobbie and Butch, eyes hooded and looking even meaner than usual, one in a blue shirt, the other in white. They're scribbling note after note on yellow legal pads, passing them to their attorney. Who isn't bad, who's fairly slick, good at cross-examination. Problem is, he's got nothing to work with. No plausible defenses at all. Not faced with Dugal, BCPD captain and head of Vice and Narcotics; Russo, chief of the Baltimore bureau of the DEA; and me, Ice Box, and several other cops saying exactly the same thing: We all personally saw the Winnebergers hand over a shitload of crystal meth to me and Russo in exchange for a couple of suitcases full of money.

The poor fuck. He should never have taken this case.

He takes his best shots. He tries calling the bust entrapment, he tries discrediting witnesses, he squirms finally into offering a plea bargain. Trotter isn't playing. The woman's a human steamroller. She just rolls right over every move, every objection, every arcane legal point the defense guy can dream up, and leaves him flatter than a dime.

The trial's over in four days, the jury takes just an hour to return a verdict of guilty on all counts. The judge sets a date for sentencing, stipulates the Winnebergers will remain in jail until the sentence is handed down.

The twins look stunned as they're led out of court, cuffed. Russo can't resist. She glides up to them, turns on her high-wattage smile. "Bobbie! Butch!" she says. "No hard feelings, right? Just part of the game. With any luck, you guys'll be back selling fertilizer in Westminster. Maybe twenty years from now."

"Fuck you, Di," Bobbie says.

"Hey! Thought you were a gentleman, Bobbie. But you're bitter, I can see it. You feel betrayed. Never mind. For me, personally, it's been a great pleasure doing business with you."

The woman's psycho, for sure. But not out of control. She grabs my arm, steers me out a side door of the courthouse. Good move. Because there on the front steps is Dugal, suit buttoned just so, knot of his tie perfectly centered, managing to look grave and triumphant at the same time as he delivers his victory speech to three TV reporters with their camera crews and a half-dozen print reporters gathered below him. When question time comes, he calls on the journalists by name, a trick of ingratiation he must have learned studying TV coverage of presidential press conferences. Give short, colorful answers. The man knows the sound-bite game.

"I believe Dugal missed his true calling," Russo says. "He should have gone into politics, not law enforcement. Made better use of his talents."

"Not too late to make a career change," I say.

"Almost never too late, if you see an opportunity and have the nerve to seize it."

"You're the best living proof of that I've seen in a while," I say.

We sit on one of green-painted wooden benches with curlicued wrought-iron arms placed here and there around the grounds of the courthouse. Russo swivels her body toward me, trying for face-to-face, direct eye contact. But I only give her my profile, stare out across the neatly trimmed turf where the very last of the tulips and daffodils are dying, and beds of summer flowers are beginning to bloom.

"Let's deal with the worst first," Russo says. She's dropped both the anchorwoman pose and the Di act. "Luther, I did not tell Phillips to do what he did to your girl. I knew nothing about it until after it happened."

"The man took your orders. Like Blizzard took your orders."

"Usually. But not this time. Phillips moved entirely on his own. You can't really believe I'd react that stupidly to your stunt with the license plates and the meth? Sure, I was furious at the time. I still am cross, for the reasons you know. But if I'd wanted any payback, I'd have gotten serious payback."

"What Phillips did seemed serious enough to me."

"And you messed him up bad for it. Fair enough," Russo says. "You have any idea how bad?"

"I know precisely. Everything I did to him was deliberate."

"And without mercy. I don't suppose he deserved any. But I did not, repeat not, order him to do anything to Helen. The retard dreamed it up all by himself. I had no idea he'd go crazed on me like that."

"So?"

"So what is your real problem, Luther? I get the Phillips thing. I even approve in a way. I do not get the point or purpose of changing plates and planting drugs in my car, considering what we discussed when you came down to the farm. Why'd you pull a dumb juvenile-delinquent stunt like that? Why the bad acting-out? Why are we having difficulties like this?"

"My problem, Francesca, is that I decided I hate the idea of being your employee," I say. "Another expendable asshole like Phillips or Blizzard. I've got a job. I am an employee. If I'm gonna bend, it's got to be for something much more."

"Christ, we've never had the chance to talk money. Tell me what you've got in mind."

"The point's not entirely money. Employees get paid. Remember risk-reward ratios? The math on this problem works out to one thing for me. Some equity."

"That's the issue?" she says. Then she laughs. "Do the math an-

other way, it works out to sole proprietorship. Since it's my operation. I conceived it. I brought it into being."

"Using me to eliminate your competition. For free. And at
fairly high risk. You forgetting the ambush at the Wynn place,
stuff like that? So it becomes very simple. You want me in on this,
you've got to give up some ownership interest. Otherwise, no go."

"And if it's no go?"

"Then I don't bend. I stay on my side of the line, and do my
job. Which is taking down people on your side. No matter how
big and bad they are. Guy named Vassily, he thought he was too
big and bad to be touched, too."

"Finally admitting to that number, huh? So impressive," Russo
laughs, mocking me. Then her voice goes icy.

"I don't respond well to threats, Luther. I don't respond to absolute demands. Reasonable negotiation, that generally works
with me. So why don't you go home, get real calm, take out your
calculator, plug in some profit projections and what you think
your share should fairly be? Given risk-reward. We'll talk again
when you've done that. Because this conversation is nowhere. So
I'm ending it."

"There you go, giving orders like an arrogant CEO."

"I *am* an arrogant CEO." She grins. "Doesn't mean I'm totally
ruling out having an arrogant chief operating officer."

■ ■ ■

One step foward, one step back. Leaves me nowhere I want to be.

That's what I'm thinking when I get back to the squad room.
I'm gaming with Russo, just made a nice move. Which, as Annie
rightly pointed out, is both dumb and dangerous. Exactly what I
shouldn't be doing. I should walk away from the bitch. Stay way
out of her way, stay clear of this whole thing. But I'm a fucking ad-

dict for the action. Even when the action looks lose-lose from every angle.

Just another stupid junkie. Can't help myself. Wired that way, I guess.

Which must be why I get a rush when Radik drops by with what should be very bad news.

"Can I get out of that bet I made involving losing my left nut, Luther?" he says, looking about as dispirited as I've ever seen the man.

"What? Your wife find out about that little waitress you've been porking on the side?"

"Shit no. I could talk my way out of that, easy," he says. "Can't talk my way out of a solid ballistics report, though."

"Oh, fuck. You're not gonna tell me what I think you're gonna tell me?"

"I am. The .44 Special we found at Blizzard's is definitely not the .44 that domed the guys in the basement, or the cookers in the Wynn trailor."

"Goddammit! I know he's the shooter."

"So do I. But not as dumb as we figured. He made the hot .44 disappear, then went out and had his sweat hog buy another one. Very nice and legal. 'Cause as a convicted felon, he cannot possess a handgun. The .44's in her name. And get this shit. Ballistics says the piece has never been fired. Not once, not a single round. New in the fucking box."

"He know about the report?" I ask. Suddenly I'm seeing an opportunity in this.

"Not yet. But he fucking knows we can't hold him much longer. Because he knows we don't have the right gun. And he knows we can't touch him even on a small thing like illegal possession, either. Knows he's not facing any trial, let alone jail.

Clever little fuck. I can't stand the idea he's laughing at us. And I fucking know he is."

"When do you have to turn him loose?"

"Later today. We drop charges, he walks. Got no option."

"Let me know when he's leaving, will you? I'm up for having a talk with him."

"You think you can do any good?"

"Maybe. Maybe I can at least cast some spooky shadows on his mind."

"The darker and spookier the better, man," Radik says.

When Eddie Blizzard leaves the station that afternoon and starts walking across the parking lot toward York Road, I pull up next to him in the TT.

"Get in," I say.

He bends, looks in the window, says "Suck my dick, Charlie," and keeps walking. I pace him with the car.

"What are you gonna do, take a fucking bus out to the sticks? Hitch a ride? Russo maybe sending a limo? I don't see one."

"Russo? Who the fuck is that?"

"Your DEA pal," I say. "Di. You know. Hey, don't tell me she's not taking care of you?"

"I got no DEA pals. And my good friend Charlie the narc wants to drive me home? Fuck off."

"I'm off the clock. And I may be the only friend you got left, Eddie," I say. "You wasted most of them, solving some of Di's little problems for her. Dig this. Ray Phillips must have become a problem for her too. Because he's been taken down."

Blizzard stops, bends, looks at me. "Bullshit. You don't know what you're talking about."

"Oh, I do, Eddie," I say. "Because I'm the one who did Ray. Kind of worries me now, though. Seems like everybody who does a job for Russo gets taken out afterward. That worrying you at all?"

Blizzard opens the TT's door, slides in. He smells like jail, clammy and sour. We head north on York.

"Smart move, ditching that .44, Eddie. Radik would have you nailed on multiple murder ones if it was still around," I say after a while.

"No clue what you're talking about, man."

"You know exactly. Also know I don't give a shit. Nice clean hits, all of them. Wonder how Radik got on to you, Eddie?"

He doesn't say anything.

"Somebody must've ratted you out. You only got a couple of possibles. Angel Dust? Don't think so. He's still shot through with so many painkillers he doesn't know what planet he's on. That leaves only one person I can think of. Our pal Di. Bet Radik told you so, too."

"Fucking bitch can kiss my balls," Blizzard snarls. "We got a deal."

"You had a deal. Ray had a deal, I had a deal. I'm starting to think they're bad, bad deals. I'm starting to get kind of edgy here, wondering who she's going to get to cap me. She doesn't like to get her hands dirty."

"Do you?"

"I don't mind a bit, kind of dig it mostly, if I can wash up afterward. Like I did after Phillips," I say. "Hey, you play chess, Eddie? Sure, you do. Everybody who does time learns chess."

"It's an okay game."

"Yeah, when it's played on a board. Maybe not when it's played for real."

"You're whacked, man. You do a lot of drugs or what? Where you heading with this shit?"

"Picture this, Eddie. Di's playing real chess. She's the queen, naturally. You think Phillips, you, me are like bishops or knights or something? No way. We're the fucking pawns, Eddie."

"You're out of it, totally."

"Hey, she gets people like us to do things she wants done. She moves us where she wants us. And what happens then?" I say. "Ever seen a queen hesitate to sacrifice a pawn once it's served its purpose?"

"Now you're just trying to fuck with my mind. She's got no problem with me."

"No? Well, if I hired some shit-kicker like you to hit eight or ten dudes, I think I'd be nervous about him. Specially since he's been arrested for the hits. The cops know, they just don't have the proof. So I'd make sure they don't ever get any. I'd give my hitter a Colombian necktie, like you and Angel gave that old farmer."

"That's pure bullshit!"

"Hey, take it anyway you like it. Long as it makes you happy."

"Why're you slinging all this shit, man? You give a rat's ass what happens to me."

"A rat's ass, that's about it. Ordinarily," I say. "I ain't gonna come to your sorry funeral all weepy, Di has you domed. I'd just laugh when I heard Eddie Blizzard got capped. Ordinarily."

"Funny, I got the same feeling about you."

"Except you're one move behind me, Eddie. I'd like you walking around alive as long as possible. I'd like Di to have two pawns on the board to sacrifice, not just me. That's why I'm bothering trying to educate you a little, asshole."

"I'm supposed to say thanks or some shit?"

"Don't give a fuck what you say, man," I say. "Don't give a fuck what you do, actually. Me, I'm gonna be busy watching my back real, real close. I'm gonna stay real alert. I hear one footstep I don't like, I'm going down to that fucking farm of hers on the Shore, maybe solve the problem permanently. Pawn takes queen, game's over."

"Heard Di had a place down there. Where is it?" Blizzard asks, the beginnings of the ugly smirk forming on his weasel face.

I give him directions.

"She only goes on weekends," I say. "Goes alone."

25.

"Ohhh, you are fuckin' evil, man," Ice Box says when I get back to Towson, fill him in on my ride with Blizzard. "You just sicced a mad dog on our bent DEA lady. Genius move. Jesus!"

"Maybe," I say.

"Sounds like more than maybe to me. I think she's gonna get bit. Soon."

"Russo's got a lot of experience with bad dogs," I say. "Odds are better than even she can get Eddie under control again. If he does go for her, which is problematic. He may not have bought into the story I told him."

"Problematic? Hell, he's crazy. You just made him supercrazy. And he's got the stones. He'll go. All you gotta do is wait for it to happen."

"Can't wait for a maybe, IB. I've got to keep playing her."

"Oh, no, Luther," IB says. "This is one you got to stay clear of."

"Nothing like the Russian thing, man. I'm not going to lay a finger on her, I swear it. I just have to keep her preoccupied for a while with me, with the idea that I'm going to go rogue, get into biz with her. Tactical diversion. So if Eddie does go, she might be off-guard. If she isn't, he's got no chance."

"I'm not liking what I'm hearing here. Not digging it one bit. You got to disengage right now, not go in deeper. I take back that 'genius' shit. You've set something in motion. Just let it happen."

"And if it doesn't?"

"Go to Plan B. You don't have a Plan B? Then spend your time coming up with one. Not fucking around with Russo."

"Sure."

"You too arrogant to entertain the notion she's playing with you? That she's got uses for you that you can't comprehend?"

"She's already played me."

"My point, numbnuts. Definitely scratch that 'genius,' if you figure because she's done that once, she isn't gonna do it some more. Especially if she's as good as you claim."

IB, like Annie, is absolutely right, of course. But I'm not admitting that to him or anyone else. Especially myself. Plan B? Fuck that. Plans always have a way of cracking, collapsing under unexpected pressures. Never met a plan in my life that stayed whole from start to finish. Not one. So it's better to have a bunch of fallbacks in mind and stay very flexible, very light on your feet. Better to believe in Gunny's old Corps saw: Improvise, adapt, overcome.

And worst case, no matter how big a goatfuck develops, there's always plan SIG. Right there on my hip. Don't even have to think to implement it. Instinct and muscle memory will do it all on their own.

■ ■ ■

I call Russo, invite her to dinner.

"Your dime? Okay, then Bleibtreu, night after next," she says. "I'm in an old Checkpoint Charlie Berlin kind of mood. A little tense, you know? Like I'm on the wrong side of the border hoping to get across, and you're the Vopo about to ask for my papers, which are forged."

"Cold war's over, Francesca," I say. "I'm more in a peace dividend state of mind myself."

"Are you now? Big dividend? Been doing projections and so forth? Come up with a proposal you think I'll accept?"

"Numbers'll wait. First I'd like to get friendlier with you, maybe get a better sense of whether we'd be smooth as a CEO-COO team," I say.

"Smooth as Di and Charlie, I'm thinking. Tight. In synch."

"Possibly."

"For sure. If you can make a very small attitude adjustment." She laughs. "Nothing major. I like you pretty much the way you are."

"Same thing I'm thinking about you."

"What'd I just say! In synch, totally," she laughs again. "Meet you there. Eight o'clock, okay?"

It's a full house at Bleibtreu two nights later, but that doesn't matter. The tables are set far enough apart that you can have a private conversation, no fear of being overheard. I'm sitting there sipping some Badener wine the waiter'd recommended when Russo swans in, wearing that sleeveless black number with the princess seams and her highest-watt smile. She spins around once when she reaches my table.

"Luther! Hey! Am I printing?" she says as she sits down. She's a few minutes late. I figure it's because she was doing a line or two of coke outside in her car. She's almost glowing with a sort of radiant energy that *has* to be artificially induced.

"Big time," I say. "But full-body, not a piece. Very, very nice outline."

"Wow, you must be really lonely with your schoolgirl gone," she says. "Talk like that is way outside the usual parameters of our relationship."

"Relationships develop, don't they?" I say, pouring Badener into her glass.

"Sure. Sometimes they get better, sometimes they get worse," she says, sipping. "Neat wine, Luther. Here's hoping our relationship is moving in the right direction."

"I think that's going to get clear pretty fast," I grin. *But not in any way you're imagining, Russo.*

"My impression, too. Perfect synch again. Charlie." She's almost giggling. Maybe it was three lines of coke in the car.

We order. Russo interrogates the waiter—charm full-on, but still a grilling—until he confesses exactly what the chef's doing best this night, what he's slacking off with. She gets one answer finally that appeals to her, chooses the dish. I take the goose.

"Guess you already know it," I say when the waiter's gone, "but, just in case, Eddie Blizzard walked. No ballistic match."

"Eddie? Blizzard?" she says, cocking her head. "Oh, who cares about that lowlife anyway? Probably he'll go back to sticking up convenience stores, now that he's off Butch and Bobbie's payroll. Since Butch and Bobbie don't have a payroll anymore."

"I care. Hate it when a mean little shit, who did an old man in his rocking chair plus eight drug runners with .44 Special wadcutters to the head and the two chemists at that meth trailer in the woods, just walks. You remember those woods, since you and ex-Ray hosed down the guys who were shooting at me and IB."

"X-Ray? Jesus, Luther, your sense of humor is so weird," she says. "I do have clear recall of that forest fiasco. Remember, too, you were very ungrateful, almost pissed at me for saving your ass. Which seemed a pretty odd reaction. So okay. It is a damned shame some scumbag got away with murder. But it happens lots of times."

"Eddie didn't get away, he just walked on the first try," I say. "Our homicide chief's a pit bull type, but smart. Like your dogs.

He's got his little ways and means. Just a matter of time before he hauls Blizzard back in. And keeps him in."

"Wish your homicide chief luck," she says, not a hint of irony in her voice. She is so cool tonight, her front's so good. But I feel sure she's hearing some footsteps she doesn't like at all.

The food arrives and Russo slides smoothly into dinner chat: how this or that tastes, how the wine's got a fine finish. She takes it further, starts getting personal: what am I doing for fun, with Helen gone? I don't dig that line at all, but I force myself to keep as light and teasy as she's being.

"Had a replacement ready way in advance," I laugh. "And guess what? I even tried that motel in Arbutus you like so much. You were right about red neon giving things a little extra kick."

"You punk!" she grins. "I must've been on drugs when I told you about that. Oh yeah, I was on drugs. Shit! Listen. If we run into each other down there some night, we're total strangers, okay?"

"No problem, 'cause once was enough for me. I won't be going down there again. Unless I get invited."

Russo hoots. "Luther! Hey! In your dreams."

I've cleared about half my plate, Russo's taken maybe two bites of her flounder and mainly just pushed the rest around with her fork, when she excuses herself and goes to the girls' room. She returns as lit up as she was when she entered the restaurant, starts talking a mile a minute. I have to break into the monologue.

"You, uh, frequently crank up so much, Francesca?" I ask. "Because I don't feel a lot of confidence in people who do that. Skews their judgment. Makes 'em very unreliable. Not the sort I care to do business with."

"Relax, Luther!" she says. "Recreational only. And don't you think I know that tonight's test night? That I've got to meet or exceed whatever standards you've set up, if we're going to go forward together on some things?"

"Sure, I knew you knew. Which is why I'm wondering so much why you'd show me what you're showing me."

"Because I'm so sure I'll pass anyway. Simple as that. You've seen what I can do, you've seen me in action. Any of that give you pause about reliability? Or competence? No. You've been impressed. You've also hated the little ways I've outmanuevered you. Right?"

"Right," I say.

"So I've deliberately handicapped myself tonight. Now let's get on with the exam, okay?"

"Why're you going bad?" I ask. "Something happen in Phoenix?"

"Sonora. I was in the field almost always. Where I like to be," she says. "The drugistas, they caught my partner. What they did to him made a Colombian necktie look like a mercy killing."

"And becoming one of them is your response?"

"My first response was to take out a bunch of the scumbags the ugliest ways I could think of. What you'd do, right? If it'd been Ice Box who'd got what my guy got?"

"Probably."

"Certainly, you mean. So it gets real personal, and private. As you well know. My chief sees where I'm going, gets panicky about scandal, about bad repercussions to his career if it leaks that he's got an out-of-control agent capping Mexicans on their side of the border. So he benches me.

"And then: enlightenment," she goes on. "I realize finally the whole thing is personal and private. Nobody cares how many of us get killed, or how many narcotraffickers we kill or jail. Americans want to get high. They really want their drugs. Millions of them. Not just city kids with no hope. I mean Hollywood millionaires and Silicon Valley tycoons and big Wall Street bulls. Everybody's got to have their coke and their smack and their grass and their speed—if they're not just old-fashioned alcoholics. We have a drug culture in this country embedded so deep it could never be cut out. If there was some kind of miracle, and suddenly you could not get any dope here, there'd be a fucking revolution."

"Don't think I buy that."

"Bullshit. I haven't said one thing you haven't already been sure of yourself for a long time. Americans love drugs. They're junkies. They'll do whatever it takes to get their high. And there is nothing anybody can do about it. So I quit trying."

"No, you decided to supply them. Big difference."

"I decided fuck them, they want their dope, they can have it. Especially crystal. Everybody knows meth's a death ride. Anybody stupid enough to take it deserves what they get. But before they go down, they're going to make me very rich, and then I'm getting the hell out of here. I've got an option on a beautiful property in New Zealand. I'm going there, raise beautiful horses. Everyone and everything else can go to hell."

I laugh.

"Find me amusing, do you?"

"No. I think you're sort of self-righteous, which is okay. But definitely deluded, which is kind of sad. You'll never make it happen, Francesca. Because you're a hard-core junkie yourself. For the action."

"Am I? How would you know?"

"You're exactly like me. You have to rock. Somebody needs to go down, you put 'em down. No hesitation, no remorse. People like us don't just walk away. We can't walk away from our own natures."

"See if I'm still here two, three years from now."

"I'm wondering if you're going to live two, three years," I say.

"Wicked point, Luther. You may be right. Things can happen even if you're supercareful and good at what you do," she says. "But maybe you've got a New Zealand of your own, and just haven't realized it yet. Anyway, what I've set up is going to happen. With you, or without you."

"IB, he collects weird little stories from the newspaper," I say. "Even though I asked him not to, he read me one the other day. A guy in Riverside, California, starts feeling real sorry for himself, gets deeply depressed, because his girlfriend leaves him. So he sticks his hand in a cage where he keeps a pet rattlensnake. Gets bit. Doesn't move his hand. Gets bit again. Keeps his hand in there. Gets bit two or three more times. Then he just lies down on his sofa. And he dies."

"So?"

"If it all makes you sick, if you only want to get away from it, just go, Francesca," I say. "Don't stick your hand in the cage."

Russo laughs, drains her wine glass, laughs some more.

"Luther, you crazy guy!" she says. "That's a fine morality tale. But you know damn well we're both good enough to reach right on in, grab what we want, and get out faster than any rattler can strike. You're digging the idea, I can tell. You want to make that grab, half for the money but half for the thrill. You're coming in on this with me, aren't you?"

"Well, it feels like it might be happening. Couple little details we need to work out, though."

"I doubt it'll take much work," she grins. "Come down to the farm Saturday. Very early. We'll go fishing. And I'll bet before you land one we'll have a solid deal."

■ ■ ■

When I get back to my place that night it feels, for the first time, all wrong. Too Zen, too quiet, too serene. And too empty, without that girl who brought so much light, life, and love to it. Helen's left a definite void. I move to fill it. Put that Reindeer Section CD she liked on the sound system, strip and toss my clothes all over the place like she used to instead of hanging each item in its appointed place, which is my habit. Slip into my yakuta, open the fridge, pop a bottle of beer, and take a few large swallows.

No good.

But Helen's also left a message on my answering machine when I check for calls. It's the first. I don't bother checking the others. I punch in her Westport number, hear two rings, then a sleepy-sounding "Yes?"

"Hello, pretty," I say.

"Luther?"

"Sure."

"Oh, Luther. I've been missing you so much, babe. Why aren't you here? Or why aren't I there?"

"Well . . ."

"Yeah, yeah, I am so stupid," she says. "Of course you can't be here. And I can't be there. For now, anyway. Are you missing me?"

"In more ways than you could know," I say. I'm falling deep into it, wanting her presence.

"Does that mean I can stay with you a while when I come down? I've got to come down in about ten days to pick up my Bug. You'll be there? You'll let me stay with you?"

I stop falling. "For as long as you can manage. I'd love that," I say. "But I'm not sure about the timing, pretty. Got some things happening that might get badly in our way. Does it have to be exactly ten days from now?"

"No. The Bug'll be ready then. At least the repair shop promised it would. It's not going anywhere. But ten days already seems way too long. I am really missing you. Didn't think it would be this bad."

"Me neither. Let me just try to take care of some things the next few days and over the weekend. I'll know Monday if I'm going to get clear. Call you then, set a date?"

"Promise? Promise you'll get clear of whatever it is?"

"I promise I'll call Monday. I promise I'll see you very soon," I say, knowing the words are empty, hating that.

"Okay, babe," she says. There's a silence. "I'm sorry, Luther. It hurts to just talk on the phone. I'd better hang up now. Monday, then? Promise?"

"Yes," I say. Click.

My mind stays on the line, stays connected to Helen. It's clear what's best, clear what I've got to do. But it's going to be hard. And it's going to hurt, I'm realizing, much more than I ever imagined. I have got to cut it clean with Helen, cut it off with one stroke. It has be clean and absolutely final. I hope I have enough integrity left to do the right thing, not the selfish one. Which would be to keep on seeing her any way we could manage and as often as we could arrange until she realizes what I know too well: There can't be a future for us. But letting it play out that way would be using her. I care for her far too much for that. It'd be a ruthless, heartless thing.

Which is why it's going to be difficult, and also why it has to be done. Because I am ruthless and heartless. I'm not going to change. Even if I wanted to, I could not do it.

Just like Francesca Russo. We're the matched pair, not me and Helen. Russo and I are in exactly the same place. Our routes may have been different, but not our ultimate destination.

I start laughing. Not happily. Only at the irony. I actually like

Russo at lots of levels. I like her smarts, the way she makes her moves, her toughness. I don't mind at all that she's bent, that she's breaking all the rules, big time. Since most of the rules are bullshit, and I bend or break them whenever I have to. There's probably even a kinked sexual thing for her down somewhere deep where I won't go, and which I'd never admit if it surfaced.

Shit, I don't even care much that she shot me. It was only a love tap. Rough, but still a tap. She could so easily have killed me, not just put a fairly minor hole in my flesh.

But there's one thing I hate, one thing I won't forgive or forget: an old man wired to his rocking chair. Maybe she never directly ordered that, maybe she was telling the truth when she claimed she never ordered Ray Phillips's move on Helen. Maybe that sadistic scumbag Blizzard did Early on his own hook, and Phillips did what he did on his. But she's responsible, because they were under her command.

So. The vertical stroke. Phillips has been partly taken care of. Blizzard will be totally taken care of. I'm going to really enjoy doing Eddie. Plus his buddy Angel Dust, if the fuck ever stops being a hospital vegetable.

And Francesca Russo is going down too. I won't take so much pleasure in it. But I'll find the way, and I will do it.

26. Very early Saturday, the sun yet to edge over the flat green horizon of the Eastern Shore but already turning the sky and the waters of the Chesapeake rosy, I take the TT smooth and fast up that long rising curve of the Bay Bridge. There's a lot more traffic even at this hour than when I last made the crossing, in early May, though the Memorial Day holiday's a week off. The weekenders, I figure, are trying to get a jump start opening up their houses for the long summer season.

I weave in and out through the heavily loaded SUVs and station wagons, push the needle higher and make the weaves more often once I've left the Bridge, crossed Kent Island, and hit Route 50 south. The TT feels good, quick. So do I.

It gets brighter fast. By the time I take a left on Route 328 just past Easton, I've slipped on my shades. I'm heading straight into the sun. Heading straight to Russo's farm.

But I'm just moving to be moving. Know where I'm going, but not what I'm going to do when I get there. I have no idea at all how to deal with the Russo problem. Only some vague hope that she'll show me a way herself. Not today, probably. Not tomorrow. Maybe someday.

Maybe if I hang with her a lot, she'll make that mistake, say or do something that will give me the key I need to put her away.

Not today, though. Feel sure of that.

The corn's thigh-high now in the front acres. Her Volvo's there, the Steyr-Puch is in its shed. But she's not around when I pull up, get out, and look around the place. I smell that river smell on the soft breeze, see a square of white paper taped at one corner to the house's back door, fluttering. "I'm down at the dock. Just follow the path. Door's unlocked if you need to go, or want some coffee first," is written on the square in neat green script.

I go in. She'll expect that, so there's no point in prowling around. Even if I did find something worth moving on, so what? I'm not geared up for any action. There isn't going to be any. I do have one accessory, about the size of a cigarette lighter, in my shirt pocket. For personal reasons. Those dogs of hers. I'm a little freaked by those dogs, I admit.

I pour myself a big mug of coffee, check the fridge for half-and-half, find some and lighten the coffee with it. As I'm leaving, my eye zeros on the cattle prod hanging from a hook on the wall. Impulse: I put the coffee mug on the counter, take down the prod, and remove the batteries. Reverse them so they won't work, reinsert them, put the thing back on its hook. Then I grab my coffee, walk outside, and amble the few hundred meters to the gap in the woods that funnels to the Choptank.

She's sitting all the way at the end of a weathered gray log dock that's built out maybe fifteen meters into the slow, turbid river. Her back to me, legs dangling just above the water. I see her right arm come back, a light rod flex with the weight of some fairly heavy rigging, then whip forward. The hook rig soars, hits the water at least twenty meters out, disappears. Nice toss.

I step onto the dock then. She turns her head, but keeps slowly reeling in her line.

"Luther! Hey!" That five-hundred-watt smile. "Great morning, huh? Come on out here and I'll teach you things I bet you don't know."

"Oh, I've done my share of fishing," I say as I close the distance and sit down beside her. There's a light spin-casting rod, same as she's using, lying there, line already weighted and hooked. I pick it up, check the tension on the reel, whip the rod once or twice.

"Where's your lure box?" I ask.

"Lures? Knew I'd have to teach you. You're a bass guy, if you're thinking lures," she says. "No good when you're after rockfish."

"So what're you using for bait?"

"These," she grins, sliding toward me a plastic gallon bucket half-full of slimy black things twisting and churning in water, watching my expression. Then she laughs that wild, free laugh.

"You pussy! Never used live eels before? Typical bass guy. Guess I'll have to bait you up. The first time. After that, you're on your own."

She finishes reeling in, sticks the butt of her rod in a socket screwed to the piling on her left. I put my rod next to her. She sticks her hand in the bucket, pulls out an eel about six inches long that's writhing and trying hard to bite something.

"Rocks' favorite food," she says, swiftly running the hook all the way through, just behind the head, so the barb's just barely protruding. The eel goes berserk, snapping and struggling. She hands the rod back to me. "Now you can just spin-cast like you would with a bass rig. And maybe have a chance of catching something. Though I'm skeptical you'll be able to land a big boy, if one decides to strike."

I make a cast, she makes a longer one. We both start to reel in slowly. I can't see even a foot beneath the Choptank's deep greenish surface, but I can feel that eel thrashing through the thin line.

No hits on the first casts. We toss out our lines again, repeat the slow reel. I stop every now and then, sip some coffee.

"You sure there are any fish in this river, Francesca?" I say after the fourth or fifth cast.

"Absolutely. You saw the beauty I landed last time you were here," she says. "What kind of fisherman are you, anyway? You've got to chill, get into the casting, get relaxed and patient. Enjoy the peace, and the process. A big rock hits, you'll get a jolt then. Your rod'll bend almost in half. And if you don't play it slow and gentle, he'll snap your line and swim away with a tasty breakfast in his mouth."

"Believe that when I see it," I say.

"Bad approach, Luther. A pessimist by nature. That's one of those little attitude shifts I mentioned. I do wish you'd try on at least a little optimism sometimes. I'm always optimistic, and I always catch what I'm after." She laughs. "Some kind of self-fulfilling prophecy thing, maybe?"

"Nah. I don't believe anybody can wish anything into being," I say. "Nothing happens because you think good thoughts. You've got to make things happen."

"Hello!" Russo shouts, her rod suddenly bent near to snapping. "Here's proof you're wrong. Just watch."

I watch her let monofilament race off that reel 'til her rod's straight, then hit the brakes so it starts bending again, then let the fish run a while, then hit the brakes and reel in a few feet. She works that way for four or five minutes or more, it's hard to gauge. Until the balance seems to shift and she's gradually reeling in more footage than the fish she's hooked is stripping off. Pretty soon her line disappears into the water very close to the dock, though it's still slicing the surface this way, then that.

"Grab that net, Luther. Stand by me," she says. "Scoop him up as soon as you can see him."

I miss with the first scoop. Miss something I can see is huge even in blurred outline through cloudy water.

"Spastic!" Russo laughs. "I'm bringing him in real close again. See if you can do your job right this time, okay?"

The weight's almost astonishing when I net the rock and heave it flopping and fighting up on the dock. This monster is nearly a meter long, and clearly not resigned to its fate. Russo pounces on it before it can power its way out of the net and off the dock.

"Ohhh, a nice papa rock! Okay, tough guy. You're busted," she says. She kneels on the fish, runs the clip of a stringer chain through one of his gills, takes a pair of pliers and eases out the hook. Then she tosses the chained fish back into the river. He'll stay alive there until we're ready to haul him out and take him home.

Russo's beaming at me. "Well? Well? Did I nail a big boy or did I not? Ye of so little faith. Stop looking stunned and start casting again or something, Luther. Me, I'm just going to sit here and enjoy a little postbust lassitude for a while."

I cast and reel, cast and reel. Pretty soon I'm into the slow rhythm of it, relaxing, gazing at the arcs my line makes, the flow of the waters, a pair of long-legged blue herons stepping gingerly in the shallows near the far bank. It is so peaceful. My mind's nearly empty. Some time passes, but I have no idea how much. And I feel I don't care at all.

■ ■ ■

Then, at some unknown point, Russo snaps me back like a hooked rockfish.

"So come on, Luther," she says. "What's your plan? Your proposal? I assume you didn't come down here without one. Care to lay it out for me? In detail, please?"

Detail? Jesus. For a second or two I'm hard-pressed to even focus on where I am and who I'm with, let alone why. Russo's timing is perfect. Jukes me at just the right moment, when she sees my mind is somewhere very, very far from business.

"The deal? Pretty simple. Based solidly on what we've already discussed. Territories, CEO and COO, that sort of thing," I say, moving fast as I can to recover.

"Luther, wake up here. God's in the details," she grins. "Give."

"Here it is, then," I say, making it up as I go. "First, my territory is everything north of Virginia and east of Chicago. I pick my own people, set up my own cookers and distribution network. I make all day-to-day operational decisions. Without having to consult you first."

"Okay," she says.

"Long-term strategy, expansion into new areas, anything else serious—say, capping people who get in the way or fuck up—we'll discuss and agree on before I make the moves."

"Okay."

"You'll watch my back for any DEA interest, any signs of heat from local law enforcement, twenty-four/seven. You'll let me know the instant you know if anything like that starts happening."

"Okay, okay. Now how about the real deal?" she says. That smile's on her face.

"You supply the start-up capital for the people, the cookers, everything I need. As soon as I've paid that back, the overhead comes out of my cash flow. The net, I take 70 percent, you get 30. Weekly reports, actual money split quarterly."

"Wow! We may have to fiddle with that ratio. But in principle, okay," Russo says. The smile's still in place.

"Jesus, Francesca," I grin back. "I'm getting a little worried here. I expected some opposition, some negotiation. Not a blank check."

She laughs. "It isn't blank at all. First, you're going to pay back all the start-up money. Then you're going to do most all the hard work. That was always tops on my agenda. What's to negotiate, except maybe a digit or two of the split? You're going to make me rich, Luther."

"Going to make myself rich."

"Good for you! Now that's exactly the right attitude, for a change. The better you do, the better I do. Seems win-win to me."

"Does this sound win-win, too? If in a year, maybe eighteen months, you've got guys like me up and running in the other slices of the country, and I'm netting minimum five million annualized, I replace myself. I become CEO, you move up to chairman, and we split the national take seventy-thirty?"

"Shit, Luther. That is completely crazy!"

"I mean seventy to you, thirty to me. If we make that move a year or so down the road."

"Now that's not completely crazy," she says. "Jesus, you had me worried there for a moment. Okay, if you deliver on that annualized five million net in your original territory, we promote ourselves and take the percentages you said. But let's do 60 percent for you, 40 for me until then."

"Nah. Has to be at least sixty-five for me. Provided I net that five million mark. I don't make it, then your numbers are good," I say. "Anything else is a deal-breaker for me."

"You got a secret MBA lurking somewhere in your dark and violent past or what?" Francesca Russo laughs. "Hell, you'll probably ask me to do your fucking laundry for you too. Through my Cayman bankers."

"I did have just that in mind," I say. "Cost me a fortune to get everything nice and clean otherwise."

"You punk! You are a real piece of work, you know that? Yeah, you do know that. You like being that, Luther. I know you," Russo says.

"Well?"

"Okay, okay, okay." She stands, hauls in the rockfish, smacks its skull on the dock to kill it. Then she puts it, bent almost double to fit, in a plastic bucket of river water. "You take the rods and the eels. We'll go back to the house, have brunch, I'll tell you what I've already got operating and where it is. Monday we'll start going to meet some people. I'll introduce them to their new boss. We got a deal, Ewing."

■ ■ ■

Jacked.

Eddie Blizzard's sitting easily at the old pine kitchen table when I walk in, pointing what looks like a brand-new Taurus .44 Special at my belly.

"Eddie! Hey! Big surprise to see you here," Russo says. "Caught a great one this morning. Didn't I, Luther?"

"Huge," I say. "Award-winning."

"Really fucking happy for you, Di," Blizzard says, that ugly smirk of his going even uglier, and evil. Got an uncertain situation here, I'm thinking, any way it goes. Very delicate one, whether he's here for her, for me, or maybe both of us. Get real cold, real clear. Now, Luther.

Now's not quick enough.

Russo, behind me, reaches under my shirt and whips the P5 out of its small-of-the-back holster before I have time to twitch. I hadn't bothered to wear the SIG today. Thought it was going to be nothing but a talk day, easy, relaxed. Thought there was nearly zero possibility of any trouble. Felt sure if something did develop, I could solve the problem easily. With my hands. Or the P5.

Jacked. Fucking jacked.

Because Russo's now beside Blizzard, both of them out of my reach. And he's got the hammer cocked on that piece-of-shit .44, which may only have a two-inch barrel but at this close range will kill me just as dead as a tuned H & K or a Colt Python if he decides to let it.

"I'm a little confused here, Francesca," I say. "The lack of courtesy and all. Not a real reassuring way of closing our deal. Kind of hostile, actually. You know?"

The bitch laughs. "Closing? Don't worry about that, Luther. No problem there. We are definitely in accord on closing. In synch. Hey! Like Di and Charlie, right? Only maybe I've got a different kind of closure in mind."

"You trusting this, Eddie?" I say. "You really believing in this, after what went down with the cops and those murder charges?"

Blizzard doesn't respond. The smirk doesn't even flicker. Neither do his eyes.

"Remember Bleibtreu, Luther?" she says. "Nice little wine you gave me? Nice little exam? Which I passed?"

"Sure. That's why I came down this morning. That's why I gave you my business plan. So where's the problem here? I'm not seeing any problem, except for the little scumbag with the .44. The dude that's going to go on unemployment the moment I take over my territory."

"He thinks I'm just a dumb shit-kicker, Di," Eddie says. "Thought he was supposed to be real smart. You said he was real smart, real good at what he does."

"He is, Eddie, so please just keep doing what you're doing," she smiles down at him. Then she turns her gaze back to me. Gives me that anchorwoman look.

"The problem, Luther, is that you've flunked all my exams, including the one you clearly didn't catch I was giving *you* at Bleibtreu, okay?" she says. "Hate to bruise you ego or anything, but you blew them. Totally. You're a poor actor."

"Cross your mind you maybe scored wrong? All that coke? Playing little games with your judgment?"

"Crossed my mind that, when I started playing with you, way back with that first mention of Bobbie and Butch, I was overimpressed with your history. Caused me to overlook a few things, make a few rash assumptions," she says. "You punk! You came so close! You were playing hard to get. I got into that, understood it. But Charlie and Di, a terrific team. The places we could have gone together."

"Seems to me that still stands. Seems to me we have a very nice deal, a very bright future," I say.

"Except you said some shit to Eddie we know isn't true. About Ray Phillips, things like that. And maybe played just a little too hard to get. Then tried a little too hard with that nice dinner, that nice wine," she grins. "And, Jesus, the moralizing!"

"You're not thinking it all the way through, Francesca. Until I was sure about you and me being compatible, I needed your hitter here a little off-balance. A normal precaution, given the possible risks, right?"

"Sure. But I *have* thought it all the way through," she says. "Definite conclusion: You are a problem, not an asset, Luther. Because at Bleibtreu I saw you're still all cop. You're on the clock with this. Probably your own clock, not the official one. But you're on the case, and you want to take me down."

"That's pure shit. That's a little too much cocaine talking, Francesca. Fuck! This is what I get for dealing with a user. No dependability, no reliability, no trust, 'cause users are paranoid."

"None of the above applies," Russo laughs. "And what you get is a tragic accident. Two respected law enforcement officers who worked as partners on a major case, enjoying a relaxing Saturday, fishing. Then this awful, totally tragic accident. I'll try for a brave front before the media, but my voice will crack, the tears'll flow. You ever see me cry, Luther? I'm good, I'm really convincing, trust me. They break hearts, my tears."

She moves away from Blizzard, careful to keep well out of my reach, and takes the cattle prod down from the wall.

"Hey! Time to play with my puppies," she says.

27.

A fast fury of slathering dogs are hurling themselves violently against the chain-link. The fence rattles and bulges with each assault.

"Fucking hellhounds, Di," I hear Eddie say. He's behind me, not close. Three-meter gap, minimum. But I'm still in his kill-zone. The shit-kicker's at least got the brains to know you never put a pistol right up against a man's back. Because if he's a man like me, he'll suddenly make a move that will leave your gun hand empty, your arm dangling broken and useless.

I've got no chance.

"No, they're sweethearts, Eddie. Adorable," Russo says. She's a couple of meters in front of me, casually swinging that cattle prod by its lanyard as we walk toward the kennel. "They love me. They'll do anything for me. Right, Luther? You've seen the darlings."

"Real sweet, Francesca," I say. "The only bad dog you've got is Eddie. His rabies shots up to date and all? Choker chain nice and snug? 'Cause I got the sense he's the kind that turns on you. Out of nowhere, for no reason. Mean bitch."

"Eat me, Ewing," Blizzard snaps.

"Nothing personal, Eddie," I say. "Just read it in your jacket. You were some big hard-timer's bitch in Jessup. Gotta be true. Says so in your jacket. You dig being his bitch?"

"Fuck you, man!" Eddie shouts.

Russo laughs. "You boys! Grow up, okay?"

"Tell me, Eddie," I say. "What do you like better? Taking it up the butt, or in the mouth? Hey, you swallow? Yeah, I bet you love to swallow."

I hear a quick step behind me. Go all loose. C'mon, Eddie. Get close, try to hit me, take your best shot, scumbag.

But it's just the one step. He doesn't come on. Fuck. Still no chance. My P5 is tucked tantalizingly into the waistband of Russo's jeans at the small of her back. Just out of my reach.

Suckered.

I don't see a move, even a muscle flex. She's that fast, fast beyond belief. The cattle prod's heavy steel butt just slams right into my solar plexus with sickening force. I double over on impact, desperately sucking air. Vaguely see her rise on the ball of her left foot and pivot, other leg arcing around so her right foot smashes into my temple. I go down. Try to scissor her legs out from under her with mine, but I'm too slow. She skips up, comes down with a hand-chop to the side of my neck. My brain jolts, wavers. Left arm goes up in pure reflex to block whatever's coming next. Somehow Russo goes under the block, rams a thumb into the base of my throat. Can't breathe. Can't move. Vision's mainly a red scrim. Things are shimmering behind it.

Then I feel hands cradling my face. "Luther, you punk! You in there, honey?" Russo's voice sounds like it's filtered through a reverb unit. The hands are stroking my cheeks.

"Ray asked me to fuck you up bad, Luther," she says. "But I guess I'm just a love tap kind of girl. Breathe easier, Luther. Don't try so hard. You're not hurt. You're getting air okay. Breathe in, breathe out. That's it. Do it slow, deep. In, out. Yeah, good. Keep doing that."

The hands go away.

I breathe in, breathe out, deep and slow. The red scrim slowly lifts. I see dirt, see Francesca's Bean gum boots for a moment. Then they move out of my sight line. Her hands slip under my armpits, her knee's in the small of my back. She levers me up to my feet, lets go. I'm standing, wobbly and weak. Try my arms. They work. Touch my trunk, neck, and head. Nothing broken. Look at my hands. Not a drop of blood.

I hear "Try taking a step toward me, Luther." The reverb's shut off now. I look up. There's Francesca, a couple of meters in front of me. She's grinning. I take a step. Feels weird, wobbly. But I don't fall.

"Nice tough boy," Russo says. She laughs. "Take another step. No? Come on, you can do that, Luther."

I just stand there, stalling. Go deep into the pain under my breastbone, linger there until it starts a fade, move to the temple, then the neck, then the base of my throat. Tense and untense muscles. Then I shuffle forward a bit, stop when I feel I've got near normal control of my legs again.

"Hey, don't pussy out on me," Francesca says. "Keep on coming, babe. Don't disillusion me, okay?"

Stall. I shake my head, blink a lot. Let my right knee bend, wobble. Like I'm going to topple over. Turn my head this way, that way, a man who doesn't quite know where he is or what the fuck just skewed his world. Blizzard's still three meters back, the .44's cocked. Turn again. I can see Russo's face clearly, see her wicked smile. But I try to keep looking dazed, glazy-eyed.

"Luther, you're disappointing me here," she says, smile fading.

"I barely touched you, and you're acting like you got completely whaled. Lame, Luther. Very lame. Now get moving, okay? I'm bored with this."

Can't put it off any longer. I start moving toward her, but keep it to a shuffle, keep blinking and shaking my head.

Russo watches for a few seconds, wheels and heads toward the dog-pen gate. She blows her whistle once; the three young dogs instantly sit, motionless. The two parents back away from the fence but keep moving in small circles, their yellow eyes fixed on the gate, growling and drooling. She keys the padlock, swings the gate open, goes into the run with the prod held out before her, its business end pointing at the two moving dogs. They snarl and snap, but they back away, back right into the kennel. She kicks the door shut, pushes the barslide to secure it. The hellhounds go nuts then, slamming into the door, barking insanely. She turns and smiles at me.

"Hey, Luther. Mind stepping in here? Exactly eight paces, okay?"

"Nah. I think I feel more comfortable right where I am, Francesca," I say very slowly, voice hoarse. "I mean, what are you going to do if I just keeping standing here? Have Eddie shoot me?"

"Actually, yeah!" She grins.

"That would be very uncool. You know it. It'd put you into some very deep shit, capping me that way."

"A little messy, true. But not too deep to step out of and clean off, Luther. I've got some things in play, some pre-dated reports to my superiors, in my computer and on paper in my office, that pretty well prove you're a bent cop. You came down here to kill me. I stopped you. I'll skate."

"You snort some lines when I wasn't looking or something? Because that sounds exactly like cocaine doing your talking for you again."

"You are getting so boring, Luther. These stupid insinuations, over and over. Choice time. Either take eight paces in right now, or Eddie puts a wadcutter in the back of your head. You pick whichever you'd prefer. I'm okay with either."

"C'mon, don't walk, asshole," Blizzard says. "Please don't walk. So I can dome you. I really wanna do that."

I shuffle in the eight. I can see the eyes of the three frozen dogs track me, see their muscles just twitching, just aching to move. Strings of drool dangle and drop from their muzzles.

I'm about in the center of the run now. Russo moves around the fence line until she's behind the dogs. Blizzard steps in, closes the gate behind him, moves over next to her. The sun's glaring into my eyes. It's hard to see their faces, deep in shadow. I smell that river smell on the gentle breeze. I smell dog shit. I smell my own sweat, my own fear odor.

The dogs scent that, too. One starts to rise. "You!" Russo shouts, smacking her palm with the prod. The dog settles.

"I hate that moment just before a tragic accident, don't you, Luther?" Russo says. "That instant when you know it's going to happen? When everything seems to shift into slow-motion, but you know there's still nothing you can do to stop it? Makes you feel so helpless or something."

"Have to disagree with you there, Francesca," I say. "There's always something you can do. You know what you can do right now."

I can't make out the grin, but her laugh is clear. "You punk! You think this is maybe some convoluted way of offing Eddie? Like you told him I'd do one day? What was it, 'sacrifice my pawns' or something? You just don't get it, Luther. Me and Eddie, we've got a business arrangement. Very solid. Very tight."

"If that's the way it is, you're never gonna see New Zealand, Francesca. Your dog pack is too big by one."

"Now I'm really, truly, terminally bored," Russo says. "Listen, Luther. Just go over to the box, take out the dummy, then go stand near the fence. Hold the dummy up in front of you if you like. That'll give you an extra thirty seconds or so. If you want an extra thirty."

I don't move for a moment. I concentrate on damping down the fear, on getting clear. Concentrate hard as I'm able. I tense and deliberately relax the major muscles of my legs and arms.

No good.

"Do it, Luther. Or Eddie pulls the trigger."

I give them my back, walking toward the box that's fitted against the kennel. The closer I get, the more furious the growling and scratching of the big dogs inside grows. I stop at the corner of the box closest to that door. The beasts are slamming against it, desperate to get out. Open the box, haul out the dummy, hold it in front of me, right hand making a quick snatch of that small accessory in my shirt pocket as I turn to face the three dogs and the two figures behind them.

"See! It was easy, wasn't it?" Francesca Russo says. "Now all you have to do is take a few steps over along the fence, okay?"

Sure.

Toss that tattered dummy over the fence, blow twice on my dog whistle, and hit the kennel door slidelock as I jump on the box. The .44 booms once, twice, sending showers of wooden splinters after me as I grab the top rail and swing over the fence all in one motion. Hit the ground hard, hear a third boom just as a double black blur bursts out of the door and slams into Eddie Blizzard, jaws wide and sharp white teeth gleaming. The bullet whangs through the kennel's aluminum siding.

I'm hurting, I'm breathing hard. Things seem to move in very small but distinct jumps and pauses now, like a DVD on slow forward. Blizzard goes down in three or four motions under the double black blur. Zoom in: A pair of fangs seems to freeze, then crunch deep into his groin. He's screaming but it sounds like reverb again.

The three young dogs recoil off the chain-link they've rushed to get at the dummy, flicker around. Russo makes stuttery stabs into the flurry smothering Blizzard with that useless cattle prod, stabs again and again, then starts clubbing the dogs with it. She's reaching back for my P5 when a triple black blur hits her from behind. She staggers, jerks up her arm toward her face. Blood spurts here and there through her white shirt. I see one hand make a skittering grab for the whistle in her pocket, see one dog's fangs clamp hard, then sink all the way in on that hand.

Russo goes down. Screaming in reverb, flailing and kicking. Jumps and pauses. Her. The dogs. Blizzard's already limp. His body only moves when a dog sinks its teeth in, shakes and rips. I see sprays of blood and what must be bits of cloth and flesh arcing slowly up through the air. Russo's still twisting and jerking, still shrieking.

Somebody cancels slow forward, the DVD goes to standard speed. I'm mesmerized, lying there in the grass outside the fence, lungs sucking air hard and fast. So this is what it looks like, being torn to pieces. Never seen anything like it before. Never imagined how savage and grotesque it would be.

I don't want to see any more. I rise, ribs aching from my fall, and sprint to the house. Check the kitchen, the living room, Russo's bedroom. Her Glock's there, resting in a Fobus holster on top of a pine dresser. I grab it, sprint back to the dog run.

I kneel at the gate, take a two-handed grip, sight in, squeeze the trigger. One of the dogs on Russo skids a meter down the run under the impact of a .40 Hydra-Shok, blood spouting from a hole just behind his shoulder. Aim and shoot, aim and shoot, aim and shoot, aim and shoot.

Then I stand. Surprised to find my left leg's trembling. Can't seem to stop it. But I walk through the gate, into the run. No blurs now. No jumps or jerks. Everything's still, so still and quiet. It's like I'm looking at a photograph in a frame on somebody's wall. Though only a psycho would hang such a horror. One of the young dogs near Russo tries to lift its hellish head. I put a Hydra-Shok through it, see the skull explode.

Blizzard's body is facedown in the dirt. It scarcely looks human. I see bone and organs through the blood. Francesca Russo is on her back. Her shirt and jeans are blood-soaked. Her face is unmarked, her mouth is fixed almost exactly the way it went whenever she'd put on that high-wattage Di smile.

I know it's only a rictus. The dead have serious problems smiling.

And the front of her throat is gone. Gone. There's just a gaping red hole, deep enough to put your fist in, where smooth pale flesh should have been. I've gazed at worse wounds, from shrapnel and bullets. Counted parts of bodies dismembered by artillery bursts. But none of that ever made my stomach churn the way this does.

I pick up my P5 from the bloody dirt. Let the Glock slide from my hand and fall to the ground as I walk back to the house. Punch in 911 on the phone. I'm sitting on the back doorstep, gold shield hanging from my neck by a chain, smelling the river smell coming up on a rising breeze now. My eyes are locked on the gap in the woods that funnels to a log dock weathered gray above turbid green water, when the first state trooper skids his cruiser to a stop and blocks my pretty view.

■ ■ ■

"Holy shit! Even you'll appreciate this one, Luther," IB says, zeroing on a headline he's just spotted in the *Sun* as I come into the squad room Monday morning. "Eastern Shore Woman Mauled, Killed By Own Dogs."

"Saw that," I mutter.

"So you reading the paper now, too?"

I don't say a word. I'm saving all my words for the moment Ice Box finishes reading the story. Feeling sure there will never be enough of them.